Sister

N.K. Murray

This is a work of fiction. Names, characters, places and incidents either are the product of the author's imagination or are used fictitiously. Any resemblance to actual persons, living or dead, events or locales is entirely coincidental.

Hey Peas,

I did it.

Love, Carrots

Preface

When I was 6, my best friend gave me the most wonderful present for Christmas. It was a journal, one of those ones that had a lock and key. It was sky blue and had a little pen that came along with it, which felt grown up to me at the time. I started writing in it January 1, 1991, and continued until that journal was full. Then I bought another, and then another, filling journal after journal with my thoughts. I'm glad I did that, because it makes this much easier for me to lay out there for each of you. I was able to look back and read what I wrote and then write what you're about to read. I'm hoping it helps you see what was going on in my head, because I realized early on that how I saw things wasn't how everyone else saw things. I think maybe I'm hoping what you're about to read will allow you to walk for a little while in my shoes, because I was how I was, and you all. . . weren't.

Taking the journals and turning them into this chronology was hard, because I know this is my goodbye to you. I need to make sure you knew how much you all meant to me. The events that follow on these pages changed me; for better or for worse, they shaped my life. They were important; not just at that moment but for moments to come.

I've come to the end now, and I'm sick at the thought that this is it for me. I want to go back to the start of everything. Back to where ignorance made me a happy little girl, reading a book under my tree, well before I knew what I know now.

I suppose I should start at the beginning.

It was one of those hot, sticky summer days where it was easier to do nothing than to move and risk heat stroke. July 19, 1990. I was 5, nearly 6, as I told anyone who asked my age. I was a weird kid . . . there's no way for me to deny that now. I wasn't active, like my sisters were. Not a tomboy like Laney, but not a girly-girl like Sophie, but just content to just chill. I always wondered if my lack of motivation should have been a red flag, knowing now what would come to pass in the future.

More often than not you could find me sitting in the back yard under my willow tree, reading a book I "borrowed" from one of the girls. I loved to read, so much so I would sneak into my sisters' rooms and grab their storybooks or schoolbooks and hide behind the couch in the family room, or behind the willow where no one could see me. I could sit for hours, losing myself in the story until my dad would seek me out for dinner or my bath. I would fold down the corners of the pages to mark them, or crack their spines so I could hold them in one hand as I lolled on my back in the soft grass. The girls would rage at my poor father, screaming that I was ruining their books. The whining and crying got so bad my dad would resort to buying multiple copies of the same titles so as not to cause World War III (otherwise known in our household as the Wee Three War).

I was forever known as the baby, despite my decided hatred of that term. HATE. LOATHE. I was NOT the baby anymore. There was a rather large age difference between Sophia Joy (known forthwith as Sophie the Dramatic) and I, and she ensured I knew my place in her little fiefdom. She and I were constantly at odds with each other. Or, she was constantly at odds with me. I couldn't do anything right and it didn't matter that I was 9 years younger than she was. (Some things don't change, I suppose.) Stuck in the middle was Laney; Eleanor Anne. Looking back, Laney had the best characteristics of both of us; my ability to watch and absorb my surroundings and Sophie's to be the life of the party. She was this amazing little human. She was the mother I never had because our mom passed away giving birth to me when she was 35 years old. I think about that now and then; how my mom's date of death is my birthday. I wonder if that's why my birthday and Christmas never held much allure for me when I got older.

I think my birth coupled with my mom's death is when Sophie began to hate me, although if you asked her she would insist she doesn't. But when it comes right down to it, I took her mom from her. It sounds so . . . blunt to mention it like this, almost in passing. I never had a mom, and she had one for 9 years, and then she didn't. Laney had just turned 4 when it happened, so it affected her but not quite as much as it affected Sophie.

Anyway, my time grows short, and I don't know if these tangents further my story.

Summer of '90 was halfway over, and I found myself under my willow reading. Sophie, being a typical teenager, had no desire to be home most of the time and was at a friend's house swimming, while Laney was riding her bike. She was this diminutive hellion who was happiest playing catch with dad or helping him work on the car. But, more than anything else, her favorite thing in the entire world to do was to ride her bike. It wasn't just any bike; it was a boy's style BMX bike in matte black, except for the shocking bright blue color of the back tire. Dad picked it up for her at a garage sale and fixed it up when it became clear she had no desire to ride the pink and purple princess bike Sophie grew out of. Laney loved riding that bike up and down the sidewalk and driveway, slamming on the brakes and leaving an electric blue skid mark on the ground. I like to think it was her personal middle finger to the world who thought she shouldn't be on a boy's bike, but that could just be me projecting my adult opinion as I look back. My dad was pretty handy and made her a rather crude ramp from some plywood and some 2x4's, which became her favorite possession after her bike. She'd place it strategically in the driveway where she could take a longish run from the sidewalk to hit the jump, then land and make a sharp turn to start the circuit again.

She was riding over her ramp now, providing the soundtrack for the book I was reading. There was something soothing in hearing the hum of the playing card she had stuck in the spoke of her rear tire as she drove up and down the sidewalk and the driveway, punctuated only by the thump of her landing from the ramp. I didn't have a strong concept of time at my age. I noted its passage by the number of pages I could make it through, rather than any actual hours elapsing. But I would swear on that day, she had to have ridden that driveway circuit for hours.

It was that pattern, that hummmmmmmm, thump! that had become ingrained in my head as the afternoon grew long. It stuck there, even after the sound ended and I was shaken out of my own little world by my dad screaming

my sister's name. To this day, I still hear it in my dreams.

My heart was pounding a staccato rhythm I hadn't felt to that point in my

life, but one I would make an attempt to avoid from that moment on. (Spoiler alert

– I fail.) I don't remember how long it took me to get from the tree to the house,

but I remember running face first into the back door of the garage because I

couldn't get it open fast enough. I became frustrated when I couldn't turn the

knob in my sweaty hands, so I ran around to the front of the garage to find my dad

cradling a limp Laney is his arms, slapping her face, and trying to wake her up. I

froze in place, not truly understanding what I was seeing. I remember her arm was

just hanging from her body, so much paler than I remembered it being earlier in

the day, and how her fingers with their chipped blue sparkle nail polish kept

scraping the blacktop as my dad tried frantically to get her to wake up. Her knees

were covered in blood and so was her head. Her blood was all over my dad's arm

as he held her like a baby, and I was perplexed by how dark red it was. But it was

her eyes that bothered me most. I still see them each night when I can't sleep.

Those gorgeous huge brown eyes, so much like my father's, were open and staring

blankly upwards.

Dad raised his head from her chest, saw me and yelled for me to run to

get Mr. Jay, our neighbor. All I could hear as I ran what felt like a mile, was the

sound of my own raspy breath in between the pitter-patter beat of my own heart.

Mr. Jay was lovingly tending to his gardens (which he was known for in our little

town) when I arrived, out of breath and starting to cry as the scene I just viewed

10

really set in. I couldn't talk . . . I don't honestly believe that any real words came out of my mouth that day. But being a father and a grandfather, Mr. Jay recognized how upset I was and ran in his old man garden shoes back to the house with me.

The rest of the afternoon is a blur. I remember getting back to the house, and Mr. Jay calling for an ambulance. I remember sitting just inside the garage, arms wrapped around my knees, rocking back and forth as I watched a series of emergency personnel and neighbors bustle around Laney and my dad, until they were both whisked away. I know Mrs. Jay went to go get Sophie from her friend's house, while Mr. Jay stayed with me in our kitchen. As the night progressed, and it became clear Dad wasn't coming home, Sophie and I went to bed. I was still awake when my dad arrived home at an hour I hadn't previously seen before in my young life. Without Laney.

I walked down the carpeted stairs, holding the polished wooden banister in my hand as I made my way to my father's hunched over form sitting on the second to last step. I patted him on the back, thinking in my head, 'there, there Daddy, she'll be ok,' but not vocalizing the words. He startled a little at my touch on his back, and I sat down next to him, burrowing my head into his side so he put his arm around me and hugged me tighter to him.

"Daddy, when is Laney coming home?"

Have you ever wanted to take back something you've said, because you didn't know the question or statement would cut so deeply? I didn't understand it then, but the look on my father's face that night was the definition of the word 'ravaged.'

I'm sorry, Dad. I didn't want to write this down. I didn't want it read and to this day, it hurts me knowing this was the moment in my life where everything changed.

My dad took a deep breath, and as tears welled in his eyes, he told me how Laney's heart had stopped while she was riding her bike, and the doctors weren't able to get it to start again. He said she was going to go and live in heaven with my mom.

How is a 5, almost 6-year-old supposed to process and understand that her sister isn't coming home?

I asked him, in what felt like a whisper, what happened to her heart. What he said is something that has stuck with me throughout my entire life.

"You know how Laney loved everything? How she loved you, and Sophie, and Mr. and Mrs. Jay and me, and her friends and how she was always happy and smiling and just enjoying being Laney? Her heart was so full of love that it just couldn't hold anymore and it stopped working. God decided to take her home to heaven to be with your mom."

I love my father. He's been a rock in my life, and I don't know what I would do without him. But from that moment on, regardless of the functioning of my heart, I swore I would be careful with who and what I loved because I was terrified God would see my heart was full and I would be taken to heaven. Or worse, He would send me to hell. I know that was never his intent and as I grew older, the science of my broken heart overtook *most* of the spiritual concerns I had. I'm not going to lie; part of me questioned if the spiritual concerns impacted the scientific ones, so I remained cautious and cognizant of that throughout my life from that point on.

My devastated father put me to bed, and I fell into an uneasy sleep, waking the next morning to the hysterical sobbing of my now, only, sister. I tended to avoid Sophie's melodramatic moments as a rule, mainly because I didn't understand them, and also because it felt as though the outburst took the focus away from whatever was wrong (or supposedly wrong in her eyes) and brought it squarely towards her. Now that I'm an adult, I see this was her coping mechanism, because she could make people focus on her and stop focusing/worrying/stressing about the real issue at hand.

I think this moment may have been my first attempt at trying to reduce my love for something on purpose. I loved my sister. I still do love her, albeit differently than I did when I was younger. I worshipped her silently to an extent, because she was the oldest and everything in the world that I wasn't, even though I had years to catch up to get to that point. I feel like I have to say this, because as these words find their way to paper, I'm certain it will come across as though I don't love her, and that I never did. She was someone I looked up to. In many ways, I still do today. I wanted to be like Sophie, even when it became apparent that we would only grow further and further away from each other in temperament than we were at that moment. The morning after Laney left me, and ever since would be known in my head as ALD (after Laney died), and it truly was the start of the beginning of the end. I wanted to be angry with Sophie, because she wasn't the only one who lost someone. Being the youngest, I didn't speak up, and I know now it wouldn't have altered the course of what happened.

Sophie was sobbing, and Mrs. Jay was consoling her while Daddy was on the phone. I walked into the kitchen and realized no breakfast had been made, and I didn't feel comfortable asking anyone to stop what they were doing and make something for me. While I think every kid knows they are small, it was then I saw how little I was, so no breakfast for me.

Heading back into the living room/dining room area, I sat down on the floor near the bay window because Daddy was on the phone at the dining room table, and I didn't want to be in the living room near sobbing Sophie on the couch. Watching Daddy, I remember hearing a bunch of words I didn't understand then, like autopsy and internment. I saw his face change more over these past two days, but this look was even different than those I'd seen. Almost like he was in shock, but more like he was unable to fully process what he was hearing. I saw him sit back in his chair, and rub his face like he was trying to wake up from a long sleep. And then he looked over at me, and I knew nothing was going to be the same.

I could give you all of the gory details about Laney's wake. I remember every second. All of the crying adults, the flowers, and the overwhelming warmth that made the room feel so much smaller than it was. But, the worst part was Laney. She was just lying there, looking like she was sleeping which was unsettling to me. I wanted to touch her, to see if she felt the same as she always did, but she looked fake like a porcelain doll. Her skin was paler than it normally was, and there was a blush that she didn't normally carry in her cheeks. My Laney was tan and freckled and I couldn't see either in the face in the casket. I wanted her to sit up and give me that huge grin that was her trademark. She had lost a tooth not long before she died, and used to spit water out of the front of her mouth when she was playing around. I wanted to see that gap. I wanted more than anything to think that my sister was playing around. I wanted anything but to be there. There weren't many kids present and those that came were there with their parents and seemed either shell shocked or curious. The adults offered their condolences to my dad and Sophie and probably would've to me had I been around. Luckily, Dad sensed my discomfort and let me sit outside in the back courtyard away from the crowd. I had brought a children's copy of Moby Dick and sat with my legs stretched out on the little park bench they had there. This felt normal to me, like I could pretend I was under my willow and Laney was alive and I wasn't at her wake.

I heard a cough behind me, and when I didn't acknowledge it, I heard a stomp, and the sound of footsteps. Another cough.

Sigh. . .so much for forgetting where I was. Another cough. Now I was getting annoyed, and glared in the direction of the intrusion.

"What do you want already?"

"Why are you out here and not inside with your family?"

Just what I wanted, someone who was curious and wanted to talk.

I put my feet down and looked down at my book sadly, and up again to see a girl who appeared to be my age with her brown hair held by a curled, pale pink ribbon which matched the trim on her black jumper-style dress.

I can laugh about it now. My first impression of meeting my soon-to-be best friend and de facto sister was how cheerful and bouncy her hair and ribbon was, and how Daddy never was able to manage the more girly aspects of pulling my hair back. I didn't want to answer her, because I didn't want her to think I was weird, so I hesitated.

"Is it because you're too sad?"

Was I sad? My sister was dead. I didn't have a mom. My father and remaining sister were both devastated, but what exactly was I?

"I miss her. She used to make us both breakfast, and now I have to make it myself." That seemed safe.

"My sister went to school with Laney. They were in the same class from the beginning."

So that's why this girl with the curling ribbon in her hair and nervous fingers twirling a leaf over and over again was here.

"I'm Laura Elizabeth Wright. But you can call me Betsy."

"I'm Merry Olivia Cameron."

"Like Christmas, or like Virgin?"

(It was at that moment I knew this girl and I would be friends. To this day, I still use that line.)

I must have looked like a fool sitting there with my hand over my mouth but she either didn't notice or didn't care, because she went on.

"If it's like Virgin, it's still kind of like Christmas, but I know they aren't spelled the same."

"No, it's spelled like Christmas." I blurted. I didn't know how to talk to this girl because I wasn't used to someone being so blunt with me. But, I would quickly learn to love it. I think it may have been as a result of being the youngest, and not having friends my own age.

Betsy sat down next to me on the bench, and we just talked. It was refreshing to be on the same level as someone instead of always being the youngest and not ever talking. Or maybe not NOT talking. Not being heard. We talked about our families and about what we liked, and what we didn't like. And on one of the saddest days of my young life, for the briefest of moments, she made me forget what I lost.

Betsy

I met Merry on the day of her sister's wake, in the back garden of the funeral home. My mom asked me to make friends, and I was resentful of the imposition at the time. I walked back there in a huff, and looked around. At first, I thought she was a statue. She was so pale. So blonde. So still. I coughed, thinking if she were real, she would move. There was a slight breeze, which rustled through her corn silk hair, and still, she didn't move. She must not have heard me. I coughed again. STILL nothing. Was she even real? So, I tiptoed my way over to the back of the bench, and coughed again.

The glare from that tiny wisp of a girl with those icy blue eyes could have melted a glacier.

It was strange, though. For as fierce as I think she thought she was, I felt and still feel to this day that Merry had this bravado, a shell she kept around her like a shawl that she could pull over her head and hide from the world. Sometimes you meet someone and just know deep within you they will change your life. That was Merry. I knew we would be friends forever. That's how I felt on that day, and every day since then.

Jeff

I found Merry and the little girl I came to love like my own, sitting with each other outside after the wake. It was so rare to see Merry animated and chattering away like a little magpie, and I hated to interrupt her. But it was time for us to go home and time for me to have a talk with my girls.

How do you bury a child? It was hard burying Liv and raising the girls on my own. For the nearly 6 years after Liv died, the girls had been my sole concern. Their happiness, their health, their everything. How had I missed this? You don't expect to lose your wife suddenly, but at the least, she was an adult. She had a chance to live her life, become a wife and mother. Laney never seemed sick. Always checked out fine at the doctor's visits. I don't understand how she had a bad heart with zero symptoms to this day. She was the most active of the girls and the last of the three I'd have thought would be sick. If anything, I would have bet Merry would have been the sick one since she's quiet and subdued and not as vibrant as her sisters.

Writing this down all these years later, it's funny how you can look back at what you think and how you felt before an earth-shattering event with such derision. Almost as if you want to smack yourself and ask how you could have been so dumb.

Laney was my little tomboy. She was Sophie's polar opposite but somehow, she did it in a way that she and Soph didn't clash that much. Easygoing. Man, she was up for whatever. If Soph was a hurricane whirling through life, and Merry was a mountain, silent and immovable, Laney was the calmest of all the seas. Fluid when she needed to be, but could be worked up into some strong waves when she wanted to. She was just as comfortable in the garage with me, as she was playing dolls with Mer, or letting Soph put makeup on her. She was so full of life.

I just don't understand how someone so alive one moment, could just collapse on the driveway lifeless. It's hard to reconcile. It's even harder to think this had happened to us again. It was easy to see how this affected Sophie, because she always wore her heart on her sleeve. With Merry, I think she got overshadowed by her sisters. Well, sister, now. She's so stoic. So quiet. When she woke up the night Laney died, she consoled ME, patting me on the shoulder. She's so much like her mother. She was contemplative, soaking up everything around her like a sponge. Losing Laney was losing any last link that might have been forged between her and Sophie.

Why didn't I force Liv to see a doc earlier when she seemed so tired, instead of chalking it up to having two kids with a third on the way? Why didn't I make sure the girls' pediatrician checked Laney's heart? Easy to say now, in hindsight. Would Liv have lived if she didn't have Merry? What if we had stopped after having Soph? I wouldn't be burying Laney right now. I wouldn't have had her, of course, but once I had her, to have to give her up like this that was almost more than I could take. A person could kill themselves under the weight of so much guilt and loss.

*****

I never comprehended why we as a culture fill our dead full of preservatives so they look lifelike, only to enclose them in a coffin, encase that coffin in concrete, and entomb the whole thing in the ground. Is it inane curiosity that makes me wonder what my mom or even Laney look like now? Morbid, certainly, but something which comes to mind as my hourglass empties.

Laney's funeral was as you'd expect. It went quickly, and for that, I'm now grateful. Back then, it felt like mere minutes had passed from me seeing her lying in my father's arms, until seeing her casket lowered in the ground. I wanted to cry out. I wanted to scream, and desperately wanted someone to give me back my sister. How could they bury my Laney? But nothing came out. I just stood there, as tears began to stream down my cheeks, watching this box holding my Laney disappear from view. My heart hurt, in a way it hasn't hurt since, ironically enough. It made my lungs feel like they were on fire and I couldn't get enough air. My head and heart just couldn't bear to see her leave me. I couldn't understand that she was gone and she wasn't coming back. I lurched forward, reaching towards this gaping hole in the ground trying to reach her that one last time, and was grabbed by my dad. He picked me up and just held me while I sobbed onto his shoulder. That feeling of being in my father's arms is something I remember every time I get sad or upset. That sense of 'It'll be ok.'

I think one of the saddest things that happens as we grow from children into adults is our increasing discomfort with finding comfort in the arms of our parents. I think we also take for granted we will see someone again. I don't know that I ever did after that day.

In the coming days, summer waned and the upcoming school year loomed. I wasn't excited, mainly because I couldn't fathom starting school without Laney. She walked me into kindergarten last year, and had promised she would walk me into first grade this year. Every time I thought about the first day of school, I began to get anxious. I didn't want to be a baby and cry, but who was going to walk me in?

As is normal, every student has to get a physical before they start school, and that year, Daddy took us to a different pediatrician because he said he just didn't feel comfortable with the level of care our old one gave us. I didn't understand it then, because he had never had any issues with the doctor Before Laney Died (BLD).

We visited the shiny, bright offices of the new young doctor my father found, and I was struck by how different it was from the comfortable, warm and obviously older offices of our previous doctor. The new doctor was different than my old doctor, and a female this time, which made me feel better about the change. My physical was also different than years past. I don't want to say invasive, but was more thorough than I was used to. She kept listening to my heart with her stethoscope, and moved me in several different positions over the course of the exam. Arms up. Arms down. Listening in the front and again in the back and even on my sides. Sophie had gone right before me and was sitting outside, so it was just Daddy and I with the doctor in the office. After she was done listening, she began writing for what seemed like hours on my chart, and began to talk with Daddy about what she had found. I didn't understand what the doctor was saying, but the gist of it was that I needed to go in for additional tests because of what happened to Laney. When I asked what kind of tests, the lady doctor told me they needed to take pictures of my heart, and record it beating because she thought she heard a funny beat when she listened to it.

"What kind of funny beat? Like how my chest hurt when I went to run to get Mr. Jay?"

A look passed between my dad and the doctor, and both got serious, and asked what I meant by that. I explained that when I ran to get Mr. Jay, my heart felt funny, like it wanted to jump right out of my chest. I could feel it trying to get out through my throat, like it was a fish flopping around when it leapt out of the water. I knew exactly what that was like, because one of my fish decided it didn't like the tank and it jumped out and was flopping all around on the ground until I ran to pick it up and drop it back in the water.

Looking back now, I think my father hoped it was just me being upset that caused me to feel like that. I think he hoped it was a fluke, and that it wasn't anything serious. But, I also think he also knew that because I wasn't the type of kid to say something fantastical, this wasn't something we could just brush off. And now, with both my mother and sister dying suddenly, my offhand comment took on new meaning. My father was told to get me scheduled immediately for further testing including an ECG, and an echocardiogram. The doctor wanted me hooked up to a monitor to read my heart rhythms once I went home. Listening to the doctor and my father speak over me as though I wasn't sitting right there scared me. It felt as though I did something wrong and they were discussing my punishment.

In short order, the appointments with a cardiologist were made for both Sophie and I. While the pediatrician hadn't noticed any abnormalities listening to *her* heart, the decision was made to be safe and have her tested as well.

I feel I should stop at this point, and say that even though I was young, I could sense something wasn't being said by everyone around me. You can tell at this point, where my story is heading. My dad, Sophie, the doctor . . . it felt like everyone looked at me like I was a ticking time bomb and no one knew when I'd go off.

After being in this state of anxiety for 3 weeks after Laney's death, I finally gathered up the courage to ask what was going on. I remember the conversation perfectly because it was the first dinner I had alone with my dad ALD, while Sophie was sleeping over at a friend's house. We had gone to a local restaurant that we still frequent to this day, known for their amazing hand cut French fries, killer beer menu (something I've never been able to fully appreciate unfortunately) and comfortable atmosphere. As we sat there, I remember sensing that he knew I was going to ask him something, because he kept bringing up everything but the doctor's visits.

"Daddy, what's wrong with me?" The look I got was priceless. Half surprise, half 'oh shit, I knew this was coming' which I'm aware seems contradictory. My dad can't hide his emotions in any way even now. It's almost comforting to know there's no pretense possible with him. (I think that's where

Sophie gets it from, although hers has more of a theatrical flair than his.) He seemed flustered and didn't seem to know how to respond, so he asked,

"What do you think is wrong, sweetie?"

"Well, you changed our doctor after Laney died. The new one was listening to my heart and the old one didn't do that as much as she did. And now I'm going for all these tests, but Sophie doesn't have to go through them anymore, so whatever is wrong with me isn't wrong with Sophie. And when you look at me, you look like you're scared. And sad. I think that I have the same thing Laney did, but I don't know what it is, because my heart isn't full like hers was! I promise!"

My poor father. There were so many times when I just think he was out of his element with Sophie and I, whereas he and Laney fit together so well. She was his little protégé, his mirror image, and someone he knew how to handle. But here I was, the spitting image of my mother in both looks and temperament. I suppose it seems strange that he didn't really know how to deal with me since I was so similar to my mom. I was different, and I know that one of the things that drew my father to my mother was that she was different than the other women he had known. Regardless, I was different from my sisters. I'm not saying that as a pat on my own back that I was this preternaturally brilliant kid or anything. I just never felt like I was like everyone else I knew then, despite the fact that my circle was extremely small. I always felt out of place, out of step, preferring to be by myself and not doing what everyone else was doing.

Was that a symptom of my broken heart? I've wondered this as the years have passed, thinking perhaps my physical limitations brought about a desire to not get caught up in the noise that consumes our lives, and just concentrate on things that were solid and stable. And then, I wondered if that was just bullshit; this was just genetics and how I was because that's how my mom was. Quiet, comfortable in her own skin, and content to just be present, without having to be a presence. I don't know if that makes sense to anyone who's reading this, because I'm only interpreting what I've heard from the few people who knew her who were still around after her death. What I know of my mother was that she was happy. She loved being a mom, and she was good at it. She loved to read. She loved to write, and had planned on doing so, before she got pregnant with Sophie. She was the calming presence in my father's life, as stable and constant as he was outgoing and vibrant. My mom was never someone you could consider to be vibrant, but more like a North Star shining in the sky, steady and always there. My dad certainly changed considerably after she died. He stopped laughing for the most part, unless Laney did something ridiculous. His smile didn't take over his face the way it did in the pictures scattered around our house. He didn't yell and he wasn't excitable anymore. He was simply there.

I'm doing it again. Sorry.

Anyway, my dad looked like I hit him on the head with a baseball bat at my explanation of what I thought was wrong. I've since heard the phrase 'Little pitchers have big ears' but I think it was the first time my dad realized how much I

28

truly absorbed from my surroundings. How hard it must have been for him to be honest with me about what was wrong, and I'm still thankful for that honesty.

"Well Mer, let me explain a few things. When your mom was pregnant with you, she was tired. We both thought it was just because she had Sophie and Laney and was getting ready to have you. They didn't tell me much after she died, sweetheart. When Laney died, and they found that it was because her heart stopped, they started looking into what happened with your mom. What they've found, is that your mom probably had the same kind of thing that Laney had, and that's why they both died."

"But what kind of thing? And when will I be ok? I don't want what they had."

I said this pragmatically because in my nearly 6-year-old mind, I was sure this was just a temporary situation and could be fixed now that they knew what was wrong.

"Well, the doctor's think you have something called HCM, which is what Laney had, and what they think your mom had. We still have to go through a number of tests to make sure that's what's wrong, and then the doctors will tell us what we can do about it."

"Daddy, *we* don't have to go through anything."

This stopped him.

"Merry, what do you mean?"

"Well *you* don't have to have any tests. *I* do. You haven't told me how to make it go away yet, either. I don't ride my bike like Laney did, so that means

I'm going to be fine, right?" I kind of laugh now about it, but I said all of this while munching away on my French fries doused in ketchup while looking up at my dad with these guileless eyes. Knowing what I know now, I have to give my father a lot of credit for telling me what he did know and promising me he would keep me informed of what was happening. I'm sure had this conversation been held with Sophie, it wouldn't have gone quite as smoothly. Partially because of our age difference and what it would mean to her, and partially because she was Sophie the Dramatic. I guess if you have to give a kid bad news, it's better to give a younger kid who doesn't understand the ramifications of the news, than a teenager who is . . .well, a teenager.

What did this mean to little 5, nearly 6-year-old me? Well, after wearing a Holter monitor intermittently over the course of the first two months of first grade to track my heartbeat, I missed so much school I think my father contemplated pulling me out entirely. What was odd, was that I wasn't missing school because I was sick. I was missing school because my dad was paranoid that I would do something at school that would make my heart fail. I was a good student, and though not the social butterfly my sister was, I enjoyed learning. It was just prior to my birthday in December that I had my first episode with my broken heart.

Daddy took Sophie and I to the mall to do some last-minute Christmas shopping about a week before the big day. Sophie was understandably upset that at 15, she had to be seen with her father and her baby sister. (A fact she beat into my head on the drive there.) Needless to say, I was exhausted by her the constant sniping by the time we got to the mall.

The mall was packed with busy shoppers, hustling to spend their money on the perfect presents for their loved ones. I never liked the mall. (And after this Christmas, I avoided it as much as possible. Thank God for the advent of online shopping.) Santa Claus frightened me, so a trip to sit on his lap was not something I looked forward to. Part of me was terrified he would put me into his sack and steal me. The other part of me was angry that he couldn't bring me the only thing I wanted to Christmas this year.

Laney.

I missed her. So much. She was the glue that held us girls together. The filling of our Oreo. Without her here, these past few months were awful. It felt like Sophie hated me more than she already did and went out of her way to be mean or yell at me for some perceived slight. I began to resent her screeching voice that interrupted my every waking moment. I began to tune out whatever it was she was saying, because it was always a complaint or a criticism.

As the three of us walked into the mall, I felt completely overwhelmed. It was cavernous and loud and filled with busy people living their busy lives. I never understood how anyone could be happy there. It was a beehive of activity; constantly moving, constantly pulsing with life. For tiny little me, it was scary. I used to get carried when Laney was alive, but now that she wasn't, and due to my vehement protestations that I was NOT a baby, my dad simply held my hand. We snaked our way through the crowd, from store to store, with Sophie at point leading the charge. My short legs were getting tired from the rush, and I was beginning to lag behind my dad and slow our pace. We had stopped to look at something in JC Penney's when Sophie began to insist to my dad that she wanted to go into another store down the way from where we were. And when my dad insisted we stick together because of the crowds, she began to throw an EPIC hissy fit. (Who was the baby?!) She began to storm out of the store yelling her head off that she was not a child and could go into any damn store that she wanted to by herself. First thing I thought was 'ohhhhhhh you are in SOOOOOO much trouble!' as I was yanked by my arm out of the store so we could follow her. Sophie was still flipping out and by this point, Dad was getting pissed.

What happened next was no one's fault. I mean that. Dad went to grab Sophie's arm and in doing so, he let go of mine. And just like that, I was separated from him. It sounds ridiculous now, but it happened easily. No one grabbed me; I was just swept away in the crowd. When I finally reached a clear area, neither Dad nor Sophie was around.

Stop for a minute and think about this: every kid has had one of those panicked moments where they get placed in an unfamiliar environment. First day of school. First sleepover maybe. You have that sinking feeling in the pit of your stomach that you're alone. Really alone. Nothing is familiar. No one you know is around you. Tears well up in your eyes, and you start getting seriously upset. You begin to hyperventilate and try as you might, the words won't move past your lips and you stand there . . . paralyzed.

I still remember how I felt even all these years later. The utter terror. The smells of the people rushing by me combined with the sickeningly sweet scent of cinnamon pretzels and greasy French fries. My heart was racing, and then, just as quickly as it raced, it stopped and I felt like I was floating. It was like I wasn't in my body anymore and the raucous commotion of the mall fell away like I had been plucked up and out of there by the Hand of God.

I know it sounds trite. One minute I was there. The next I wasn't. I know now I passed out. I hit the ground in the middle of all of those people, and the rest I heard from my dad when I woke up in the hospital nearly two days later.

Jeff

I had thought my worst day came when Liv died.

And then Laney died, and I thought that was my worst day.

And then I let go of Merry's hand at the mall. The anger I felt with
Sophie was second only to the panic that raced through me as I screamed till my
throat was raw for my youngest. It felt like an hour had passed, although my
watch showed it had been less than 5 minutes. By this time, it was apparent I had
lost her, and mall security was called and an announcement was made that a little
blonde girl had gone missing. I don't know if I took a breath the entire time she
was gone. I still don't know how she got so far away from me.

Suddenly, a low murmur ran through the crowd, and through the noise I
heard a woman's voice, shrill and loud piercing the air.

"Call an ambulance!"

As bad as I had felt before, it was nothing compared to how I felt now. I
had the Sahara in my mouth as I grabbed Sophie by the arm and made my way
down the concourse in the direction the voice had called from. I had no idea how I
had heard the yell above the din of the mall, but I was grateful that whoever yelled
had some massive pipes. When I got there, it was like Laney all over again. Part
of me cursed God, while begging Him to save her.

My baby girl was laying there on the cold terrazzo floor, legs splayed
with a woman over top of her, loosening her jacket and shirt, and putting her head
to her chest.

Oh God.

Merry's lips and eyelids were blue. The lady on her knees next to her looked up at me, and said she was breathing faintly even though she was ice cold.

It's hard to be relieved in a circumstance like that, but I was relieved. So fucking relieved. The next hour flipped by quickly. The ambulance came and Soph and I went with her to the hospital. She was whisked away. Just taken from me.

Hours later, the doctor sat me down. Asked if I was aware of how her heart condition affected her, to which I blindly shook my head no. She had just been diagnosed, just started the testing and we were still in the process of figuring out what we needed to do with her, I told the doc. I quickly found out how bad off she had been at the mall. The oxygen levels in her blood were at 86%. Low enough to be considered dangerous and a concern for brain damage. They had intubated her in the ambulance, and she pinked up. Well, as pink as she ever was, as she had inherited Liv's pale features. He went on to say that the stress of being separated triggered the fight or flight response which gave her an adrenalin rush. It caused her heart to be overwhelmed which caused the syncope; the passing out. They had started to run some more tests, and would run several more over the course of the next few days, but everything pointed to Merry having a heart attack.

My 5-year-old daughter had a heart attack. Those words washed over me like Niagara Falls during the coldest winter, and my breath left my body. A heart attack.

He took me to the curtained off area where they had her, and warned me that she was sedated and had a tube down her throat. Nothing could have prepared me for how lifeless she looked. How small she appeared in that big hospital bed. The doctor said they would slowly bring her out of the sedation, and she would be in the hospital for at least the next few days. I had forgotten Sophie was next to me, and I heard her startle at that. I couldn't think of that then. Couldn't think of what that would mean for Soph, as awful as that might sound.

<u>Sophia</u>

That first Christmas after Laney died was terrible. It was clear my dad was preoccupied with everything that was going on with Merry. Of course he was. Being normal in this family was a flaw. It got you nothing. Merry was always quiet. It was creepy. Anytime she said anything, it felt like she had contemplated it over hours until it was exactly the right thing to be said at the time, which made her everyone's favorite. It just felt so fake to me. And I called her out on it. How could anyone be so dispassionate about everything that was going on in life? Dad always said I wore my heart on my sleeve, and you know what, I'm glad. At least then you could see when I was happy, or sad or angry, and there was none of this bullshit about not being able to tell anything about someone. They said Merry was overshadowed by me. Overshadowed? Why is it a flaw that I have a personality? Why was it such a good thing that she was so damn quiet all of the time? And of course, being the little church mouse that she was made me look like a grandstanding drama queen.

Ugh. Christmas. We went to the mall. I wanted to go shopping with my friends. For presents for my father and Merry, not that it matters now. For what it's worth, I was PMS-ing, but of course, that's no excuse according to my father. All I wanted to do was run to a store down the mall where I could get a book for Merry. She always stole all of mine and Laney's so I wanted to get her one of her own. Maybe I made it into a big deal, and maybe that brought about her getting lost. I get it. All MY fault. But my intentions were good and that's something everyone seems to forget in light of what happened.

We got to the hospital and I heard what they said about her. I *could* listen when I wanted to, contrary to popular belief. The doctor said she had a heart attack. How the hell does a 5-year-old have a heart attack? Is that even possible? How is it possible that she was so sick, that Laney was dead, that my mom was dead, and I was perfectly healthy? I was completely fine. It scared the shit out of me. And when the doctor said she was going to be in the hospital for a couple days, all I could think of was how she would miss the birthday party that we were going to have for her. I'm sure Dad thought I was pissed about Christmas. But let's be honest. Christmas was fucked any way I looked at it. Things were never going to be the same ever again, and there was nothing I could do about it.

*****

I woke up in the hospital just over a day and a half after I passed out in the mall. They had taken the tube to my throat out while I was sedated, and then slowly reduced the meds I was on so I would come out of the coma-like sleep I was in naturally. 'When I was ready' I had heard the doctor say. My throat hurt, my head hurt, I was hungry and I was out of sorts to say the least. Daddy was sitting there next to me, and I don't know that I had ever seen him so happy up until this point in my life. I started crying the moment he walked over to the bed. I was certain he was going to be mad at me for getting separated from him. He just sat beside me and picked me up from my spot on the bed and rocked me like a baby. And I didn't mind. It's terrifying as an adult to not have control over your body; to not have any idea that something could affect you to the point where you almost die. It's even more terrifying when you're a kid.

The doctor came in shortly after I woke up, and we went through what had happened in the mall. Hearing my 'Hand of God' story only served to confirm that I had gone through syncope, and that at this point, leaving me un-medicated was no longer an option. Unfortunately, with HCM there was no cookie cutter treatment they could put me on. To prevent blood clots, I was going to be put on blood thinners. They were also going to try to put me on beta-blockers, which would slow my heart rate. I laugh about this now, but I was confused and kept thinking they were going to give me Legos and I couldn't understand how that would fix my heart. My diet would have to be completely revamped, and more important than anything, I would not be able to be stressed out at all. My heart was clearly sensitive to stress and the last thing anyone wanted was another incident like we just had.

I figured that meant I wouldn't have to go to the mall anymore.

Instead, it meant that my dad thought I shouldn't go to school anymore. I was at an age where I loved school. It meant I could learn and be part of a group, even if I wasn't a social kid. Taking it away from me so soon after losing Laney was devastating. I just wanted to be like everyone else, and this was another example of how different I was becoming. I couldn't stop crying when he told me. When was I going to see Betsy? How was I going to have any friends? The decision felt reactionary rather than based on logic. I think he was just scared to lose someone else that he felt this was the right course of action to take.

I got out of the hospital on my birthday, December 22nd. It didn't feel like a gift. It felt like I was being sent home to a prison cell. I couldn't do anything. If I tried to walk down the stairs, my dad would come rushing up them and pick me up and take me where I wanted to go. I'd see Sophie standing there, watching me in his arms with this *look*. This barely concealed look of hatred, and sometimes, I'd see her mouth 'Baby' like it was some sort of dirty word she didn't want Dad to hear. This isn't how I wanted my life to be.

When I blew out my candles on my cake that year, I wished for Laney to come back. In the 4 months since she died, everything had changed. I missed her, the way you miss the blankets when it's cold. At first, it didn't feel quite so bad, like you could deal with it if you had to, but then the longer you went without them, the colder you felt and the more you wanted to feel comfortable and warm. She didn't think I was a baby. I think I knew deep down she wasn't coming back, but there was nothing else I wanted.

The weeks from Laney's death leading up to Christmas 1990 will go down as the worst ones I had in my life. So much had happened in a short amount of time. Merry's diagnosis took the focus off of grieving for Laney and pushed me to make decisions which, at the time, seemed to be right. I had just brought Merry home from the hospital, and she was flat out dejected. Sophie was just being a miserable beast of a whiny brat instead of what I had come to expect from the teenager she was. And of course, I was looking at the first Christmas without Laney. While I'm not saying that Laney didn't have her temper tantrums and quirks, she was the most easygoing kid of the three of them. Not stubborn and silent like Merry, not contrary and snotty like Sophia. God, I missed her.

Bringing Mer home from the hospital to a quiet dinner and just Mr. and Mrs. Jay over for some cake wasn't what I wanted for her birthday, but I also didn't want it to go unacknowledged. I remember looking over at her, with her chin on her hands on the table staring blankly at the 6 candles on the cake as we all sang. When we finished, she squeezed those big blue eyes shut, scrunching her face up in concentration, and blew the candles out as though she wished she could blow the entire house down. She opened her eyes, and looked up at me as I went to cut the cake, and I asked her what she wished for when she blew the candles out.

"I can't tell you, Daddy. If I tell you, it won't come true. I don't know if it can come true anyway, but I asked just in case." She said gravely. She looked so much like Liv then. It broke my heart to see her so damn sad. I knew what she wanted. I knew she wanted Laney back. When Laney was alive, everything was normal for her. Now, the only life she knew was gone, and so was her sister.

Sophie and I had planned a birthday party for Mer before all this happened, and was going to invite her little friend Betsy over, and Betsy's parents and then a couple of Sophie's friends (to keep her quiet) but because of the hospitalization, the party didn't materialize. I'm glad she didn't know about it because that would have made her feel worse than she already did. As it was, I was having New Year's Eve at our house this year, but in light of the hospital stay and getting home so close to Christmas, most of the people I invited outside of the neighbors and Betsy and her family decided against coming. I was secretly happy because I had started to become frazzled.

Can men get frazzled? Is that a thing? I had no family, and lost my parents before Liv and I married, and Liv's father was somewhere out on the West Coast and remarried after her mom died. Other than the few friends who stuck around through me losing Liv, and Mr. and Mrs. Jay, there was no one to help. Raising three girls without a wife is hard. Raising two girls after the death of the third, combined with dealing with Merry's heart condition was close to impossible. I wasn't sleeping well at all. Sophie was perpetually pissed off. And Merry was equal parts sad and silent. It was exhausting trying to put on a happy face for the girls with everything seemingly starting to crumble around me. I hadn't even had time to put up a tree, decorate it and the house and wrap the presents I had bought (thankfully) early.

I put Merry to bed on Christmas Eve, and went downstairs and just flopped down in my recliner looking at everything I hadn't done yet. I heard Sophie walking around in her room, and then come rushing down the stairs like something was wrong, so I stood up quickly and went towards the stairs to see her flushed with a smile on her face.

"Is Merry in bed now?"

Odd question from her. She normally didn't care about Merry's bedtime. Or much of anything that had to do with her unless it impacted something she wanted to do. Upon hearing she was, she ran back upstairs into her room, emerging with a huge box.

"Can you grab this? I have 3 more up here and they're not easy for me to carry."

It's not often I'm surprised by something. You could have knocked me over with a feather to look inside the box she had handed off to me to see it filled with wrapped presents with mine and Mer's name on them. I brought it downstairs and came back up to 3 more sitting there, each filled with more presents, stockings, stocking stuffers, and decorations for the living room and the tree.

"Soph. How?"

She looked like the cat that ate the canary as she grabbed a box and started walking down the stairs. I grabbed the other two, which was a feat since they looked like they could fit an adult crouched down in each and followed her down. She had already deposited her box on the floor and made her way into the

44

garage where the artificial tree we owned was. I was completely shocked. Who the hell was this kid, and where was Sophie the Dramatic?

She managed to wrestle the box into the house and into the living room where I was standing, and started giggling.

"Mrs. Jay took me shopping for you and Merry's presents, and I was able to get some wrapping paper and decorations on sale when we were out. I know you haven't had much time to decorate or wrap, so I figured I would wrap hers."

"But, how? How did you know where her gifts were?"

"You always put hers in the basement since she's afraid of going down there by herself. You keep mine in the attic in the garage because you know I won't go up on the ladder. And I've been saving my money from babysitting and my allowance. And... I didn't have to buy presents for Laney, so I spent the money I would have spent on her on Merry. She's had a rough couple of months, you know?" She said all of this with a straight face, which Soph never has, so I knew this was something she was being completely serious about for a change.

I grabbed her in a big hug and said to her,

"That's a pretty amazing thing you've done there, sweetie. Thank you. You have no idea how much your help means to me." I was glad she couldn't see the tears I had in my eyes, because I'm sure it would have embarrassed us both. We got to work and in short order, got the entire living room and tree done. I sent Sophie to get ready for bed, so I could wrap the presents I bought for her, and when I was done, grabbed a beer from the fridge and looked over the room. The weeks before this had been bad, but that night, I felt like those days were behind me, and my family and I could start healing.

*****

I woke up Christmas morning and lay in bed for a minute. Why rush? Laney wasn't going to be there, no matter how much I prayed or wished or asked Santa to bring her back to me. Sophie hated my guts. Dad looked at me like I was going to break into a million pieces if he wasn't there by my side every second. Is it possible for a 6-year-old to be clinically depressed? I'm sure the answer is yes. It was quite a bit for someone young to go through, even if I was precocious. I remember sighing loudly, and getting out of bed to pull on my ducky slippers and make my way downstairs. Of course, upon hearing my ducky shuffle on the floor walking towards the stairs, Dad came rushing over and picked me up and carried me downstairs into the living room. I was stunned silent. Overnight, it was as though elves had been hard at work decorating. I looked up at my dad with wide eyes wondering how this could be. I had no idea how he was able to wrap the hundreds of presents (to my childish eyes there seemed to be presents from floor to ceiling), get a tree and decorate it and the rest of the living room. It was fantastic.

Sophie was already sitting up prim and proper on the floor with her legs crossed Indian-style and patted the spot next to her where Laney always sat, for me to sit down. I didn't know what to think. I didn't know what else to do, so I shuffled over there, my jaw still dropped and sat down next to my big sis. She put her arm around me, and asked which present I wanted to open first. I was still surprised, so I just shrugged. She stood up, and reached around the back of the tree, and picked one that she appeared to have been looking for. It was about the size of a large shoe box, more the size of the boxes winter boots come in.

"Who's it from, Merry? Read it out loud."

The box was wrapped in this deep blue metallic paper that had the most beautiful stars on it, and I took it from her gingerly, and looked for the tag. When I saw it, I took a deep breath and yelled,   "Daddy, it's from LANEY! Laney got me a Christmas present, Daddy!" I was so excited. It was then I KNEW that even though she wasn't going to come home anymore, that she was watching me.

I opened the paper delicately so I could save it. My pudgy little fingers struggled to open the box, as the sides were taped. I stomped my feet impatiently as I stuck my fingers between the lid and the box, and finally peeled the tape back. The tissue paper was a deep midnight blue, my favorite color, to match the wrapping paper on the outside. I set the box down on the floor, and kneeled down next to it, and gently opened the tissue. Inside, was the most beautiful doll I had ever seen. She had deep brown eyes, and freckles and her reddish-brown yarn hair was pulled back into a ponytail with a royal blue ribbon. She had on a black tee shirt that had what looked to be a faded logo on it, and jean shorts with sneakers. Around her wrist was a blue plastic swatch watch.

She looked just like Laney. I pulled her out of the box, and held her up, and heard my dad make a sound like a cough. I looked at him, and saw him wiping his eyes.

"Merry sweetie, bring me your doll so I can see her." I got up and walked over to him sitting in his recliner, cradling the doll and crawled up on his lap. "Wow, she's a pretty little thing, isn't she?" My dad said in a cracking voice. I saw him glance over at Sophie, with this look on his face I hadn't seen before.

"What's that on her shirt, Daddy? It's pretty."

"It's a prism. White light comes in the one side, and the prism turns the light into a rainbow. It's an album cover from a band that Laney and I like." I saw him look over at Sophie again, and clear his throat.

"Daddy, look, her knees are scuffed up like Laney's used to get all the time. She looks just like Laney." I looked over at Sophie, and scooted off of my dad's lap and walked over to where Sophie was sitting on the floor. I kneeled down next to her, and gave her a hug.

"Thank you." I whispered in her ear.

"For what? I didn't do anything." But I felt her hugging me back, which was something she hadn't done in a long time.

"You gave me Laney. That was what I wished for when I blew out my candles. And even though I knew I couldn't get her back, you gave me the next best thing."

"I don't know what you mean," she said with a small smile. "Your doll came from Laney."

"I think she told you what I wanted. You're way better than Santa Claus any day, Sophie. He's scary."

I heard my dad laugh from his chair, and I sat back down next to her, with my Laney doll in my lap. We finished opening the masses of presents, and spent the rest of the day playing with the toys and trying on the clothes we got. I think maybe it was a Christmas miracle that it felt like it used to, even though Laney

wasn't there any longer. But, she kind of was again, now that I had my Laney

doll. I had no idea how she did it. Or who made it. But that doll was the best

Christmas present I ever received.

<u>Sophia</u>

It wasn't a big deal. And it wasn't totally my idea anyway, as much as I would love to take credit for all of it. During the time Merry was in the hospital, I spent my evenings with Mr. and Mrs. Jay. I loved them so much. They listened to me. I wasn't Sophie the Dramatic with them. I was just Sophia. Mrs. Jay taught me how to crochet and we were sitting there the one night and she asked what I had gotten Dad and Mer for Christmas, and I must have looked at her blankly. Being the great lady that she was, she tut-tutted, and bundled us both up against the cold Western New York winter. We went out shopping for everything from candy to clothes to toys to books. I protested that I didn't have enough money to pay for it. And I didn't. We weren't well off by any stretch and the money I saved from my allowance and babysitting I usually spent on myself. She paid for the entire lot after taking what little bit I had brought with me. As we packed everything into the car and started the drive back to her house, she turned to me.

"Sophia dear, I know this isn't easy on you, having your sister sick. But I want you to think of something every time you start to get upset or angry with her. She didn't ask for this. She's only 6, and she doesn't have your years or maturity behind her to help her deal with things. She needs you to be a big sister to her, and help her with things."

"Mrs. Jay, what about me? What about what I need?"

"Sophia, there will come a time when the only people in this world you can depend on will be your blood. Your father and Merry are all you have. For as much as they need you, you need them too. Your dad is struggling to make sure Merry is okay right now, and I know it seems like you're being forgotten about. I promise you, you're just as important as Merry is."

We pulled in the driveway to my house, and began to move all of the gifts and decorations to places I knew I could keep them hidden from my dad and Mer.

"Mrs. Jay?"

"Yes?"

"I know how much I miss Laney. But as much as I miss her, I know Merry misses her more. Laney was like a little mom to her."

"She was, probably because Merry is the youngest and you've got other things on your plate with school and such." I loved how Mrs. Jay never blamed me for wanting to have a life. She was diplomatic and that's probably why I would have done nearly anything she asked.

"I was thinking about what you said. Do you think we could find a doll that looks like Laney and we could dress her how Laney used to dress, so Merry could have Laney with her all the time? Maybe it would make her feel better." I think my question both startled and surprised Mrs. Jay. It was something I had been thinking about for a little bit. Probably since I saw Merry in that big hospital bed. I know it scared me to see her hooked up to all of the cords and tubes, but it must have been terrifying for a 5-year-old. I had thought if she had a doll that looked like Laney, maybe it wouldn't be as scary for her if she had to go in the hospital again, because it would be like Laney was there with her. It was somewhat childish logic, I'm sure, but it made sense at the time.

"Of course we can. We can put a little pair of jean shorts on her, and find a Pink Floyd tee shirt like she used to wear, and put her hair up in a pony. Oh, isn't that just a lovely idea Sophia! Come come, we simply must get back into the car now."

We hopped back in the car, and made our way to the local sewing shop to gather what we needed to make the doll. We couldn't find a small enough Pink Floyd shirt, but Mrs. Jay and I had gotten the supplies to paint the album cover from 'Dark Side of the Moon' onto the shirt, which was the album Laney used to play ALL the time. If I hear a song off the record now, it brings me right back to hearing her play that on my dad's 8-track player in the garage while he worked on the car, and she rode her bike. It was fun, spending that time together making the doll.

When we were done, and we sat back and looked at the doll, I started to tear up a little bit. Laney and I were so different from each other, but she was such a cool little kid. She used to let me put make up on her, and braid her hair. It didn't matter to her what we did, she just liked hanging out. I guess she was like that with Merry too, because she used to tell me how smart of a little kid she was. Merry would sneak books out of Laney's room and sit behind the couch or under the willow to read them and when Laney found out she would yell at her at for not asking to borrow it, but then sit there and talk about the book with her. Laney was always amazed how much she got out of the book, things she hadn't even thought of when she had read them herself, and would tell me that there were times Merry was reading books that Laney hadn't even read yet.

I knew Mrs. Jay was right about taking it easy on Merry. It just wasn't that easy for me. First I lost Mom, and then I lost Laney, and then to lose Merry and my dad to an illness was more than upsetting to me. I felt like an orphan. I have to say though, making the present for Mer and seeing her face when she saw it was from Laney and how carefully she held it, was enough for me. It sucked to have to grow up, and with as much as I'd lost, it wasn't easy for me to put that aside to think about how it affected Merry or my dad. I was just so damn angry all of the time. The anger fueled me. The only time I'd felt good since Laney died was doing the shopping and making the doll for Christmas. Guess there's something to be said for that.

*****

Christmas was over, and New Year's Eve was here. I was excited to see Betsy again after not seeing her for several weeks because I was sick and in the hospital. I couldn't wait to show her my Laney doll and tell her all about it. Since getting her, I spent my days carrying her everywhere with me. When I read my books, I sat her next to me with a book of her own, so she could read with me. Then, when I was done, we would 'talk' about the story and what we thought about it. While it wasn't like having the flesh and blood Laney with me, it was better than an imaginary friend.

Dad had started to calm down a bit with the carrying me everywhere, and had taken me to the store earlier in the day so I could buy Betsy a Christmas present, since I wasn't able to before. This time he took me to the local department store, where I could walk without being swept away from him. I wandered around and around trying to figure out what it was I should get her, and finally settled on a pair of froggie pajamas that had a kelly green long sleeve top with the eyes and mouth of the frog on the front, and yellow pants that had frogs hopping all over them. Since I had some money left, I got her a matching little frog pillow for her bed. We got home, and Dad helped me wrap it and we waited for Betsy and her parents, and Mr. and Mrs. Jay to come over. Dad had decided to let Sophie have a sleepover at her friend's house that night which was fine with everyone involved. Sophie had gone back to being Sophie the Dramatic after Christmas, although not quite as bad as she was before.

When Betsy and her parents arrived, she and I went into my room so she could open her presents. The look on her face when she opened the pajamas was priceless. She started laughing to the point she had tears rolling down her face, and I couldn't understand why.

"Merry, you don't know this, but I'm scared to death of frogs and toads. I mean I don't want to be anywhere NEAR them."

"Well, these aren't real frogs anyway. You can wear the pj's and use the frog pillow to keep the real ones away from you then!" My logic seemed sound to me at the time, and even now, I laugh about it every time I see a frog outside, thinking of Betsy tiptoeing around in her pj's warding them away from her.

"Here, open this!" Bets thrust a small present in my hands. I turned it over in my hands as she squirmed impatiently, and finally started to carefully unwrap the gift.

"Why are you taking so long? Just unwrap it already!"

"I like to save the paper." I muttered as I carefully unwrapped the box. Inside was one of those lock and key style diaries, in a baby blue color, with a matching pen and pencil.

"I thought you might want to start writing in a diary, and then I saw this one and I knew blue was your favorite color, so I thought you might like it."

"I love it! I can't wait to start writing in it." I was excited about the idea of being able to write down what little went on in my life, but more, to use it as a substitute for Laney. It was nice to sit there and talk to the doll, but writing it down seemed like a good way for me to be able to go back and read it after the fact. It was a great gift, and it became a form of therapy for me throughout the years.

We went downstairs, and showed her parents and my dad and Mr. and Mrs. Jay our gifts and drank Shirley Temples while we watched the ball drop with Dick Clark on TV. It seemed to be an indicator of things to come, that perhaps 1991 was going to be better than 1990.

I wish I could say that being home was the most fun thing I've ever had the opportunity to do. I wish I could tell you that it was the best idea my dad ever had, but in fact, it was probably the worst. At first, he thought he would be able to keep up with the coursework the teacher sent home, and we would sit at the dining room table and go through it every night when he got home from work, and I got home from spending the day with Mr. and Mrs. Jay. I learned quickly that while my father is one of the smartest people I know, he wasn't the best teacher. (Not a criticism, more of an observation.) His patience with how fast I was going through the exercises decreased as the amount of time it took me to go through them increased. He never yelled at me, but I could tell he was becoming exasperated when I didn't pick up on something the way he thought I should. There were many times I felt like telling him that I was doing the best I could without anyone teaching me the material, but I didn't think that was a good idea. I also felt like telling him that he could just send me back to school, but figured if I kept mentioning it, he would decide against it, much like he decided against things Sophie would harp on him about.

The weeks progressed, and the homework being sent home from school was becoming more and more difficult for me to get through with him. He even tried to enlist Sophie's help. Let's just say if my father was a poor teacher, Sophie was no teacher at all. She just yelled at me when I didn't get something right. The only reason I was doing decently with any of the work is because I spent the entire day with Mrs. Jay reading and going through certain exercises. I still don't understand why Dad just didn't ask her to take over, since she was a retired teacher. I know she offered. But I think Dad felt like this was something that he should do because it was his decision to pull me out of school. In practice though, it was a horrible idea. I was learning, yes, but it wasn't as easy as it had been for me when I was physically in school. And nowhere near as quick. While I was still advanced for my age in reading and comprehension, I was only barely keeping up with Social Studies, Science and Language Arts, and lagging behind in math. Back in 1991, there were no internet pages for my dad to go to and get lesson plans, or for me to do exercises on. Instead, he would go to school week after week picking up the following week's homework and dropping off the work I had completed. We muddled our way through, keeping both of our heads above water until the end of May, when a meeting was set up for the second week in June with the school to discuss my progress and talk about his plans for the following year.

It was no secret to anyone I talked to regularly that I wanted to go back to school. Bets, the Jays', Bets' mom. Thankfully I was able to keep in regular contact with Betsy throughout the year, and we spent most of our weekends together, with a sleepover (at my house only) every couple of weeks. We talked on the phone every night, and we would write each other letters that we would mail to each other, if for no other reason than to say that we got mail. At my age, that was a big deal, even if the letters were in crayon and had some major misspellings in them. Sometimes, we would draw each other pictures of this or that, and the other one would have to guess what it was we were drawing when we spoke next. (Bets, when you read this, go in the chest at the foot of my bed. I kept all of our letters. I had a few good laughs throughout the years reading through them!) To me, those letters were more than just two kids being pen pals. They were a lifeline to the world. Some semblance of normality.

Throughout the weeks and months that I was out of school, my heart didn't act up. I had doctor's appointments every other month, with blood taken monthly to verify that everything was the way it should. I wore a Holter monitor 3 times throughout the remainder of the school year, and while my heart wasn't normal by any means, it was considered stable on the medication. My dad attributed that to his decision of keeping me out of school, and showed no signs of making any sort of change for the following school year. He brought me with him to school for the progress meeting, and I stopped walking once I got through the front doors. He didn't realize I had until he was halfway down the hall, and turned to see where I had gone off to. The meeting was held after school, so the halls were quiet, and he called to me to come along so we weren't late.

"Daddy, I'm just trying to remember this, since I won't be back again." He slowly walked towards me, and I thought for a second he was going to be mad at me.

"Sweetie, it's for the best, you know that, right?"

"I don't think it's the best. I think the best would be for me to come back to school. I don't have to take gym! And I promise I won't run anymore, and I'll be super careful and make sure my heart doesn't break anymore, I promise!" I pleaded with him, with tears starting to pool in my eyes. I missed the smells, and I missed the structure, and I missed being around people who weren't always worried I was going to break or die. I missed every single thing about being in school. And I was just so tired of being at home all the time.

"Let's go to the meeting, Mer." It was then I knew I had lost the battle. He wasn't going to let me come back. It was hard for me to walk with him without dragging my feet, knowing that there was nothing more I could do. We got to the little meeting room where my teacher and the principal and another lady I didn't know was, and my teacher stood up, and came around the table to give me a big hug. She knelt in front of me and asked how I had been doing, and told me that she missed having me in class. I admit, I got a bit more teary-eyed at that, because she was a nice lady, and a great teacher. I was upset that, not only was I not coming back, but that I hadn't been in her class with her. She genuinely cared about her students, and had made a point when I started school to make sure I was settled in okay. She also knew about my heart condition as we progressed through the testing, and made certain to keep an eye on me throughout the day, and report back to my dad regularly how I was doing. It's one of those things that still bothers me a little bit to this day, that I had someone who was keeping an eye on me while I was at school, and yet, my dad wanted to keep me out of there. (Note - I have no kids, so I suppose I can't completely understand his reasoning.)

We sat down, and the adults went through my grades and the news wasn't good. I went from being near the top of the class before the mall incident, to being near failing. I wasn't failing yet, but it seemed like the general consensus was that without some sort of intervention, I would not be successful in the second grade. I know that's not what my dad wanted to hear. The school advised him they felt he needed to hire a tutor for me, and that would need to start immediately in order to prepare me for the second grade, and then to hire a home school teacher for the following year. I felt my dad deflate next to me. Even though I was just a kid, I had a feeling this wasn't something we could afford to do, especially with having to pay for Laney's funeral expenses, and my medicines and doctor's visits. My dad had a great job, with amazing benefits, but with only one income, there was only so much he could justify doing. I had assumed at that time, he would ask Mrs. Jay about taking over my tutoring, and sighed in my seat with my head down thinking of all that I was going to continue missing.

"If I were to send her back to school, what sort of assurances could you give me as to her health? Could we ensure to the greatest extent possible she wouldn't be overtaxed? She would have to be watched. All the time." Wait. . . what?

"Mr. Cameron, I can give you my word that all of the faculty and staff of Gilmore Elementary will be apprised of her condition, and of what to do should a situation arise where she needed medical attention. We will also have a discussion with the students in her classroom next year detailing what it means to have a heart condition, and what to do if they notice Merry having difficulty." I could hardly believe what I was hearing from the principal and my dad.

"Does this mean I get to come back to school in the fall? I can be with Betsy?" I was wiggling in my chair with so much excitement; I almost squeaked the words out instead of saying them.

"Would it be possible for Merry to be in the same class as Betsy Wright? She's aware of Merry's condition and knows what to look for." Well, that was news to me. It wasn't something Bets and I had ever talked about before, which was fine with me. I didn't like thinking about it, and wanted to talk about it even less. I had no idea she even knew the details of what was wrong with me, let alone had a conversation with my dad about what to do and what to look for if I didn't feel well. It wasn't something she ever brought up to me over these past several months.

"We will certainly talk about it with Betsy's parents, but if they have no objection, I don't have an issue with placing them together. I think having another student as support for her, especially in light of the loss your family suffered last year would be a huge help, and would probably relieve some of the stress you feel about placing her back into class. Are you planning on having Merry take summer school to bring her up to speed for the 2nd grade?"

"No, I'll make sure we buckle down and work hard this summer so she's not behind when she starts. My neighbor is a retired teacher and has been helping here and there, but I didn't want to place any sort of pressure on her to teach Mer. Perhaps in this circumstance, she wouldn't mind helping us out." The day just kept getting better and better! I wanted to bounce right out and run to the car so I could go home and call Bets, but figured Dad would get mad about that, so I just kept smiling until we left. Once we got outside, I gave him the biggest hug ever.

"Just promise me you'll be careful Mer. Your health is nothing to mess around with and if I start getting reports of you getting all wild and crazy, you're going to have to come home and let Sophie teach you math again." He said with a smile on his face as we got into the car. I don't think I could have promised any faster or with any more certainty that this was a promise I wouldn't break and jeopardize my chance to be back in school.

That summer was the best one of my life. I got up in the morning, and grabbed a book, and sat under my willow almost every single day, until Mrs. Jay would call me in for lunch. She would make me Kraft American cheese sandwiches on wheat bread with Miracle Whip, and slice up an apple for me to eat while I read my books until Daddy came home. I would spend my day alternatively reading and then writing in my journal, with my Laney doll at my side. For an hour or two every afternoon, Mrs. Jay and I would go through some of the school work that I had been given to prepare me for next year. Having her as a teacher was much more pleasant than Dad or Sophie, and I picked up much of what she said like a sponge in water. If the weather wasn't cooperating, I would sit in the bay window in the front of the house with my book, watching the rain drops race each other down the windowpane. The coolness of the glass felt wonderful against my head, and I'm sure there were times when I fell asleep book in hand, cheek pressed against the glass.

When Daddy would come home, he and I would go through the series of exercises for the work I had reviewed earlier that day. I think he was surprised how much easier it was once I was being taught the material, instead of just trying to figure it out as we went along. On the evenings and weekends, I would hang out with Betsy, much like we did during the school year, except without the constraints of having to make sure we went to bed at a certain time.

Despite my happiness at settling into a routine, and the freedom to be a little girl (albeit one with heart problems), I started to become conscious of certain things. Sophie wasn't home much, and when she was, she chattered on and on about all of these amazing things she was supposedly doing. Going to the beach, going to the mall, getting excited about getting her permit in October so she wouldn't have to ride her bike or depend on a ride, just generally being a teenager. For me, as much as I loved my routine and the things I could do, I started to find that there were things I missed. I missed the sound of Laney on her bike in the driveway or listening to her and Daddy talk about music or the car. Her bike was still hung on the garage wall, and every time I passed it, it seemed to cry out to be ridden. Of course, that wasn't something I could do. Her room was as it was when she left it that morning, the drawers still hanging out, and bed unmade. Dust had built up on her dresser, and I could see the sunbeams shining on the fading carpet. There were times I just sat in the sunbeam, on the floor with my back against the wall. I could forget for a minute that she wasn't going to come in and wonder why I was sitting there.

There were other things too. Laney was the little mom of the house, and especially now that the weather was nice, it was clear the housekeeping had suffered in her absence. The basics were done. Meals were usually whatever we had in the fridge slapped between two slices of bread, or cereal. Don't get me wrong, I loved eating cereal, and still resort to eating it when I don't feel like making anything, but it wasn't a real dinner. Laundry was done regularly out of necessity, but I know Sophie wasn't running the vacuum, and the one day I tried, it didn't go well. I could barely manage the beast of a thing, and I certainly couldn't get it up and down the stairs. The house wasn't ever dusted or wiped down. I remember Mrs. Jay coming in and she and I went around the house singing and wiping things down, but there wasn't much overall cleaning done since Laney died. It wasn't a priority and I suppose we were all lucky we weren't complete slobs.

I missed her. I missed her presence. I missed her laugh. I missed feeling like I was loved. Not that my dad didn't love me. But she loved me and took care of me as much as she could, and listened to me, but most of all just accepted me and let me be myself around her. I always felt like I not only had to act okay, but believe I was okay around Dad and Sophie, because there was so much scrutiny on every single thing I did all of the time. The closer I got to the anniversary of her death, the more I missed her. There were times when I would close my eyes and swear I could hear her riding her bike. Or hear her call to me and ask if I wanted scrambled eggs and bacon for breakfast. Or at night, when I was in bed, I could almost feel her lying next to me, reading me a story the way she used to.

How could it have been a year already? 365 days. That's an eternity to a kid, but it didn't change how I felt. That morning, I got up and went to the window and noticed it was gray out. It looked like a wicked storm was coming in, and I thought, well that's perfect. Almost like I wasn't the only thing in this world that felt sad about Laney not being here anymore. I kept wishing I would see her outside in the pending rain, candy cane striped umbrella in her hand being twirled around, and her feet in her bright red rain boots kicking up the puddles. I imagined her singing her favorite Pink Floyd song in the storm, without a care for how wet she was getting. I stood with my hands pressed against the window, almost hoping that I could keep the illusion up if I waited there long enough. How I wished she was there.

I heard someone walk into my room, and I hesitated to turn around, knowing if I did I would lose that vision of my sister in a rain that hadn't arrived yet. I figured it was my dad, and was surprised when Sophie kneeled down next to me to look out the window. She was already so tall like Dad, and towered over me normally. When she kneeled, she was nearly my height, and it was strange to feel her next to me on my level.

"I look for her too." She whispered, as though reluctant to break the quiet of the morning. I felt my eyes start to fill with tears, because not only was I not the only one who missed her, but I wasn't the only one who looked for her. "She would be mad at us that we were standing here looking for her, instead of doing something productive with our day."

Sophie was right.

"I can picture her stomping her foot, and yelling up the stairs that we were going to be late, even though we didn't have to go anywhere." I said smiling, picturing mornings when she used to do that during the summer when Sophie and I were still in bed. "Sophie, do you think she visits us? I could swear I feel her near me sometimes." I hoped this wasn't a stupid question, because I needed to know that I wasn't the only one who felt her near me.

"Awww Mer, I know so. I think she watches over all of us honestly. She makes sure you're taking all of those horse pills for your heart, and makes sure Dad remembers to eat, and makes sure I remember to do my homework. I think she keeps an eye on all of us." She said this so matter-of-factly that I broke my gaze away from the window to look at her. She had the dark chestnut brown hair of my dad, and his easily tanned skin tone, but her eyes were like mine, and our mom's. It was a shocking combination when you first saw how dark she was with these flashlight bright blue eyes that could cut through you like a laser beam. She had gotten so much older looking in this past year, and I could see even as a kid, she was going to be stunning once she wasn't so gangly and grew into her limbs.

"Promise me Sophie. Promise me we won't forget her. I'm scared I'm going to forget her when we grow up and we'll forget we were the Wee Three." I looked into those eyes like mine, and she looked back and nodded.

"We won't forget about her, Merry. She's a piece of us. Without her, we would have never known about your heart. She'll always be the filling in our Oreo, just like Dad said she was. Come on, kiddo, let's get you dressed and go downstairs, before we're late." She started to get up from her knees, but before she could, I gave her a hug. Having her on my level, it meant I could throw my arms around her neck like I did with Daddy and squeeze, hoping she knew how much I loved her. She squeezed back, and for a moment, I could swear I felt someone brush my hair on the back of my head. I'd like to believe Laney was there, and that she knew we missed her. I'd like to believe that.

This should be the time that I tell you how I went back to school, and on with my life, and everything was wonderful. It would be a lie. I went back to school in September of 1991, and I kept my promise to my dad that I wouldn't run or get excited or anything of that nature. It was as wonderful as I had hoped it would be, and I quickly regained the ground I had lost being off the year prior. In late spring of '92 near the end of the school year, I found myself outside in my yard after a particularly harsh winter, and decided it needed work. Dad was having Sophie's high school graduation party at the house, and the yard just looked barren. I couldn't play like the other kids did over the summer, so I took it upon myself to make my yard pretty. I could do the light work. Weeding, and planting flowers my dad took me to buy, while he did the heavy work of mulching and cutting in the beds. I had a clear vision of what I wanted, and my dad let me have my way, not questioning when I wanted a stone border, or an old raggedy bush pulled out. He just let me go. Probably because he could keep an eye on me, and what I was doing was more productive than sitting under the tree and reading and writing. It became my greatest accomplishment. Taking the barren landscape present after winter and turning it into a lush, vibrant, and visually arresting setting wasn't just a job for me to fill my time. It was a challenge. A puzzle. What worked? What didn't? How could I find things that made my gardens unique, and make someone who walked through it say 'Wow.'

I may not have been able to do the heavy work, but I could design and plan out a beautiful 4-season perennial bed by the time I was 9 years old with the help of my dad and the local library. It became obvious early on that I had rather grandiose ideas of what I wanted to do, and how that conflicted with what I could do based on the budget my dad gave me every year. I didn't get much of an allowance, which was fine since I couldn't do too much around the house. I dusted, and I vacuumed once we got a smaller vacuum cleaner, and did mine and my dad's laundry. $20 a month saved up in the 3 off seasons only translated to less than $200 and my dad would match what I had saved, and I had to make do from there.

I learned how to plant my gardens in a way where from the pop of the hyacinths and the tulips, to the last vestiges of stone crop and black-eyed Susans, they were always filled with color. I learned to pull the tubers from the dahlias I planted and put them in mulch in paper bags to plant next year. I bought flower and veggie seeds and through trial and error, got enough to grow so I didn't have to spend money on pricey plants that wound up dying at the end of a single season. I harvested the vegetables and fruits I planted, and made pickles and salsas and sauce and jams, and gave them away to the Jays, and Bets and her parents. My poor dad would take strawberry rhubarb jam and peanut butter sandwiches every day to work so as not to waste the fruits of my labor. And I sold the extras at a tiny little wooden stand under an umbrella, so I could buy more seeds and more plants the following year. It got to the point where I was so excited at the prospect of the planting season; I could hardly keep myself from starting my seeds in January, and would count down the days until I could plant them in peat pots and lovingly tend to them. It was something easy enough for me to do that was active, but not too taxing. And the overwhelming scent and sight of what I planted filled me with such pride.

Through the passing days, I still had the storm cloud of my heart hanging over my head. There were days when it was like I was never sick. And then, there were days where I was scared of what my body was doing to me. It seemed as though when it was cold, it was worse and my fingers and toes were perpetually chilly, and I had a harder time making it through the day because I was so tired. And when it was hot outside, during those dog days of summer, my energy levels were near non-existent. It was all I could do to muster the energy to lay under my willow, and I would wait until the cooler evenings to weed my gardens. Dad would watch me out of the corner of his eye when I got like this, and ask if I was okay. I would always respond that I was, and I was just tired. I didn't think about it. I didn't want to think about it. I suppose in some ways, I was lucky, because I had such little responsibility that I could just drop down and take a nap on the couch or under my willow. My dad would mention it to the doctor when I had my quarterly appointments, but there was nothing outwardly wrong with me and my tests were coming back as expected, so things were kept as they were.

I realize now that being tired was a symptom of my heart growing weaker. The meds I was on were working to an extent, but I was noticing more and more that my heart seemed to have instances where it skipped a beat, or worse, where it beat so fast I thought I was going to pass out. My toes were constantly cold. More often than not, my hands were too. I admit, I didn't tell my dad when this happened all of the time. I didn't want him to worry. I didn't want to be pulled out of school. But most of all, I didn't want to hear that it *was* actually worse. I could convince myself I was getting better when I wasn't having the symptoms, and when I did, I could just say that it was because I did this, or that.

Life has a way of intervening in ways you wish it hadn't. I had just celebrated my 11th birthday, and made it through the end of 1995, and looked forward to what 1996 could bring me, when my world turned upside down again. I woke up one night around 2 in the morning, to red and blue flashing lights on my wall. I wasn't the most solid of sleepers and had dreamt of sirens and ambulances, which woke me up. I guess it hadn't been a dream, because when I walked to my window that looked over Mr. and Mrs. Jay's house, I saw the ambulance from my dream. My dad was standing out front talking with a policeman, as the ambulance closed its doors and sped off. I went downstairs, as fast as I could, where I saw my dad come back in the house.

"Daddy, what happened? Who was in the ambulance?" I felt déjà vu wash over me. Hadn't we had a conversation like this before? At this exact spot, and near this exact time of night? How was this happening again?

"Sweetie, they took Mrs. Jay to the hospital" he said in a tired, almost weak sounding voice.

"Is she going to die like Laney did?' Hell of a question for an 11-year-old to have to ask her father, don't you think?

"I don't know, Mer. We'll know more in the morning. You should get back to bed, little girl. You have school in the morning." He picked me up in his arms, almost as easily as he did all those years before, and got me back into bed. I couldn't sleep of course. I had been through this before, and I had this awful feeling that it wasn't going to end well.

Morning came, and I still had no news before I left for school. I was a nervous wreck most of the day, and could barely stand to wait for school to let out for the day. Walking out to the car, I felt my heart start to drop. I only had to open the door and look at my dad to know that Mrs. Jay was gone. I sat down in the passenger's seat and just started crying. She was the closest thing I had to a grandmother and she was gone. My dad didn't say anything until we got home, and Mr. Jay was waiting for us, sitting on his front porch in the cold. I got out of the car, and ran over to him with my dad yelling at me to walk, and threw myself into his arms. Much like the comfort I received from my father's arms, I had always gotten that same sense of security from Mr. Jay.

"I didn't get to say goodbye to her, Mr. Jay. I didn't even get to tell her I loved her. We didn't get to finish our puzzle and I didn't get to tell her goodbye," I sobbed into his chest.

"Miss Merry, she knew how much you loved her. Her last thoughts were for you; did you know that? She told me before she went to bed how much she loved you and Sophia and how happy you made her. She didn't want to leave us, sunshine. It was just her time. She was getting pretty tired, and she hadn't been feeling well lately, so now she's in heaven with your mom and Laney and she's not tired or hurting anymore." He said this, as though he was trying to convince himself, rather than convince me, and I appreciated the gesture. It didn't change the fact that I had now lost another person who loved me. Another person I didn't get to say goodbye to, and who would no longer be in my life.

"Come now Miss Merry. Let's go in the house and have a glass of milk and a cookie before dinner time." He picked me up and walked me over to my house and into the garage, where we walked up the stairs into the kitchen. Sophie was sitting at the table with swollen eyes, an untouched plate of cookies in front of her.

"Why are we all crying so much? Mrs. Jay would be upset to know we were crying over her. She had a wonderful life and she had wonderful people in her life who loved her much. She would hate to see those people crying over her. Miss Sophia, what was your favorite memory of her?" Mr. Jay asked while pouring me a glass of milk.

Sophie looked like she wasn't going to answer at first. No longer the gangly teenager, she had morphed into this beautiful creature, who at nearly 6-foot-tall could look both Dad and Mr. Jay in the eye. But in her grief, she reminded me of the Sophie of 5 years ago, sobbing over her sister's death into Mrs. Jay's arms. Now, with no arms to comfort her, her grief felt more solitary, almost as though she didn't want to share it with us. Just when I thought she wasn't going to answer, she looked up at Mr. Jay.

"She helped me buy Christmas presents the first year after Laney died. We went to the mall, and went around from store to store, and got coffee. And she made your Laney doll, Mer. It was my idea, but she made it happen. There was no way I could have done that without her. She was so creative and crafty. She was willing to do anything for us. It was my favorite thing about her. She just loved us, just like we were her own." Tears started to make their way down fresh tracks on Sophie's cheeks. She wasn't looking at us, almost as if she did, she wouldn't be able to stand seeing our grief on top of hers.

Sophie used to make everything about her, and made sure everyone knew exactly how she felt. This was a different Sophie. She seemed to internalize her grief this time, and I didn't understand why. I couldn't get past the difference in her, and while I wanted to attribute it to her being older and growing up, I just couldn't reconcile the different Sophies that popped up all the time. It made me sad to realize how different things had become from that summer day 5 years ago. How far we had all come since then, yet, not far at all.

We buried Mrs. Jay on a cold, clear winter day in January. Sophie hadn't gone back to school for the semester yet, and Dad pulled me out of school so I could go. We stood by Mr. Jay, and he had his arms around both Sophie and I, and as the graveside ceremony ended, I remember thinking to myself how tired he looked. How old he looked. It was funny, I never thought of him as old until Mrs. Jay died. And now, I wondered how much longer we would have him in our lives.

Six months to the day Mrs. Jay died, Mr. Jay and I were sitting in his backyard drinking lemonade, and looking out over the fresh planting we had just done. It was one of those impossibly beautiful, idyllic, almost summer Saturdays. I had learned so much from him over these past few years and I looked forward to learning more from him as I got older, and a little more comfortable propagating my own seeds. We had discussed trying to graft roses at one point, but decided that would wait a few years until I was a little bit older and it wasn't such an adventure for me to hold such a sharp knife.

I was supremely content. I hadn't had any palpitations or extremely cold hands in a couple months now, and I finally felt like I was going to be okay. I was hanging out with one of my favorite people in the world, I only had a couple of weeks of school left for the year and I finally felt good. I would have even gone so far as to say I felt normal.

"You know what, sunshine? I think this year we are going to have our best gardens ever. It usually takes a couple of years for things to set in, and if the almanac is right, this will be a banner year for both of us." He wiped the sweat from his brow and squinted up at the sun, like he always did.

"Mr. Jay, why do you look up at the sun all the time? You're going to hurt your eyes!" My heart medication made me sun-sensitive, and I was always slathered in the highest SPF available, with a big floppy hat on so my head wouldn't get burnt, and sunglasses to make the summer sun bearable. I used to think it made me look ravishing like Audrey Hepburn, but in reality, I probably looked like a little kid who had gotten into her mother's closet.

"Well, Miss Merry, I look at the sun because it reminds me of Mrs. Jay. When we first met, she had the most beautiful blonde hair, just like yours. She was such a spitfire, and a fine dancer. And she loved the sun. I used to sing 'You are My Sunshine' to her, and she would dance around me while I did. She was a mighty fine dancer. You remind me of her, sometimes. She was always tickled that I called you sunshine, just like I called her." He took a large gulp of his lemonade after this, as though he wanted to say more, and didn't want to, at the same time. The deep-set lines of his face seemed deeper than ever, with the rivulets of sweat running down them, and for a moment, I felt a brief frisson of concern that perhaps being outside doing work as we had been wasn't good for his health. While he never discussed how he was feeling, I felt myself more conscious of his age lately. At times, I felt like I was older than 11, because of everything I had been through. While not quite a badge of honor, how many 11-year-olds could say they had a heart attack? With no more filling to the Oreo and a gaping 9 years between Sophie and I, I felt like I needed to act more mature in order to be taken seriously. This was one of those times where I wondered if what I was about to say would carry more weight if it came from Sophie or my dad.

"Mr. Jay, are you feeling ok? Is the heat getting to you?" Sophie probably would've made it about herself so as not to alarm him that she was worried about him, but I was more direct than her it seemed.

"No Miss Merry, I'm doing okay. We should discuss what we're gonna do in that corner bed in your yard this year. Last year's plants didn't fare so well in all that sun. Maybe a rose would work there." He stated this as he pulled out his ever-present spiral bound notebook and pencil from his breast pocket on his short-sleeved button down shirt. I could always count on him to be wearing a different color of the same shirt during the summer, with the buttons undone showing his old man tank top and whitish chest hair. His chest seemed redder than normal but my brain attributed it to the sun we had worked in and his assertion he didn't need anything stronger than the Coppertone SPF4 that came in the chocolate brown bottle and smelled of coconut. To this day, that smell brings me right back to his backyard, and the sight of a fresh-cut lawn next to the furrowed soil in his vegetable garden.

I never wanted that day to end. But soon enough, it did, and he went home after I gave him a big hug and told him how much I loved him. I made sure I told him every time I left him now, because you never know.

I'm forever glad I did that.

Chester Jay went to bed after having dinner with us that night, and never woke to see the beautiful Sunday that followed. He was found in his marital bed, having passed peacefully in his sleep. My father went to gather him when he didn't make it over for Sunday brunch, after noticing his car was still in his garage, and he wasn't answering the phone. I told him I would go and get him, thinking that he forgot what day it was, but luckily, Dad stopped me and went himself. I think my dad knew what happened.

He was an amazing man.

I still remember him every time I step outside into my back yard and see this year's incarnation of plants we planned. I see him in the tiny blooms of my heirloom cucumbers and in the sunflowers that sway back and forth in the breeze. And I see him in the sun, much like he saw Mrs. Jay, because he helped me grow and gave me guidance to make my yard the sanctuary it is now. It comforts me knowing he's up there with Mrs. Jay, Laney and my mom, waiting for me.

We live. We love. And we lose. It's a vicious circle. You can't fully live and not love. And once you love, you're going to lose. I had lost my mother before I knew her. I had lost my sister not long thereafter. Then Mrs. Jay. And now Mr. Jay, all before I hit 12 years of age. I suppose you could say I lost the ability to have a normal childhood as well. Lost the ability to move through life without worrying if my broken heart would stop beating and leave my dad and my sister without me.

I had felt the losses weigh heavily upon me summer of 1996. School ended shortly after Mr. Jay died, and with it, my desire to do anything that reminded me of him. I didn't want to plant or weed or reap or sow or anything that had anything to do with my gardens, because who was there but me to appreciate them? And not just appreciate them, but love them as I did? They became my neglected children. I didn't want them to die. And spending time with them was merely a reminder of what I had lost. I couldn't help but watch them wilt and crumble, like poking a bruise. I became more withdrawn than I had been before, sitting out on the back porch with a lemonade nearly every day, watching the slow decay of what I had built. My dad let me go on like this for a couple of weeks, doing the bulk of the work himself when I wasn't looking. I came outside one July day, and saw him out there digging a hole in the back-corner bed. The one Mr. Jay and I were going to plant this year.

"Stop it. Daddy, stop it. What are you doing? Stop it." I tried yelling at him, but couldn't get the words out. "That's my garden and I don't want you digging in it. Stop it RIGHT NOW!" By this time, I was becoming a little hysterical, feeling that familiar clenching in my chest that came from getting emotional.

"Sorry Mer. I have to get this rose bush planted in there so it has time to set in before winter comes."

"I don't want a rose bush there. I don't want anything there. That's my garden, why are you ruining it with your stupid rose bush?" I couldn't help but be upset. I didn't want anything planted there. It was my special project with Mr. Jay and now Daddy was ruining it.

"Merry Olivia, I'm surprised at you! Here I thought you'd love the rose that Mr. Jay helped me pick out for you to be the centerpiece of your garden. It's going to give you some gorgeous flowers." My legs gave out, and I sat abruptly in the mulch and dirt.

"Mr. Jay helped pick it out? Why didn't he tell me?" I started crying in earnest, throwing these questions at my poor dad like accusations.

He set the shovel against the fence, and sat down in the dirt next to me and put his arm around my shoulder.

"He wanted it to be a surprise for you. He knew you wanted to get more roses in the garden, and he had been searching for this one high and low. He died before he could get it for you, but I went and found his notes on it on his pad when I was helping clean out the house, and thought I would get it for you. It's called Always and Forever. It's a tea rose, and you're going to get long stemmed ruby-red roses. He said this one was just like the roses he used to give Mrs. Jay every year for her birthday and their anniversary." My dad's words were intended to make me feel better, but I just couldn't stop crying. This went deeper than just feeling sad over Mr. Jay's death. I was sad he wouldn't be there to see everything we created year after year. I was sad that Laney would never be there to see it. I was sad that I would never again sit on the porch with lemonade and listen to Mr. Jay tell me how Mrs. Jay reminded him of the sun. I was sad that I would never again sit with Mrs. Jay and make cookies for us to eat when I got home from school. I couldn't feel anything but sad anymore. My poor dad. I didn't melt down often. Actually, I don't know that I ever melted down, but here I was, sitting in the dirt in my ridiculous floppy gardening hat, next to a hole in the ground sobbing. I bet he wished he had boys more than once throughout the course of his life with us.

"Sweetie, stop crying. You know how upset Mr. Jay would be if he knew you were crying over him. How flustered he used to get, and then would reach and try to find his hankie to give you girls. He's probably getting all sorts of worried up in heaven looking down at you right now."

"Do you think they are all up there watching us? Mom and Laney and Mr. and Mrs. Jay?" I felt him hug me closer and my crying slowed a little.

"I do. I know it's hard right now. Just like it was hard after Laney's death. But one day, you'll come out here, and you'll smile knowing Mr. Jay helped you pick out your flowers, and helped you with your veggies, and it'll be okay. It'll never be how it was. But it will be okay, I promise. Now, come help me plant this rose bush, so I make sure it's exactly where you want it." He got up from sitting and went to grab the shovel again, and turned back to look at me. I sat there for a minute; my head bowed, and then pushed myself up onto my knees and started to look at the rose bush. It had glossy dark green leaves that looked like they were coated in car wax. There were seemingly a hundred buds on it, with some just about ready to burst, as I could just see the pinky red of the petals peeking through.

"Does it pass your inspection, Miss Merry?" I could nearly hear Mr. Jay ask as he watched me look over each part of the bush. I sighed, knowing the voice would only ever visit me in my head and looked up at my father, standing there in the beating sun shovel in hand.

"It's going to be pretty Daddy. Thank you for getting it for me. I just need the hole a little deeper so I can give the roots room." He quickly got the hole dug to my specifications, and we removed the rose from the plastic pot and went to work loosening the dirt around the root ball. Once I had placed the rose into the hole and we filled it back in and tamped the soil around the base of the plant, I stepped back to take a look at it.

"That's going to be one mighty fine bush, Mr. Jay. Maybe you can ask Mrs. Jay to make sure it gets enough sun for me, okay?" I mumbled, not wanting my dad to hear me.

My dad was right. Things were never going to be the same. And in the months and years to come, I would have settled for okay any day.

Time went on. Life progressed quickly and slowly at the same time. Sophie started her senior year of college, and I went into 7th grade. Betsy and I were still two peas in a pod, and I felt incredibly fortunate to have her in my life. It made living without Laney manageable. There were days when I would forget and go to her room to tell her something and only when faced with the empty bed and dresser which still had her headbands on it, did it come rushing back like a tidal wave.

It also made living with Sophie more bearable, especially since she decided she was going to go to law school. It was an admirable goal to have, albeit one I didn't quite understand, as I hadn't gotten to the point where I was going to think about my life after school. Sophie became a beast again, in the politest of terms. We were never quiet enough, despite the fact that I wasn't a naturally loud kid. It took too much effort and energy, neither of which I ever had. I had become incredibly weak. I tried to hide it, making sure my homework was done right after school or in school if I could manage it. I'd eat dinner, and fall asleep on the couch until 9:30 or 10 at night, when Dad would wake me up and I'd drag myself to bed. On Fridays, I would take a nap before Betsy came over, or I would go over there, just so I could be somewhat functional when we were hanging out.

Clearly, something wasn't right. The cardiologist I had been going to felt my fatigue was a symptom of growing pains and adjusted my medication according to the increasing needs of my body, since I was no longer quite as tiny as I once was. I wasn't an Amazon like Sophie, but I was starting to grow some legs on me, as my dad mentioned constantly. They were monitoring my heart, so I had a false sense of safety, and trusted them when they said I was as normal as I could be under the circumstances.

I turned 12, and just like that, 1996 was over. 1997 brought an end to Sophie's undergraduate college career. She had been an English major and received excellent grades all through high school and college, and applied to multiple law schools. She was accepted at several, but declined to choose any of them, and decided to attend the University at Buffalo's School of Law. I wondered about this on more than one occasion. Why would a girl with excellent grades, and a stellar LSAT score stick around and not attend any one of the multiple schools she got into? Why wouldn't she get away from here? Leave the painful memories and move somewhere she could start fresh? I think if I had been in her shoes, I would have more than seriously considered it, but I didn't ask. Not then. It was better not to poke the bear as finals approached for her.

I felt like shit. There's no way for me to sugarcoat it. I was always pale, but I became practically see through after the holidays. I had massive black circles under my eyes and I started getting questions from my teachers at school about my health. Luckily, Betsy's mom took me to the drug store and I was able to get some makeup to make myself not look so scary all of the time. I can laugh about it now, but I probably looked worse for a little bit until I finally got the hang on how to apply the blush and concealer.

Sophie's college graduation took place on May 17th, 1997. I woke up to a blinding headache, and my heart racing. But there was no way in hell I could miss the graduation. I took a shower, popped a couple of Tylenol and covered my dark circles with makeup, and hoped it wouldn't be obvious. I had no color. My lips were white, nearly blue in color. A little lipstick, just to offset that was in order. I had to find something to wear which wouldn't make it obvious that I wasn't feeling well, and picked out a pair of black dress pants, with a baby pink dress shirt. I made it down the stairs, barely. Hurricane Sophie was in full effect, and I was glad, because it took the attention off of how I looked and felt. We bustled into the car after a quick breakfast, and I settled into the backseat hoping my head would stop pounding before we got to Alumni Arena. And praying that the scary beat of my heart would calm down.

Dad dropped Sophie off in front of the Arena so she could go in and get prepared to walk, and drove us around trying to find a parking spot. I prayed he'd find one close, but seeing as how there was a ridiculous amount of kids graduating today, we were forced to park what felt like a mile away. The walk to the ceremony seemed interminable, like standing at the bottom of Mt. Everest looking up and thinking 'No way in hell could I get there'. But get there I did. We found seats, and I had to keep pinching the back of my thigh to keep from passing out. I had to make it through the ceremony.

Even today, I couldn't tell you what went on during the graduation. I couldn't tell you when Sophie walked. I couldn't tell you what any of the speakers said. I honestly don't remember any of it. I remember standing up, and starting the walk outside, making it to the parking lot and turning towards my dad to tell him I wasn't sure I could make it and that was it. Blackness.

Jeff

I suppose I'm glad Merry made it through Sophie's graduation before she collapsed. I can't imagine the shit storm that would have happened had we missed it. I know that sounds terrible, but I also know my eldest daughter. Graduation day was to be about HER. About her accomplishment in spite of everything that *she* had lost. I'd have given everything to see what Sophie would have been like if she had Liv here. And if Laney was still here. Would she be so hard? I would look at her some nights studying in the dining room, and she seemed much older than she was. She was driven to succeed; almost to the extent she was obsessed. I fully expected to hear that she was going to go away for law school, but she made the decision to stay local and go to UB for law school.

I think I know why. And I didn't ask, because I didn't want to bring attention that I thought she was staying because of Merry and I. She may not have been close to Merry, and I didn't think she understood Merry much, but she was the only sibling Sophie had left. I had tried to tell her that even though there was such a huge age gap between them that Merry was the only other person in this world who knew what it was like to lose Laney as a sister. Blood was thicker than water, and ultimately, Merry was going to be the last family she had once I was gone.

Mer, when you asked me to write this, I thought back to that. That I was going to be dead before you, and you and Sophie would be left. Your kids aren't supposed to die before you. I was 43 when Laney died and you were diagnosed, and I never thought for a second I would ever lose you too.

I'm sorry. Went off on a bit of a pity party there. I know why you wanted us to write about certain things. You wanted us to tell you what it was like. You wanted to learn what it was like from our perspective. Guess what baby doll? It fucking sucked. You're an adult now, and I can be bluntly honest. I knew something was wrong with you, more wrong than you let on, and more wrong than the doctors thought. You were so tired all of the time, but you never once complained. I think that comes from living with Sophie. Everyone knew when Soph was upset. Or sick. Or mad. But you just kind of went along with life, and didn't say much about how you felt. I always had to pry it out of you, and when you answered, you always said 'I'm okay, Daddy, don't worry about me' with this little smile on your face. Maybe I wanted to believe you and that's why I didn't push it. You were always so strong, so stubborn. You may not have been a hurricane like Sophie, but you were stubborn when you wanted to be.

I should have parked closer. Honestly, I didn't think about it. Sophie wanted to be dropped off because we were running late like usual, and parking was non-existent at the college. The graduation class was several thousand strong from what she told me, and from my parking spot nearly a mile away, I could believe it. You were so quiet in the back seat that I didn't think about it until I went to get out of the car, and saw you through the window with this pinched look on your face. I almost asked you if you were okay. But I didn't, because you saw me looking, smiled and said we better get up there before Sophie threw a tantrum. And out of the car you went, and started this slow but steady walk through the sea of parked cars.

Throughout the graduation, I would sneak a look over at you, and if you caught me looking you smiled at me. You usually have the sweetest smile, but this one was different. It was scared. I almost asked you again, if you were okay and did you need anything, but you looked away, and stared intently at the program. I should have gone to get the car for you afterwards, but you just got up, and started to walk out like nothing was wrong. It amazes me to this day, with everything you have going on inside of you how you just go. No excuses, no whining. You see what's in front of you, and you might sigh, but you just go. I think you got that from your mom to be honest.

You made it to the parking lot. Sophie was going out to lunch with her friends, so it was just you and I. I'm telling you, it's amazing you haven't given ME a heart attack. You didn't say a word; you just turned towards me, touched my arm and collapsed. Just thud and you were down on the ground. Smacked your head pretty good on the sidewalk. I'm glad it happened there, and not deeper into the parking lot where there weren't as many people, because I don't know what I would have done. A couple of the families that were heading to their cars stopped and one guy ran back in to have security call for an ambulance.

It was different but the same as the mall. You had no color to your face except for your lips which were blue, and you were clammy to the touch. Your breathing was shallow, and so fast. I was holding you in my lap in my arms which wasn't as easy as it used to be when you were little, and I realized your head was bleeding from when you fell. Where were Mr. Jay's hankies when I needed one? One of the moms had tissues in her purse leftover from crying at her child's achievement, so I packed those into the back of your head to try and stop the bleeding and waited anxiously for the ambulance. I kept patting your cheek, saying 'come on baby, wake up' but got no response.

I don't get it, Mer. Why did you want me to rehash this? Why do you need to hear how I felt? I felt horrible. I still feel horrible. I'll feel horrible until the day I die. There's no way for me not to feel horrible. I'd have given anything to have this happen to me and not you. I wanted to scream and rage at God for doing this to you. For doing this to us. I hated feeling helpless sitting there holding you.

*****

The ambulance came, and Dad and I were rushed to the hospital. I started to come to while we were on the way, but I felt foggy and out of it. Almost like when you get hungry, and your blood sugar drops and you can see what's going on around you but you're not able to interact with anyone and make any sense. This time was definitely different than when I passed out in the mall. I knew it was coming, and I don't know if there was anything I could do to stop it. The doctor in the ER seemed to think it had to do with my oxygen levels being low, which caused the short, fast breathing. What we didn't need him to say was that this episode was a sign that my heart was growing weaker. Not just that I was getting older and we needed to adjust my medication. We needed to go through another battery of tests to determine what was going on.

I was sent home after a day in the hospital with an appointment set up for an ECG, an echocardiogram, and a cardiac MRI. I had had the first two before, but never the MRI, which was supposed to give my doctor a clearer idea of what was going on with my heart. I can only imagine how much this would have cost my father in 1997, because I know how much it costs me *now* to go through this. We were incredibly fortunate to have excellent insurance through his union, but I know the medication, tests, doctor's visits and the emergency visits were a massive hit to his bottom line. I remember telling him not to worry, that I would get a job once my heart was fixed and I would give him what I made to help recoup the costs of my treatment. It sounds so naïve now, but I truly believed I would get better. I had to believe I would get better.

I went in for the tests the following week, and waited anxiously for my cardiologist to consult with one of the other doctors at the practice. It's frustrating how slowly time passes when you want it to go by quickly, and how you'd give anything for those minutes and seconds once you realize how little time you have left. The doctor called, and we had to go in for the appointment because they wouldn't tell us anything over the phone. I realize why they do that; however, I have to say that I still don't understand how my father didn't lose his job any of the multitudes of time he had to take off of work for me.

(Hey Medical Community, there has to be a better way to do this in the future, okay? We have to progress beyond this in-office notification and if you don't want to do it by phone, what about Skype, or some other sort of video conferencing? My sister can have a damn meeting on the internet, but I have to go in and be out in public when you give me bad news?)

But I digress. Getting a bit ahead of myself actually. (Is it just me, or is the pace of what I'm writing picking up? I feel like I'm at the crest of a big rollercoaster hill, and I'm just about to reach that point where I start rushing towards the bottom screaming bloody murder because I'm terrified.) I still firmly believed at this point that I was going to eventually be okay. That my heart was going to be fixed. And that I would eventually be normal. I was almost 13, not quite a teenager, but also, I was never really a kid.

The mood at the doctor's office was somber. Previously, I would walk in, and everyone was cheerful and always positive about what was going on with my heart and prognosis. This time was different. I remember asking my dad if everyone was having a case of the Mondays, and he gave me a rather forced laugh at that. Was everyone in a pissy mood that day? After what seemed like an endless wait, we were called back to the doctor's office, rather than an exam room. Well that was certainly new. My doctor at the time was a pediatric cardiologist, and his office was filled with jovial artwork from his patients, stuffed animals for the amusement of the kids while the consultation was going on, and a chessboard. I always wondered why the chessboard was in a different position than how it had been during my previous appointments. Today, I saw the white king lying down, and I wondered if he knocked it over.

"Well Mr. Cameron, we've gone through the scans, and reviewed all of her test results, and my colleagues and I believe Merry should start seeing an adult cardiologist from this point on," he rambled without so much as a 'hi, how are you.'

"Were you going to tell us why that is, or was this just going to be your proclamation without any explanation as to why?" Clearly my dad was as anxious as I was about the results of my tests.

"Mr. Cameron, perhaps we should allow Merry to step out of the room for a moment while we discuss what we found," the doctor wheezed out as his face turned deep pink. He looked like he was going to have a heart attack, and I felt like telling him it was a good thing he was sitting down, so he didn't crack his head on the ground like I did.

"Merry stays. I promised her long ago that I wouldn't keep anything having to do with her treatment or condition from her," my father stated bluntly with his arms crossed. I could tell he was starting to become a little frustrated with the lack of immediate information about what was going on with me.

The doctor looked at him. And then looked at me. He was a larger man, which seemed contradictory with all of his talk about how my diet was so important to my health. I wondered how many cheeseburgers HE got to eat while I was stuck munching on freaking carrots all the time. "Merry's heart is almost 50% larger than a typical heart of a child of her age. Due to the increased heart size caused by thickening of her heart muscle, her heart's ability to pump blood throughout her body is severely decreased. Currently, it's nearly 30% less than what it should be. We expect that will worsen if nothing is done. The thickening is causing her ventricle to be reduced so much in size that the blood is blocked from exiting her heart. She also has some thickening of her septum, which is bulging into her left ventricle, and is also blocking blood flow. We were aware of the left ventricle abnormality previous to this most recent issue as that's what is primarily seen in pediatric HCM cases, but the septum thickening is a new development. This is unfortunately something we were aware could happen, but were hoping that we would be able to preclude in her case."

I remember sitting there thinking that if my heart was 50% bigger than it should be, pretty soon, my entire chest would be filled with it. Looking down at my still relatively flat chest, I felt a bit of fear at the idea that my ribs would get pushed out of the way by the mammoth growth that was my heart. My father interrupted my ponderings, and I forced my attention back towards what was going on between the two of them.

"What exactly does this mean for her overall health? What do we do at this point? It's nearly impossible for us to keep her any more sedentary than she already is, and she follows the diet you placed her on with nearly zero deviation. She takes every single pill you've prescribed for her, so please tell me what the hell else we are supposed to do at this point?" Whoa. . . I hadn't seen my dad get so fired up, yet so calm at the same time before this.

"At this point, Merry needs to be seen by a cardiologist that deals with adult patients. She is of an age right now where her condition is likely being affected by her going into puberty. While HCM can be managed by what you're doing, and some patients don't have any further symptoms or episodes by staying the course, that isn't the case here. Merry's heart is unfortunately getting worse, and I would feel more comfortable having her treated as an adult, with a cardiologist who deals with HCM on a more regular basis than I do here," he said with finality. My dad sat back in his chair, and I could see how badly he wanted to say something and didn't. It was then I could see where Sophie got her fire from, even though he refrained from saying what it was he was thinking. For the first time, I could understand where that could be a benefit, instead of a detriment, because I was still stunned at the idea that my heart was so enlarged.

"Doctor MacPherson, can I ask a question?" My voice seemed squeaky from disuse when I spoke up, but I had to get something off my chest.

"Of course you can, Merry." Deep breath.

"At what point does my heart become too broken to fix?" I was trying not to get upset at this question, but after hearing and understanding what was going on during this consultation, I couldn't help but wonder at what point they would start giving up on me.

"Merry, I can promise you something. The doctor I am referring you to is the best in this area. He's well-informed and concerned with making sure each of his patients has a good quality of life. He will fight to keep your heart working for as long as you fight with him."

I didn't understand the gravity of that statement then. But I do now. Sometimes, you can fight to the death. But ultimately, the fight ends in death. Whether you're 9 or 12 or 35 or 80. It doesn't matter. We all die.

I didn't like my new doctor.

He was brusque. Cold. Blunt. Talked over me as though I wasn't there. And he didn't look me in the eyes. He treated me as though I was a broken heart. Not as though I was Merry with a broken heart. His clinical approach was so different than my previous doctors that I immediately detested and resented having to deal with him. However, my father LOVED his approach. There was no bullshit with him. He came right out and advised my father that my diet wasn't going to cut it anymore, and the medications I was on were older and not what was currently being subscribed to adult patients. I wanted to insist that I wasn't an adult, but my physical age didn't seem to matter with him. What mattered was that my heart was broken and it was his job to fix it.

My medication was immediately changed. My diet plan was evaluated and revamped. I had to keep an exercise diary, which was laughable because I didn't exercise. But I had to log how many minutes a day I walked, or gardened or did anything other than breathing it seemed. I wore the Holter every other week for nearly two months through summer of 1997, as they tried to determine what meds were working and what exactly I was doing that made my heart act up.

This process went on through the end of 1997, all through 1998 and into 1999. It sucked. I felt like Mr. Jay, having my little notebook with me all the time. When Betsy would come over, we would doodle in the margins, in an effort to make my notebook less of a chore and more of a masterpiece. I began to resent the intrusion into my daily life. I could usually make it to school in spite of everything, and keep my grades pretty decent, but it was a struggle.

At yet another monthly doctor's appointment, with my father in the waiting room, the nurse had the gall to ask what consistency my bowel movements were, and what differences there were as though relaying this information to a complete stranger was normal. Even though I was used to the indignity of having to bare my chest to everyone and their brother, this was by far more intrusive than I felt comfortable with. I sat there, stone-faced as she insisted she needed to know this information for the chart. Every answer was written in the damn chart, and I had no idea what the damn chart even said, because half the time it seemed as though way more or way less than what I was saying was being transcribed into the damn chart. I was done. DONE! She wasn't getting another answer out of me and there was nothing more that she could do to convince me otherwise.

She walked out of the room in a huff, and I was left to sit there in a thin paper gown, shivering in the chilly exam room. I contemplated getting dressed and sneaking back out to my dad, and had just about convinced myself that I should, when the door opened and the doctor walked in. I can say now that he was an attractive man physically. As a 14, nearly 15-year-old, I didn't see the salt and pepper hair as anything but old, even though he wasn't more than mid 40's. He was tall, and imposing with these deep-set hazel eyes that were always intense but never warm. He scared me. Not because I felt he was mean, but because I felt like he didn't care about me as a whole.

"Ms. Cameron, I understand you decided against giving the nurse information she requires for your chart. May I ask why?" His voice was nearly monotone; as though he was reading from a set of questions they give to doctors showing them how to interact with patients. I admit I wasn't feeling polite at that moment.

"I am sick and tired of being ignored when I come here. You don't treat me like a patient. You treat me like a condition," I spat out at him. "My old doctor used to look me in the eyes, and tell ME what was wrong with ME, and all you do is talk over me like I'm not even there. Last time I checked, I was the one who had to deal with my condition. The least you could do is treat me like I'm human instead of some organ." My voice got increasingly loud with every word, until I felt like I was almost screaming.

That certainly made him look at me. Grabbing the chair across from the exam table, and putting my clothes that had been neatly placed on it on the floor, he sat down right in front of me. From my perch on the table, he sat below me. It was a strange sensation, and the first time I had a doctor do that in all my years of going through treatment.

"Merry, let me be honest with you about something. Other than your family, there is no one that is more concerned with your health and well-being than I am. My complete focus is on making you better. I am aware that some of the questions you have to answer are more in-depth or even more personal than you've had to answer before. I'm not going to apologize for that. The answers to these questions aren't just written down on your chart and that's the last they're dealt with. With your condition, in many cases, certain seemingly unrelated answers to these questions give us the ability to know how the medicine is not just affecting your heart, but the rest of your organs. It can tell us prior to you having an episode of syncope, that you could be heading towards an episode if we continue down that same path of treatment. It can tell us if there is anything else we have to be concerned with, like a side-effect that affects you differently than it would affect an adult because of your size and age." He paused here, and looked at me when he said, "Merry, your case is serious. I don't want to lie to you. I'm going through all of these tests, and all of these questions in an effort to find a way to keep your heart beating. If my staff and I are asking you a question, it's for a good reason."

"Then why aren't you talking to ME about it? You talk over me. Above my head. You never say my name. I see your nurses more than I see you. Your bedside manner sucks," I said rather vehemently, and then thought, 'oh I shouldn't have said that' as I realized I sounded like a brat.

"You're the youngest patient I currently have, Merry. By almost 10 years. Your case is complicated, because of the history of sudden death in your family, combined with the significant and recent worsening of your heart's output. I'm not used to dealing with someone of your age, coming in with his or her parent. I'm used to dealing with adults. That's not an excuse," he clarified as he sat back in the chair. "It's a justification, I suppose, that I'm learning you're not like them. Both in personality and in your treatment."

I hadn't considered that I was the youngest patient of his. I didn't understand until much later that when kids died from this condition, it was just sudden, and then that was it. Most of the time the cause either wasn't immediately identified, or it was a one-off event. I learned much later on how many adults died suddenly from this. And more recently, I've learned how frequently athletes die from it. Both Laney's and my mom's death placed a spotlight on Sophie and I early on, and in some ways, I was grateful for that.

"Can we work together through this?" Dr. Scanlon's question brought me back to the exam room, and I took the briefest of seconds to contemplate what he asked.

"We can, but only under one condition. No more BS." I was feeling rather ballsy by this point.

He laughed and nodded.

"No more BS. You help me, and I'll do my best to be a bit more conscious of the fact you're still just a kid."

"Well, Dr. Scanlon, I don't know if I have ever been just a kid. And I am almost 15 now. Going on 9 years of dealing with this," I replied.

"Merry, tell me something. What do you want to be when you grow up? What do you want to do more than anything else in this world?" Wow. I don't think I had ever been asked that question before.

"I want to be an adult. I want to live longer than my mom did. I want to have a little girl, and name her after my sister. But mostly, I just want to be an adult. I can make career decisions when I get there. I just want to get there first." I believe that was the first time I had vocalized the fear that had been growing over the past few months that I was going to die young like my mom and my sister. I don't know if he expected that answer from me.

"I can't promise you anything more than I will do my best for you. That's all I can say. I need you to be completely up front and honest with me about everything. If my nurse asks you a question, as uncomfortable as it may be, act as though it came from me, and know it's for a good reason. If you don't feel well, you need to tell your dad, or you need to call me yourself. No more hoping it goes away and telling everyone you're okay. Your heart is not strong enough to withstand attacks like the one you had at Sophie's graduation on a regular basis and we need to prevent them, rather than dealing with the aftermath," he warned. "Now, do you have anything else you want to discuss with me, before I send my nurse back in to finish getting what she needs from you?"

I told him he could send her in, and I don't quite know what he said to her, but she was a bit kinder on her re-arrival in the exam and we got through the questions as quickly as we could. Having an understanding as to why they were being asked made me feel better about having to answer them, even though it was still embarrassing for me. We made it through though, that time.

The appointments were a constant in my life. I could ensure I would have at least one a month, when my dad felt I was looking a little more Violet Beauregard than normal or when my blood pressure was outside of my baseline. I turned 15 in the midst of this flurry of appointments, and started the new year back at the doctor's office for my year-end review, as I liked to call it. I was becoming quite sarcastic as I aged, and my personality was definitely that of someone who had 'been there, done that,' and wasn't interested in revisiting whatever IT was again. I got through the litany of diagnostics and chit-chatted with the nurse at how I could probably save her the trouble and just do them all myself. My dad was called back in, and we sat there waiting for the doc to go through everything.

The news wasn't what I had hoped for. Despite the different medication, the revised diet, the exercise journal, keeping me quiet as a damn church mouse, my heart was showing signs of worsening. While I hadn't had any further attacks, I was exhibiting symptoms of ischemia in my heart itself, which was the cause of the almost daily chest pain I had long become accustomed to as being 'normal'. My skin was always mottled and blotchy, and my fingers, toes, and lips were more often than not, tinged blue. I had become rather adept at covering up these signs, which I had again attributed to the normality of my situation.

We were at the point in the treatment of my condition where something aggressive needed to be done. My idea of aggressive was some sort of clinical trial, but my Doc Scanlon didn't think that was a great idea for me. His idea of aggressive was intervention in the form of a surgical cardiac septal myectomy. It meant an open-heart surgery where my heart was stopped, cut open, and the overly large septum was dissected to allow my left ventricle to have more room to function more normally. I say more normally, because my heart wasn't just enlarged in my septum, but also had a thickened left ventricle wall.

My first thought was hell no. My second thought was HELL NO. (If I could, I would have those words in flaming red font that jumped off the page to fully express how I DID NOT WANT TO HAVE OPEN HEART SURGERY.) The idea of having my chest opened, and my heart carved like a thanksgiving turkey was not one I was willing to consider at all. Even at the cost of saving my life, because I was certain there was something else that could be done. There had to be something else that could be done.

This was before the Internet we have today, boys and girls. That meant there was no ability to Google my condition and see what some hospital or doctor across the country was doing for my condition. There weren't chat rooms or online forums I could go to and inquire how other patients were dealing with HCM and its fabulous side effects. I could go from doctor to doctor, taking time and money and come up with similar responses, or I could trust the doctor I had. While I wanted to trust Dr. Scanlon, I wasn't willing to take the huge step of having this surgery just yet.

"Is there no other treatment available? What happens if I don't have the surgery?" I whispered. Dr. Scanlon looked at me, and I couldn't tell what he was thinking, but I could sense he was disappointed in my question.

"There is a treatment that was developed in England that is being introduced into the US now. However, I don't know that I feel comfortable with this treatment over the myectomy. It's called alcohol septal ablation. A catheter is inserted into your vein, traced to your heart and alcohol is injected into the septum to essentially kill those abnormal heart cells. It induces a heart attack. It's less invasive, but the complications are different than those stemming from the myectomy. If your septum is not thick enough, there is a risk the alcohol will get into tissue they don't want to kill. There is a risk of stroke. The procedure is currently only done in a few hospitals, and you have to meet certain criteria in order to be considered. The myectomy is a better choice, because the offending tissue is removed. With the ablation, you'll have a scar on your heart that theoretically could raise your risk of a severe cardiac event." With this, he paused for a moment. He looked at both my dad and me. "Merry, I'm going to be quite frank with you. The myectomy is the best option right now."

"How long will she need to be out of school for the surgery? And how quickly does she need to have it?" I looked to my dad as he asked these questions gratefully, because I hated the idea that I was going to be have to miss school, possibly to the extent of screwing up my ability to pass 10th grade. I was starting to consider what I wanted to do for college and the extended absences would certainly hinder my grades.

Dr. Scanlon picked up my chart and pulled out a graph he had made detailing my progress, or regression I suppose in this case, of my cardiac output.

"Mr. Cameron, as you can see here, there has been a steep drop-off of Merry's heart's production from when I first took her case until now. There isn't much more room for it to drop further before we start to see neurologic issues, severe circulatory damage causing tissue damage and a greater risk for sudden heart death. I would recommend we do this sooner, rather than later. If your heart continues to weaken, Merry, you're going to wind up in congestive heart failure. It's not a matter of if, but when. At that point, you would need to be evaluated for a heart transplant. Once that happens, there is no guarantee you'll live long enough to get a donor heart."

Shit.

Even writing that now, all these years later, I still remember how fucking terrified I was. I remember wanting to scream how unfair it was. I still do.

I was 15-years-old. Open heart surgery at 15. It was at that moment I stopped believing I was going to be ok. I stopped believing in there being a tomorrow for me where I was going to be ok. Where I was going to be normal.

<u>Betsy</u>

When Merry told me they were scheduling her for open-heart surgery, I thought she was kidding. We were both 15, and young enough to want to rule the world, and old enough to realize we had some work to do to get there. I was always more of the optimist than she was, I admit. And I don't know why that was. We had been friends for nearly 10 years at this point, and I had been there through everything she had gone through up until that point. I couldn't imagine not having our Friday night sleepovers. I couldn't imagine not being in her classes. Even in high school, the district made some pretty unusual concessions to keep her in school, including the manipulation of both of our schedules so I could be there for her. On more than one instance, Dad Cameron asked me if I minded. I still remember exactly what I told him.

"Why on earth would I mind? Merry is my best friend." I replied to him, matter-of-factly. And the truth was that I didn't mind a bit then. I'm not saying that I'm some altruistic saint by any stretch. I'm definitely not a hero in this story. She wasn't the easiest person to be friends with. Where she was quiet, I was loud. Where she was content sitting there not doing much, I wanted to be doing something. I felt the need to perpetually move and she would sit as still as a statue. But when we were together, it just clicked. Over the years, we had become so comfortable with each other's presence that we just did stuff. It was strange that two people, who were so different from each other, were so utterly complementary. We balanced each other out so perfectly. We still do. She makes me stop and think, and for her I'm there for her and I'm not Sophie. I'm not Laney either, but I don't think she ever wanted that. I don't think anyone could ever be what Laney was to her.

The thought of open-heart surgery terrified her. She had the appointment where her doctor told her she needed it in end of January of 2000, and it was scheduled for February 18th. They originally offered the beginning of the week, and she adamantly opposed that. Said it was cliché for her to have heart surgery on Valentine's Day. And looking back now, I tend to disagree with her. I think it would have been kind of awesome to have it then. Conversation starter to say the least!

But she wasn't like me. She didn't want more friends. She didn't want anyone else in her life than the people that were already in it. She would rebuff anyone who tried to talk to her in school. She wasn't rude, but she wasn't friendly either. She would answer questions with just enough of a response to fulfill the request without the need for any follow-up, and that was it. She didn't care who talked about her, and she certainly didn't care what people thought about her. People did talk about her, mainly because she just wasn't like everyone else. She didn't much care how she dressed; as long as what she wore covered her nearly see through skin. She still wore the heavy foundation and dark lipstick and I'm sure some people thought she was just weird. I could've easily been tarred with the same brush, but I would like to think I acted as a mediator between her vault-like silence and the judgmental masses. An interpreter of sorts. One who couldn't tell the people she was talking to exactly what the other person was saying, not because she didn't understand, but because she knew they wouldn't understand. Kids don't comprehend loss until they've dealt with it. Merry had been dealing with it since she was born and it changed her. Not just the loss of her mom and sister, but the loss of who she could have been had she not been hampered by this defective heart of hers.

The closer she got to the surgery, the more upset she got. If you didn't know her, you probably wouldn't think anything of it, but she was agitated. As I'm sure anyone would be, but Merry doesn't get agitated ever. She's the most even-keeled person and that's because that's how she's always had to be, to keep her heart from acting up. This was different. She looked like she was on the verge of crying nearly every day. Her eyes darted around nervously whenever she didn't have something to do, as if cataloging everything around her. She didn't want to talk about it. At all. I knew Dad Cameron talked with her teachers and somehow smoothed out the fact that she was likely going to be out of school for a month or more. For her, it was like going into isolation and I knew that even though the surgery worried her like nothing else she had gone through; the idea of being alone for a month in the hospital was almost more than she could take. Strange for a girl who wasn't known to talk much and didn't have many friends right? Merry, I know you probably hate that I'm writing this. But you lived vicariously through her people watching. You were constantly watching everyone you came into contact with. Not in a creepy, voyeuristic sort of way. But in a sad, 'I wish I could do that' kind of way. Back when we were in grade school, you'd sit at the edge of the playground on the benches they had there for the parents, and just watch everyone. You had promised your dad you would stay still, and still you would stay. I told you to tell people that you had a bad heart, so they understood why you weren't participating in anything, and the answer you gave me resonates with me even now.

"I don't want anyone to know I'm sick. People pity sick people. They pity sick kids even more. And then, they want to know more about what's wrong with you. Why you can't do this, or what the prognosis is, or if you're going to die. I'd rather them think I'm weird for not talking to them, than pity me and want to know more only to fulfill their morbid curiosity when they don't give a damn about ME. I don't need them in my life, Bets." Hard to argue with that logic.

When you spend so much time with someone doing nothing much at all, you learn things about them. You learn their tells. I may not have gone through what she was going through physically, but at times, I felt how she was feeling emotionally. Sometimes it oozed out of her and I don't think she realized it or she probably would've hidden it better. She did this thing with her eyes where she was seeing things around her, but then it was as though she was seeing right through them. I suppose to some people it looked as though the lights were on and no one was home, but to me it was her own 1000-yard stare. She would lose herself in her head, imagining that she was the one on the swings. That she was the one dancing. That she was the one playing baseball in the summer. Her breath would catch when she realized that she'd been gone awhile, and she'd shake her head just the tiniest bit to clear it, and then she was back.

Bet you didn't know I knew you were doing that, did you Mer? As much as you hid from everyone, you never could from me.

*****

The morning of the surgery I felt like I was going to throw up and pass out at the same time. Apparently, that was normal for someone going through what I was about to go through. Lovely! I was finally NORMAL! It only took 10 freaking years.

They could have their normal back. I didn't want to do it. I didn't want to have a scar on my chest. I didn't want to have a piece of my heart removed. I didn't want to die.

And that was just it. In order to not die, I had to have the surgery. I couldn't even drive yet, and I had to have my heart cut open and apart. Appropriate, since my heart had been broken since I was 5 and lost Laney, and then Mrs. Jay and Mr. Jay. This wasn't fixing anything. It was putting a Band-Aid on an amputation and eventually, I would bleed out.

Jeff

The day Merry went in for surgery was scary for me. The doctor kindly scheduled it for a Friday, so I only had to take a day off of work, and would give Sophie a chance (I had hoped) to come visit her. It also meant that Betsy would be able to spend the weekend with her, and get her ready to be in the hospital for the next couple weeks.

She was as quiet as I had ever seen her. She looked like she was walking towards the gallows, or the firing squad. I had faith that her doctor was going to bring her out of the surgery better than she was before. But she's my baby. There were several times over these last 10 years where I thought I had lost her, or was on the verge of losing her, but this time, I felt like I was the one walking her into the lion's den covered in steak.

I don't think she believed she would come out of it. Betsy told me Merry was telling her she expected not to come out of the surgery, not because the doctor wasn't talented, but because she knew her heart was that bad off. She could feel it in her chest that her heart wasn't right and she didn't think it would ever be right. I have to give Betsy credit. Most teenage girls take their best friend's secrets with them to the grave, but I think Bets knew when it came to Merry's heart that I needed to know because Merry wouldn't say anything. She didn't want to be a bother. I hate that she thought she was, ever. And it didn't seem like anything I said or did could convince her of any different notion.

When they wheeled her back and through the doors of the operating suite, Bets started crying. I hadn't ever seen her cry in 10 years of being Mer's best friend. I put my arm around her and hugged her to my side as she just stood there sobbing. Times like that, I wish I had Liv here.

*****

I woke up from the surgery in recovery, and felt like I had an elephant sitting on my chest. Not because of my heart, but because I had about 2 inches thick of gauze padding covering my incision. I had a tube in my throat and I had to fight a bit with myself not to panic about it. I wasn't in pain, and felt terribly dazed. I closed my eyes to try to rest some more, and when I woke up, I was in my room in the Cardiac ICU, and Dad and Bets were there. I didn't realize it at the time, but I had been in surgery and then recovery for nearly 9 hours. It was dark by the time I was awake, and was able to realize that I was starting to hurt. A LOT. My chest felt constricted, and while it wasn't how I normally felt, it was scary.

Jeff

Doc Scanlon told Bets and I after almost 6 hours that the surgery went as expected. He said her septum was the thickest he had seen in all of his years of practicing, and he was surprised her cardiac output was as high as it was with the amount of obstruction she had. He also mentioned that her left ventricle was severely thickened, and while this surgery fixed the septal abnormality, she still had to combat the effect of that on her overall health. The doc didn't want to remove any more heart mass after dissecting as much of her septum as he had, so he had left her ventricle the way it was. Dependent on how everything wound up, she would likely still be a candidate for a pacemaker or cardioverter defibrillator since she still had the ventricle deficiency.

Poor kid. Can't catch a break at all. I'm not saying I expected this surgery to be the magic elixir that cured her. But I admit, I thought it would fix most of the issue, and she could just medicate for the rest of it, like she had for years before this.

When they brought her to her room in ICU, I almost lost it. She had all these tubes coming out of her, three from her chest, one from a catheter, a couple of IV lines and had a trach tube in her mouth where she was being ventilated. Her chest was covered, but you could tell there was a ton of gauze on it, because it looked like a pillow under the sheet. Her eyelids were so pale; I could count the veins in them. It was strange to see her without all of the makeup on that I knew she used to cover her face. I never said anything. I knew it was her way of dealing with her illness and I didn't mind. She looked so damn young lying there in that bed. I know she was 15, but for a minute, I flashed back to seeing her in the hospital when she passed out in the mall. She filled out more of the bed this time, that's for sure, but she still had the softness to her face that indicated how young she was.

I had called and left a message for Soph at her apartment letting her know Mer was out of surgery. I wasn't surprised she wasn't there. She was never there, and even though I knew she was busy with law school, I was surprised she hadn't checked in to see how her sister was doing. Maybe I wasn't that surprised. Sophia hadn't been the sister I had hoped she would be for Merry, the one she could depend on, or go to for those situations I couldn't help her much with, being a man. Soph had grown into this beautiful and accomplished woman and I was proud of her for that reason. I loved her, but I didn't like her much. She was hardened. Abrupt and almost elitist in how she acted. Not quite that she was better than us, but that she looked at what we were, or more to the point, where we were in our lives and realized that she was beyond that. In some respects, I couldn't blame her. She had built herself from scratch and had every right to be proud of what she had become. So damn smart. I just wish she realized how important it was to hold onto those ties at home. She had become incredibly contradictory in recent conversations where it felt as though she was arguing just for the sake of arguing rather than actually believing the point she was trying to make. It was frustrating for her to try to argue with Merry in those few instances she spoke up, because Merry just didn't care enough to fight with her.

I was worried that Merry didn't care enough. She had been restricted so much these past 10 years that there were times when I wondered if she wasn't telling me when she wasn't feeling well because it didn't matter if she was healthy. She was going through the motions these last 18 months or so, and when she smiled, it didn't reach her eyes. She was quick to let you know she was fine, because she didn't want you to worry. But she wasn't ever happy and nothing I could do could change that. I couldn't fix her heart. I couldn't make her better. I'd have given her my own heart if I could have.

Betsy

My best friend is a fucking gladiator. She came out of the myectomy like a champ, waking up in the ICU and motioning to get the trach tube out. She wanted nothing of it. She had a morphine drip, and for as much as I was there, I never saw her use it. I found out later on in that hospital stay that she felt strongly about not using the pain meds, because to her, she would have this false sense of feeling better. I'm a 'damn the torpedoes and give me the pain pills' kind of girl, but not her. I'm not sure if that's because she's been in varying amounts of pain throughout her entire life, and her tolerance was just that much higher than mine was. To me, she was amazing.

I was there every day, as much as I could be. When the nurses tried to kick me out, I would hide in her bathroom, and wait for them to leave, and then just sneak out to sit with her. Dad Cameron told me the nurses knew what I was doing, but because I seemed to be helping her spirits stay up; they turned a blind eye on it. She was determined to get out of the hospital as soon as possible. Her doctor told her it was likely a week in the hospital and then a week in a rehab facility, but she told him she didn't want to go to the rehab facility and would rather just stay in the hospital. I know why she said that. She didn't want to be somewhere I couldn't come visit her. (Is that egotistical of me? I don't think so!) Luckily, the hospital she had the surgery in had a rehab wing, and while it was filled with old people, it was still better than being sent somewhere else.

The first time they changed her dressing, I was there. I almost shrieked, it was so horrifying to me. She had this massively angry red incision held together by metal staples running from the notch in between her collar bones, to about 4 inches above her belly button. She looked at me when I gasped.

"Guess I'm going as Frankenstein for Halloween this year, huh Bets?" she commented weakly without much humor in her voice. I know she had gotten used to baring her chest to the various people that she had come in contact with over her journey to this point, but I was still shocked. How the hell did someone live through having their chest sliced open, their ribs spread apart and their heart cut into? How was she so fucking calm about having all that hardware in her skin and in her chest? And how the hell was she going to wear a bra? I was 15, and rather healthy in that area so the idea of not being able to wear one was a big concern.

I must have stopped talking much, because once the nurse and doctor left, she threw her ice chip cup at me. It was a weak throw. I mean, the girl just had her chest cut open, but the intent was clear.

"Hey, stop it," she croaked.

"Stop what?" I replied, wiping my eyes a little bit.

"I'm still Merry. As in Christmas, not as in Virgin. Although the virgin part still applies and likely always will. Ain't no man gonna want to have anything to do with me with all this fabulousness going on in my chest area." She laughed silently at this as she motioned weakly at her sternum. She was always the biggest fan of her self-deprecating humor. "Bets, seriously, I'm fine. Stop worrying about me. I already have one parent. I don't need another." She closed her eyes and winced, which got me up at her bedside.

"What's wrong? Do you want the nurse? Do you need pain meds? What can I do?" I threw questions at her like a major-league pitcher and she did the silent laugh thing again.

"Dude. Chill. You're gonna give me another bloody heart attack with all your worrying. I'm fine. It's just a little bit uncomfortable. Kind of like someone gave my heart to Edward Scissorhands to play with." Leave it to her to come up with that kind of analogy. "If it hurts, it means my heart is still beating. And I'm still alive. No idea who decided that was a good idea, but if they were in front of me, I would give them a stern talking to." Ugh. Did she have any idea what talk like that sounded like to me? Did she care?

"Merry, stop it. I hate when you talk like that." I know I sounded whiny, but I didn't care if I did. She was my best friend and I didn't want to think of life without her.

"Didn't you ever wonder if there was someone up there holding the marionette strings? And why that someone cuts the strings of some people, and keeps tying others in knots to screw with them? And then there were others who are just allowed to go through life as easy as pie? Because I've been thinking about that a lot lately, and I have to be honest with you. Sometimes I DO wonder if it would be easier to have the strings cut." She trailed off at that and looked at me. I wanted to blow it off. I wanted to tell her she was crazy, but I knew she wasn't. She had more reason than most people to contemplate her demise and I couldn't just dismiss this as her being hopped up on pain meds, or just flat out being in pain. She was serious.

"Is it fair? Not at all. It's not fair that Laney and your mom died, and Sophie gets to be a bitch and walk this earth and do whatever the hell she wants. It's not fair that you have to go through this. The meds, the surgery, the inability to do what you want, and eat what you want and be like a normal teenager. But I have to believe there is a reason for this. I don't know what it is. I don't know WHY it is. I don't know who the hell you pissed off in your former life that they decided whatever you did needs to be brought as this sort of punishment against you in this life. I know if there was something your dad or I could do to help make it better, in any way, we would." I confessed.

"But why? Why would either of you do that? Let's be honest with each other, Bets. Even if this surgery fixed my heart and I was now normal, I've already lost 10 years of experiences and memories and I've lost the ability to do the stuff that I couldn't do then. I lost my childhood. That time is gone. I can't ever get it back. And my heart isn't fixed. This was a finger in the dam. The dam is still going to break. We just don't know when. No idea why either you or my dad would want to lose what you have to help fix what's unfixable," she muttered. Oh no. That was not going to fly in my world.

"Your daddy and I would give anything in the world to fix you, because we love you. WE LOVE YOU. Now you get that through that thick, stubborn skull of yours, because that won't ever change. I don't know where this pity party came from all of the sudden, but I don't like it," I snapped back at her. "I get it.

This sucks. It's never going to not suck. And you're right, you may never get better, but you're here for a god damned reason."

"Yeah, we just don't quite know what that reason is, other than for the sheer purpose of seeing how much torture and abuse I can tolerate," she declared. My god, she was so frustrating!

"Mer, I love you, but I swear on the baby Jesus if you weren't in that hospital bed, I would smack you. Someday, someone is going to want to be with you and then you're going to open that mouth of yours and talk them out of it with that sparkling personality of yours," I threw at her.

"Yeah, you know all those guys who want to fall in love with terminal heart patients." She closed her eyes and winced again, and I wondered how much pain she was in that she wasn't telling me or the doctors or her father about.

"You're not terminal. Terminally stubborn maybe. But you're not going anywhere anytime soon," I insisted.

"In case you haven't noticed, I just had a chunk of my heart ripped out of me because it was the most defective piece of an overly defective piece of shit organ that doesn't work properly in any way. Sometime in the near future, they're going to put a piece of metal-covered electronics in my chest to make said piece of shit organ work better, which will be in addition to the metal that I already have in my chest holding my rib cage together. All of this to stave off failure of said organ which is inevitable, unless they can replace said organ with one of someone who's dead from something other than said organ failing. My prospects sound fantastic. We should take bets on when all of this is going to happen. There's got to be a bookie willing to take my pity allowance for a sure thing." For the first time in nearly a year, she uttered this whole statement without gasping for breath. I was going to mention it, but I didn't want to point out that she was already doing better when she wasn't feeling better. I pulled my chair closer to the bed, and grabbed her hand.

"Someday, we're gonna look back at this and laugh. And you know why? Because I'll be right. No, no. Don't say anything. Let me finish. I'm going to make a bet on something. Someone will find you. You won't look. Someone will find you, and love you just how you are, even if you're a sarcastic, stubborn pain in the ass with a busted heart. And that person will give you a reason to want to keep living." I squeezed her hand as I said that, and she looked over at me. She looked defeated.

"That's so cliché, Bets. You're better than that. You may as well have said a tall, dark and handsome stranger would sweep me off my feet and I would bare my soul to him and we would live happily ever after with the caveat that I'd love him forever with an asterisk. You know, because forever is a relative term in my world," she smiled when she said that, so I knew the storm had passed for now. I knew I would have to try to keep her spirits up, which wasn't easy when I hated to admit she was probably right on much of what she said. She was wise far beyond those 15 years of hers. And maybe as a result of knowing her, I had lost some of that innocence as well.

I went home that night, and went to my room, where my mom found me crying into my pillow. I told her the whole conversation between Merry and I, and said that I didn't know what I should do to help her. I was afraid she was in so much pain, that I was scared that she would stop fighting. "How much can one person go through? What more can she lose, Mom? I don't know what I'm supposed to say to her, because I think she's right and she is terminal and she's going to die," I hiccupped my way through this as my mom hugged me.

"Betsy, everyone dies. But not everyone lives."

"Mom, did you just quote Braveheart?" I sat up straight and looked at her, and we both started laughing.

"Well I guess I did. But it's true. All you can do is be there for her, much like you've always been. You're her guardian angel here on earth, and in conjunction with her angels up in heaven, you need to just be there for her when she needs you, and even when she doesn't. Make her laugh. Give her a purpose. Make her want to live. It's not an easy job, but if anyone is up for it, it's you."

"It's not fair, Mom. It's not fair to her, but it's not fair to me either." This was the first time I had vocalized my frustration with being her friend to anyone. "When we first started being friends, we were little kids. It wasn't a big deal that she couldn't play or ride her bike or go to the park and run around. She was sick, but it wasn't like this. Now, she's talking about how she's going to die, and that she doesn't know why Dad Cameron and I care so much. Doesn't she realize how that makes me feel, and if her dad knew how it would make him feel? When she gets like this, I don't want to be around her. I hate being around her because I'm afraid she's right, and I'm putting all this effort into being friends with someone who doesn't want to live, and probably won't live."

"Laura Elizabeth Wright! I'm ashamed of you right this moment. This isn't about you. This isn't about her dad either. This is about Merry. And how she feels. And while it's not easy to be around her when she's feeling so down, just imagine what she would be like if you weren't there. How poorly she would feel then. Being a friend is hard work. Being a good friend is even harder. But being a best friend is the hardest thing you can ever do. Because it means that Merry chose you to be the number one friend in her life. She trusts you enough to be honest with you, and that's a huge responsibility. Instead of judging how what she said made you feel, judge how what she said made HER feel. And the reason she said what she did. Put yourself into her shoes, instead of thinking of yourself." With that, she stood up in front of me and crossed her arms. "I want you to think for a moment. Think of how you would feel if she wasn't there for you. While I know you and Merry have a rather unique friendship, unlike others you could have had, it's a blessing. Because you have a friendship built on truly knowing each other, instead of silly, shallow things that you'll love today and hate tomorrow. You've been given an opportunity to do something special here. Don't screw it up."

As she left my room, I stuck out my tongue at her. Childish I know, but I was emotionally exhausted and frustrated and it was my only way to rebel against what she said. I knew what Merry and I had was special. I had seen other friends fight and stop talking, talk behind each other's backs, then make up with each other in big displays of 'oh I'm so sorry, no I'M so sorry'. We hadn't ever fought, and I'm sure that was because she was the least confrontational person I've ever met, more than it was because we disagreed. It wasn't that she wasn't opinionated. She was. She just wasn't the type of person to fight with anyone about it. She thought was she thought, and you could think what you wanted to and that was it.

I know you're reading this Mer, and I still felt it necessary to admit this. Do you know why? Because I realize now how it feels to lose someone I love. To lose a piece of yourself you won't ever get back. And how you still have to keep going. Not for yourself, because at first, you don't want to feel all that pain. You just want to feel nothing. But you keep going for the ones who love you. Because you mean the world to them, even if it's not always apparent. It takes experiencing a loss to understand and I'm sorry I didn't get it then.

*****

I'm gonna jump ahead a little bit here, because time is short and I still have so much I have to say. 5 months after the myectomy marked 10 years since Laney's death. How could time pass so quickly? She'd have been 20 years old in August of 2000. I constantly looked at my now slightly raggedy Laney doll and wondered what my sister would have been like at 20. Would her hair have darkened from the ruddy brown it was to the deep chestnut like Sophie's did? Would she be the tallest of us three girls? What would she have gone to college for? I thought about her nearly every single day since she died, and I laid in bed every single night and hoped she and my mom were looking down on me. I needed to believe in something, because I couldn't believe in a God that took away my mother and my sister and put me through this hell on earth. I imagined Laney when she was 9, laying on her stomach on a cloud keeping watch over me, while my mom sat and drank lemonade with Mr. and Mrs. Jay.

Moving on. Twenty months after the myectomy, I still felt ravaged. Instead of being exhausted and unable to focus, I was exhausted, unable to focus and in pain. The wires holding my sternum together and I didn't get along so well. Some people joke about having thin skin, but I could finally say I legitimately had it, because the wires kept popping through my scar after surgery. Five times actually. I noticed the first time when I got out of the shower, and the towel got stuck to my chest. When I pulled it away, I snagged one of the threads on the piece of wire and pulled it nearly two feet out of the towel. I had a hole in the skin of my chest. There wasn't much blood. It just looked like a piece of paper that has ripped away from a spiral notebook. Almost fainted from fear that first time, (BECAUSE THERE WAS A HOLE IN MY DAMN CHEST! I COULD SEE MY STERNUM FOR CHRIST'S SAKE!) and then, once the doctor shrugged and explained that 'these things could happen', it became less scary and more frustrating. I swear, it did. It's amazing the things that become no big deal when you're sick. I underwent a relatively minor procedure where they took skin from my back and grafted it to thin spot on my chest so that I wasn't popping through the scar anymore.

I also had multiple pleural effusions, (fluid buildup in the space between my lungs and the tissue that surrounded them) and while the doctors assured me I wasn't in congestive heart failure, I had to keep coming to the hospital to have thoracenteses. That's a big fancy word for sticking a needle in my chest cavity to suck out the fluid. Not a little needle either. A BIG FUCKING NEEDLE. At one point, I had 3 in a month, and they put a chest tube in because my lungs kept producing so much fluid. I was on antibiotics and diuretics, and was even more restricted with the amount of liquids I could drink, and what food I could eat. The lack of liquid meant I was constantly thirsty. And constantly had a migraine. When the fluid was in my chest, I felt like I was drowning, and when it was removed, and I could breathe again, I was in almost constant chest pain.

They adjusted my medications AGAIN, and said how normal this was. I can tell you it was anything but normal. My heartbeat raced for no reason, then slowed. It hiccupped and made me feel as though I had John Bonham in my chest playing "Fool in the Rain" most of the time. One day I thought I had counted

wrong or gone crazy when my heart rate went from nearly 250 beats per minute,

down to 50 in the next. Went to the ER for that one. Sorry to all of the esteemed

professionals out there telling me these side effects were something I could expect

and were unfortunately typical. They most certainly were not.

Throughout this whole ordeal, I kept going to school. When I was feeling

'good' the days flew by. I loved learning. I loved learning about things that

happened in the past and how they colored the future. I loved learning about

chemistry and biology and physics. I loved learning anything I could get my

hands on. For being out so much, my grades were decent. I couldn't manage

straight A's, but I was holding down a solid B average that I was pretty happy

with. My secret was out at school, and I was given a wide berth as I shuffled

slowly from class to class.

When I was feeling badly and couldn't make it into school, Bets brought

me my homework and I was able to keep up. It wasn't the same as being there,

but it was the best I could do under the circumstances. Keeping up on the work at

least meant that I could expect to graduate in May. I had plans to go to college.

Pretty stupid huh? Girl with a terminal heart condition, who had at least one heart

attack and one open heart surgery under her belt wanted to go to college. The

concept was laughable to me even, but it gave me a goal. A moment in time to

aspire to.

I woke up one morning, feeling particularly off. I had been sleeping like

crap for the past month or so, but I figured it had to do with being back in school after summer. I was 2 months into my senior year of high school, and on this particular Saturday, I just couldn't get myself functional. I'm always off. But this was way more off than usual. Foggy brained. Tired to the point of sitting down on the stairs, resting my head on the banister and waiting for my dad to find me. When he did, he brought me down to breakfast and I just couldn't eat. At all. I wasn't a big eater to begin with, but being a good little soldier, I always ate my dietician approved meals with a minimum of complaining because I had perpetually hoped one day they would be replaced with something tasty. Dad called my new doctor, and being the wise man that he was, he attributed the lethargy to the shifts in medication after the myectomy and hormones, and advised my dad I was just going through a phase. Like I was some sort of average teenager. He constantly insinuated I needed to 'toughen up' because his other patients didn't complain as much as I did. He seemed to think that I was just not trying hard enough to want to get better. That I wanted to feel like shit all the time for the sympathy. I still don't know why my dad didn't boot his ass, but I think it stemmed from the fact Doc Scanlon recommended him to us, and we trusted what he thought. I missed Doc Scanlon, who moved his practice to North Carolina where his family was from shortly after my surgery. This new guy was a putz. That's the nicest description I could come up with for him.

Days went on, and I just pushed through it. This was 'normal' and I just needed to try harder. Despite the lack of appetite, I felt puffy and constantly thirsty. I had lost some weight, and figured it had something to do with the Oreos I kept sneaking when my dad wasn't looking, which made me not want to eat as much at dinner. If there was one thing I broke the damn diet for, it was Double

Stuf Oreos dunked in skim milk. One morning, I slithered my way downstairs

dragging my feet, and sat down for breakfast. I looked at my dad when he asked

me how I was feeling, and I couldn't speak. I felt the words in my head, but what

came out of my mouth was just gibberish. Freaked my dad out pretty good, that's

for sure. My dad called 911 and I was hurried to the hospital. It was pretty

obvious to the ER personnel, but the tests were run regardless, and they discovered

I had a large amount of toxins built up in my blood. I was admitted to the hospital

immediately. Once admitted, I was whisked away to have dialysis because I was

so mentally out of it, and they needed to clean my blood ASAP. After the junk

had been cleared from my blood and I was coherent, I found out what was going

on.

Acute renal failure.

Why did nothing in me want to work?! And how the hell did this

happen? While not completely unheard of, it wasn't something my father and I

were even aware could happen. Because I had been restricting my liquid intake

because of the effusions, and still taking the massive amount of heart medication,

combined with the diuretics, my kidneys decided to quit on me. They had had

enough. The dialysis was going to continue, and I was going to be in the hospital

for the foreseeable future, until they could stabilize my heartbeat and blood

pressure. While there was a small chance my kidney function would come back after being on supportive therapy like the dialysis, it was more likely that my kidneys were shot. Dialysis was something that could feasibly continue for an extended period of time, but for all intents and purposes wasn't changing the fact I needed a kidney transplant.

My cardiologist finally made his way to my room a couple of days later, and I saw my dad go into Papa Bear mode. I wish I had felt better, because I may have initiated a slow clap to show my approval. Unfortunately, I could barely keep my eyes open. There were f-bombs, thinly veiled threats followed by an eventual, extremely uneasy détente which I can assume was only reached because the dialysis machine had reached my bedside. In my stupor, I remember being hooked up to the machine through one of the veins in my neck and thinking here I was, not quite 17 years old. Broken heart. Dead kidneys. How much could one body take? Would I even survive the transplant? These were all questions asked and supposedly answered affirmatively that while not ideal; this wasn't an unexpected side effect of my situation. Best shot for a transplant match for me was family, so Dad immediately got tested, even though he knew he wasn't the same blood type I was. He amazed me. Despite knowing he wasn't a match, he still went through it anyway. He's always been willing to go the extra mile for me.

When I was first brought in with the kidney failure, I still just figured this was another bump in the road on my way to getting my stupid heart stable. Once it was determined what was wrong, I would either get a kidney or they would get better, and I would go home and be my abnormally, normal self. I was going to insist that I got a new doctor though.

When Dad got tested and was found not to be a match, the hospital asked if there was a sibling that would be willing to be tested for donation. That left Sophie. There was little chance that conversation was going to go well. Sophie had graduated from law school, and landed a job with a local firm who was known for their high-profile defense work. While she was hired at the bottom rung of the ladder, it was only a matter of time before she became the hot shot lawyer she always wanted to be. It suited her. The responsibility. The prestige. She was always a force to be reckoned with and being a defense attorney was perfect for her. In my opinion, there was no way in hell she would give me one of her precious kidneys.

Dad had called her the day I was taken in, and called her again to let her know I was admitted to the hospital (again) and asked her if she would mind stopping in so he could talk about something important with her. I was surprised when he told me she would be in later that day after work.

She arrived late. She was always late for everything that wasn't work. They had just hooked me up for dialysis and I tended to doze during it, because it made me uncomfortable to read with a tube in my neck. I wasn't awake, but not quite asleep when she made her way over to the window where my dad was. He liked to stay with me in case I got restless or uncomfortable. (I can say now that I appreciated him being there. The whole process was terrifying and I was always freaked out at the idea that if I moved wrong, I would rip the catheter out and blood would go spraying everywhere. My nightmares were made of such visions.)

He was blunt with her. I had no kidney function, and it wasn't likely to come back. I needed a transplant. He had gotten tested, and wasn't a match, but a sibling was more likely to be a match and he wanted her to get tested.

And silence.

Still, nothing.

Then, almost as an afterthought, I heard Sophie softly say no.

I expected that. I still don't know why Dad was so shocked by the answer. I give him credit though. He didn't get angry. Anger didn't work with Sophie anymore. He explained to her that without the transplant, I would die. I wasn't considered a long-term dialysis patient because of my heart. I was already being treated for pericarditis, a serious inflammation of the sac that was holding my heart. It was likely the case of much of my chest pain over the course of the past two years, and in my humble opinion, something they should have caught well before this. A transplant was supposedly something they could absolutely do despite the arrhythmia I was having, as they would stabilize that before I went in once they treated the pericarditis. (ummm why didn't they do that at any point over the past nearly 2 years?!) It was also a sign of kidney failure that my doctor missed. I was so exhausted, I couldn't even get angry.

"I can't leave work right now. I was just given my first case and the trial has been scheduled."

I think that's when Dad started to get upset. He didn't yell, probably cognizant of the fact I was only a few feet away in bed.

"You'd let your sister die, so you can defend someone who broke the law? Some criminal means more to you than your sister? You would choose work, over your family?" I could hear the ice in his voice from my bed. I don't know if she missed the tone of his voice, or she just didn't consider the dangerous territory she had just walked into, but what came out of her mouth next sealed her fate.

"I think you're being a bit unfair, don't you? It's not like she can't get one from someone else."

"Wow, Sophia. This is your sister we're talking about. Don't you care that she could die?"

Silence.

Was she thinking about Laney? Was she wondering if this nearly 12-yearlong saga that started with Laney dying would end with my death as well? She was always the analytical one, so I would imagine she was calculating the odds of me actually dying vs. what would happen with work if she stepped away to give me her kidney.

"Sophia Joy Cameron. I don't even know what to say to you right now. I didn't raise you like this."

"No, Dad, you didn't. You didn't raise me much at all once Merry was diagnosed. I've been on my own since I was 14 and Laney died. And I need to consider myself and my future before giving a kidney to someone who is likely going to have it ruined just like the two she has were ruined. I might as well just throw it away." She snapped back at him.

Tell me how you really feel, Soph. I hated confrontation, so I knew I needed to break this up before my dad started getting vocal. I startled in the bed, and the movement brought my dad over. He looked upset, but by this point, more pissed. I can't say I blamed him. Her attitude was all her, like normal.

"Oh hey, Soph. Didn't know you were here," I said weakly.

She walked over slowly, almost like I had a communicable disease.

"Hey Mer, you look good. Where's your Laney doll? What's that thing in your neck?"

"She's at home. It's not a good idea for her to be here, since I'm prone to infections apparently. It's my catheter port for the dialysis."

"Oh."

Yeah, oh. Part of me wanted to be nasty to her. Part of me wanted to make her feel guilty. As much as she and I didn't get along, part of me understood why she didn't want to and part of me didn't want her to.

"How's the new job, Soph? Do you love it?"

"Yeah Mer, I do."

"Good, I'm glad. At least one of us will make something of ourselves. Thanks for coming to visit me. I know you hate hospitals." I closed my eyes, dismissing her.

Definitely don't think she expected that. She kind of looked at me for a minute and then quietly and quickly said goodbye.

I have a confession to make. I was, and still am to this day, tired of being sick. Tired of the meds. Tired of the diet. Tired of not being able to do anything. Tired of living my life as a fraction. I didn't want to do this life anymore and I was somewhat relieved Sophie said no. The idea of going through another surgery, another recovery and coming out the other side still feeling like shit on a daily basis because my heart was still messed up wasn't just daunting to me. I was just done. Done with it all. Sophie being Sophie and declining to donate was a relief I wouldn't share with anyone, but one I was surprisingly grateful for.

Does that sound terrible? I knew if my dad or Bets had learned that, they would've been furious with me for giving up, but the truth of it was, I was tired of being poked and prodded and wearing monitors and not being able to do anything without fearing I would keel over from a heart attack. I was tired of seeing my father worry that I wouldn't come home every time I left the house. I was tired of my best friend having to put up with having a best friend like me. I was tired of being an outcast and I was tired of being looked at like I was sick. I was tired of being tired and in pain all the time. I was just so tired of it all.

Which leads me to address the obvious. I'm still here.

I had been in the hospital for almost 5 weeks, so nearly a month after Sophie's visit when they had finally cleared the pericarditis. Still hooked up to the dialysis machine to clean my blood, with no foreseeable end in sight, when my dad came to me and told me they had a kidney for me from a live donor. I was going into surgery the following morning. I hadn't even realized that they were considering a live donation from anyone who wasn't a family member, but my dad was insistent it wasn't from someone who had passed away. He looked so damn happy.

I started crying. Dad thought I was crying happy tears, but I was crying because I simply didn't want to go through with it. I was so weak, and so spent, mentally and physically that all I could do was lie there and sob. Why couldn't they just let me go?

The next morning came quickly, and they came to prep me and got me ready to roll in. They placed the gurney in the hallway, so I could see the donor being brought in for surgery and thank them. And like a freaking Lifetime movie, coming down the hall on a gurney was Sophie.

Well SHIT. I was never going to hear the end of this. And not like I could be pissed about it, you know? She was giving me an ORGAN. It wasn't like she had given me a doll. This was a piece of her. She looked scared, absolutely terrified. And pale like I am, without her daily war paint on. In the whole time I've been alive, Sophie never looked scared. That glimpse of fear stayed with me as they wheeled her, and then me into the surgical suites.

The surgeries went well. I was kept in the hospital for another couple of weeks while they got my heart acting relatively normally, and ensuring the new kidney was doing its job. My dad and the asshole heart doctor had come to an agreement that my dad wouldn't kill him if the doctor transferred my case to another doctor without commentary. Sophie went home a couple days after. She was back at work before I was out of the hospital.

How could I not admire a woman who gave me a piece of herself? I always thought you could stand Sophie up at the gates of Hell and she would stand there in her stiletto heels and power suit and flip off the Devil if he didn't give her what she wanted, and then go ahead and do whatever it was she wanted to anyway. After I got home, and I could reflect on what happened, and I was feeling "better," I was glad she decided to go through with it.

After the surgery, she became distant. Well, more distant. I was there, but not there. There was a disconnect between us, almost as if she consciously decided not to care one way or another. It was this lack of emotion and interest that permeated our interactions from that moment forward. I hated it. I felt like I kept losing more and more the older I got.

Sophia

My sister is the strongest person I know. An absolute trooper. I don't know that I ever told her that. I don't think I could tell her that. I had imagined her sometimes as a healthy nearly 17-year-old. I feel like she would have been that kid that did everything. Sports and dancing and straight A's. Driven to be the best because it came easy to her, but not needing to be anything more than herself. Not having to fight to be exceptional like I did. She'd be the person that everyone would turn to because she was so competent and capable, but so laid back that you wouldn't mind turning to her. Quiet, but so comfortable in her own skin that it didn't matter if she wasn't a talker. I imagined her healthy, much like I imagine Laney if she had lived. Merry is this quiet, unassuming pillar, but Laney, she was this whirlwind and would've been everywhere all at once. She would have been the one who snuck out of the house, and did all the things that Dad said she couldn't. A daredevil. So full of life. It was thinking like this that made me sad for what they were now; one sister dead, and the other dying a slow death. It pushed me to do more. To BE more.

Merry had been through so much. So, so much. What was I supposed to do? I was stuck between a rock and a hard place. If I didn't give her my kidney, and she died, my father would never have forgiven me. If I give it to her, and she dies, it was a waste. Either way, I lose her, my dad loses her, and our family is thrown into turmoil again.

I love my sister. I know it doesn't seem like I do. I truly do love her. But loving people comes with a cost. I loved my mom. And she was taken from me. I loved Laney, and I always will. And she died. My dad has basically been gone since Merry got sick. Mr. and Mrs. Jay. Loved them too. They're both gone. And I just don't have it in me to show Merry that I love her the way I loved them. Because she's going to die too. That much is clear. As strong as she is, and as much as I see her fight through things that would fell Superman, she needs a new heart and if she doesn't get one, she's going to die. And what will that leave for me? I won't be a sister anymore. I'm barely a daughter as it is. I just can't be as emotionally invested with Merry as I should have been because losing another member of the family that I deeply loved and cared about would kill me. I can't go back to her and my dad now and say how much I care because it'll ring falsely with them. It wouldn't seem true now and it wouldn't have seemed true then. All I could do was to give her my kidney.

I had made up my mind to walk away and deal with the consequences of my actions. Figured there was something they would be able to do. I left the hospital and walked out, thinking of what she said to me laying in that hospital bed, so weak and so tired. 'At least one of us will make something of ourselves.' It felt like she intended to punch me in the stomach with those ten words. 'At least one of us will make something of ourselves.' I went out to my car and lost it. I cried and I screamed and I punched my steering wheel and threw my purse and just got so angry at God and this world and how unfair this is. I hate that she thinks that of herself. That she's nothing. Those months after the myectomy, she was so weak. More than she normally was. And defeated. Merry never looked defeated. It was almost as though she was done being sick. It felt like she was giving up. I couldn't allow that to happen. She doesn't get to give up just because she was faced with this. Her giving up was like Sandy Koufax retiring at 30 because he was worried about his arm. Just because it's not going well now, doesn't mean it's going to be like this forever.

But after the transplant, I couldn't face her. Or my father. I didn't want to hear a 'thank you'. I didn't want my dad to pat me on the back. I didn't want to see how Merry fared after the transplant, because my kidney didn't fix her heart. She was still going to be sick. She's still going to die. I couldn't make her better. I couldn't do anything to make her be normal. I hate that she compares herself to me. I didn't want her to see me back up on my feet and back at it after I had the surgery because she doesn't have that ability.

Do you know what it's like being the normal one? How guilty I feel every single day knowing I went to school and played sports and was ridiculously healthy? I can have kids. Merry can't. I can go to the gym and exercise. Merry can't. I can go to a bar and have a drink and dance and be merry, while my sister can only be Merry. I can do whatever the hell I want, whenever the hell I want, and Merry will forever have to worry if what she's doing will kill her. Do you realize all of the questions I've had to face? How people appear to care more for Merry and what's going on with her than what's going on with me? How difficult it is to grow up with no mother, a sister who dies suddenly and a sick sister who consumes all of your father's time, leaving none for you.

I know it sounds selfish. But I made myself what I was in spite of that, and if I come across cold or dispassionate, it's because that's what I need to be so I don't break down and be an emotional mess. I work hard, because there, I can make a difference. It doesn't break my heart. I hated having to ask for time off to donate my kidney, not because I was ashamed of what I did, but because I didn't want the focus to be on ME for it. And I didn't want to answer questions about why my sister needed my kidney. I didn't want anyone to know I even had a sister. I was lucky my trial got delayed and I could take a couple of weeks off without it being a big deal. As it was, I worked from home once I got out of the hospital. It soothed me. It let me forget how unfair the situation was. And if I'm going to be the one making something of myself, I needed to focus on it, so she could be proud of me.

*****

I got out of the hospital and made it home in time for a quiet birthday and Christmas. It was vastly different than Christmases in the past, as it was just my dad and I. Sophie wasn't able to make it, and when I asked why, all my dad did was shake his head. I spent a quiet New Year's Eve with Bets over, and let my dad take the night off from baby-sitting me. I thought it was needed, as he was so worried about me all the time. I think the night off was a relief for both of us. He could go out with a couple of work friends and have a drink or two, and I didn't have to deal with being watched like a hawk. I wasn't in any condition to do much anyway, but it was just like old times to have Bets over and to eat popcorn that I wasn't supposed to have and drink Shirley Temples like they were cocktails. She and I hadn't discussed my minor (major?) breakdown since I was in the hospital for the myectomy and I was glad. Because I still believed what I said. I could see the road in front of me, and while it had twists and turns, it was still going to be much shorter than the one everyone else I knew was on.

I started back to school in late January of '02. With as much time as I had taken off of school, getting back to the routine was nice. After the transplant, I considered not going to college. And then I realized that if I was going to die, I was going to die with my boots on, and I was going to do the best I could to make something of myself. I was going to be the most accomplished invalid I could be, and that's all there was to it. I was so different than everyone I went to school with, and sometimes, I would watch them when I was sitting at lunch. They were like bees in the hive, buzzing around and visiting each other's honeycombs. They each had their own stories, their own triumphs and sadnesses. It made me realize that as much as I made a point to isolate myself, I was lonely and missed all of the little things. I missed passing notes in class. I missed going to gym class and being picked or not picked for team sports. Dating was non-existent in my world. There were no cutesy flirtations in the hall, and no late-night phone calls from a boy I had a crush on. Dances were missed, because why go to a dance to stand there not able to dance? Prom was coming up, and I had already decided against going. There was no way in hell I could justify spending a ton of money to go by myself. And there was no way I could find a dress that would cover all of my scars. There were so many of them. One in my neck from the catheter port from dialysis. My chest scar which was mangled because of the wires popping through it. My arms from all of the needles. My abdomen from the kidney surgery. A faint rectangle scar on my back from where they took the skin to fix my sternum scar. I couldn't wear clothes like the other girls, with cute crop tops and low cut blouses. I avoided shorts because my legs were so pale and I always wore long sleeves. There was no way I could find a dress that was suitable to go.

But what I could do was to help Betsy get a dress, and get ready. I was starting to feel okay now that the pericarditis had been eradicated. My chest skin still hurt, and there was some talk about removing the wires since I had so much pain from them, but for the time being I wasn't interested in another surgery. I was still on meds for the transplant, and for my heart, but for the first time in a long time, I was doing relatively okay. Bets and I started shopping for a dress for her in March and it was nice to do something someone my age would do. Knowing my fear of the mall, we stuck to places we could get into and out of without walking through. I was normal for those brief moments, even though I wasn't going to the prom myself. I think part of her was happy I was partaking. But I know there were moments when she felt badly that she was getting to do something I wasn't. We had done so much together over these past 12 years that it felt strange that she was going to be doing something this major without me. Or at least that's what I thought she thought. I was fine with it. The whole idea of prom was abhorrent to me. That's what I kept saying to myself. I didn't need to pomp and circumstance of the social ritual to make me happy.

I didn't want to go to prom without my best friend. But I also knew that there was no way in hell she would go, and she insisted that I attend. It felt so weird to be planning this huge event, and know she wasn't going to be there. I had been asked by this guy in my chem class, and I was excited, mostly. We had gone dress shopping, and it was wonderful to be doing something that everyone else did with their friends. We were like peas and carrots, as my mom said. (Actually, it was Forrest Gump, but Mer and I let her think it was something she came up with.)

On the day of prom, we got out of school early, and I drove us both to the salon where I was getting my hair and nails done for the night. Little did Mer know that my mom set her up for an appointment to get a manicure and pedicure, and then a haircut as well. Even though she wasn't going, Mom wanted her to have that experience and was meeting us there for a surprise girl's spa day. Merry and I walked in, and I checked in, knowing that she was going to be checked in under my name. I wanted to keep the surprise up as long as I could. Not even 2 minutes later, they called Merry's name, and the look on her face was priceless. Confused and assuming it was a mistake, she started to protest, and then Mom and I were called, and we herded her to the pedicure chairs where we had her sit in between us.

The salon was wonderful. They brought over sparkling apple juice, and a platter of fruit, cheese and crackers for us to snack on, and as we finished with the pedicures, moved us to three consecutive tables for our manicures, and then three chairs in a row for our hair. Merry was so animated. I don't know if I had ever seen her like that before.

All too soon, the experience came to an end, and we had to get going so I could get dressed and ready for pictures. For the briefest of moments, I think I noticed Merry looking a bit wistful about leaving, and I put my arm around her as we walked to the car.

"Thanks Bets. I don't even have the words to tell you how incredible that was," she said as she squeezed me back. "That was the most fun I think I've ever had." Made me stop and think for a minute how sad that was. The smallest of gestures on mine and my mom's part, and it was the most fun she had ever had? It made me resolve to be better about finding things we could do that were fun, instead of just hanging out all the time. I was a creative soul. I could do this.

I got dressed, and my date came to the house to pick me up and we rolled our eyes through getting our pictures taken, and I was again struck by how happy Merry looked. She gave me a big hug, and whispered in my ear as we were leaving to not do anything she wouldn't do. It made both of us giggle, and I hopped into my date's car with a big smile on my face. She waved good-bye and I saw my mom hugging her as we pulled away.

*****

I kept it together until she pulled away. And then I burst into tears. I didn't want to go. But I was sad that I couldn't be there with her. Or rather, that I chose not to be. If I had told her I wanted to go, she'd have agreed in a heartbeat. I didn't want that for her. She had given up so much to be my friend, that the least I could do was to give her this experience without her having to worry about me tagging along. That she and her mom included me in the manis and pedis was amazing. But tonight was for her. Mrs. Wright gave me the biggest hug, and told me that she thought what I did was wonderful, but that I should know I didn't need to do that. That I wasn't a burden on Betsy as a friend. Friends weren't burdens. I knew what she was saying, but there was so little I brought to the friendship that I needed to do this for both of us. I needed to show I could be away from my crutch, just like she needed to be free from me always being there.

Mrs. Wright drove me home, and upon my arrival, I told my dad all of the details of her dress and showed off my finger and toe nails, and he complimented me on my new haircut. I felt like a normal kid. I grabbed a book, and curled up on the couch, and took my mind off everything for a while. Even all these years later, I could be transported away from my reality in a book, and get lost somewhere else even when I wasn't feeling well. My dad always said that he could tell whenever I was feeling badly, because I didn't want to read. It's funny to me now to see that as a sign of my health, but I guess he had to look to something when I wasn't telling.

I went to bed around 11, and had just gotten to that point where I wasn't quite asleep and wasn't quite awake, where things have a dream-like quality when I heard a noise downstairs. I didn't think much of it at first, and then I realized my bedroom door had been opened slowly, probably so as not to wake me. I quickly pushed through the sleepiness and opened my eyes to see Bets standing over the bed.

"Wait, what the hell?" I creaked out, shocked to see her there. I had thought she was going camping with the rest of the kids after the prom breakfast, and couldn't quite wrap my head around the idea that she was standing in my room. With a sleeping bag. And a big bag that looked suspiciously like a sleeping bag. In her dress.

"Hey there Carrots, get your ass out of bed and come downstairs. Bring your pillow and your blanket, while Dad Cameron and I get the tent set up in the back yard." She walked out of the room, with her prom dress hiked up to her knees in one arm, carrying everything else in the other, leaving me half-propped up on my arm wondering what the hell the just happened.

This was bizarro world, and I was living in it. I pulled my slippers on, and grabbed my pillow and comforter and shuffled sleepily down the hall to the stairs and stood at the bottom wondering what was going on. Walked to the kitchen and looked out the back window, and saw my dad setting up this massive tent in the backyard, while Bets was nowhere to be seen. I didn't understand what was going on, and then saw movement out of the corner of my eye. Bets walked out of our downstairs bathroom, no longer in her prom dress but in stretch pants and a tee shirt, with her curled hair no longer in an up-do, but in a bouncy pony-tail. I was reminded of the day I met her, and how I've always thought she had the best hair. Thick and pretty, not pin drop straight and lank like mine.

"What are you doing there standing there with your mouth open? Come on, we still have to build the campfire! Grab the bag of marshmallows on your way out" Bets exclaimed as she whisked by me. I was always jealous of her ability to make an entrance or an exit. It was always so theatrical. I grabbed the marshmallows conveniently sitting on the counter, and made my way outside. It was a warmer night for May, probably somewhere in the high 60's, so the campfire would be welcome once I cooled off from being cuddled under my covers. Which reminded me. Why was I outside again?

My dad had just about finished setting up the tent beside the fire pit he had built a couple of years after I had started my gardening out here. It had been a few years since I was able to be outside with my hands in the dirt, but I was thinking I was well enough this summer to manage doing it. I had missed the feeling I got when planting. How proud I got watching my seeds transform into lush plants over the course of a season. I missed the smells of the dirt and the peat and the scent of green that you can only fully experience when you were right up close to the garden. He waved me over and I stood around the fire pit, with my blanket wrapped around me. By this time, I was fully awake, and I looked over at him and Bets and just thought how lucky I was. Still had no idea why we were outside past the witching hour, but it wasn't unpleasant. The sky was bright with stars, and I could pick out the constellations easily among the midnight blue backdrop.

"Does anyone want to let me in on the secret here? What are you doing here, Bets instead of at the prom breakfast? And why are we putting up a tent and building a fire? Is this some sort of sadistic no-prom attending torture, getting me out of bed when I was all cozy and such?" I asked with a slight smile on my face.

"You didn't actually think I was going to all of that without you, did you? Jeeeez. . . what kind of best friend do you take me for? I talked with Dad before tonight and we set this up, so you could go camping, without leaving all the comforts of home. I know how you get when you're sleepy. It's really not one of your finest moments. You turn into Captain Crankypants. We have air mattresses in the tent, and I went and pulled some branches off the willow so we could roast marshmallows and hot dogs, and then we can tell ghost stories and it'll be just like we're camping!" She exclaimed.

I have to say something here, before I continue along with this tale. People read these stories of these amazing friends who remain so over the course of years and years, and you think to yourself, man, I wish I could have a friend like that. I never had to do that. Because Bets was the best friend I could have asked for, or dreamt of. With everything that came along with being my friend, and everything that we were restricted from doing because of my condition, her spirits were never dimmed. Or if they did, she didn't show it. She truly had a sparkling personality, and I don't know if I would be here today without her. She reminded me I could be me, and it was okay. That I didn't need to apologize for my heart. That I could be Merry and even at times, be merry, and it was alright. Even throughout all of the lows I had that far; the highs I was able to experience thanks to her, and my dad and Bets' mom far outweighed them. I truly was a lucky girl.

I gotta admit, I was pretty damn happy when Bets called me to see if it would be okay for her and Mer to put up a tent in the back yard after prom to go 'camping'. The bouncy little girl had become a force to be reckoned with, and I was putty in her hands when it came to doing something she asked. I'm sure she could have exploited that if she weren't such a peach, but she never did. She never pushed the envelope when it came to the ground rules I had laid down for Mer, and the past couple years, I didn't even have to mind them much when they were at the house because I trusted her with Merry more than I trusted anyone else. She knew what to watch for with her, and more than that, she understood the consequences of what would happen if things went south. Strange that I was able to have such an ally in a 17-year-old kid, but I was grateful for the support Bets and her mom had provided over the years.

I knew better than to convince Merry to go to prom, but for the first time ever, I felt pretty guilty that she wasn't taking part in something. For the past 12 years, I had been the warden, restricting her from partaking in the things normal kids take part in. And this time, I didn't have to do it. She had been conditioned too well by this point. It made me sad to think of all the things she wasn't able to do, in comparison to Sophie, who was a cheerleader and was constantly involved in some extracurricular activity when she wasn't in school or home. Or over at her friends' houses or having them at ours. There was always a bustle of activity with Soph that was so contrary to the bustle of activity that came with Mer.

Standing there as I set up the fire, with her blanket wrapped around her, I realized abruptly that she wasn't a kid anymore. She looked older than Sophie did at her age. Not in a bad way, but it was noticeable. She did grow into her legs, and was nearly as tall as Soph was. The scar on her neck from the dialysis was a slash across her throat and reminded me daily how close I was to losing her before the transplant. Her hair shone like polished platinum in the starlight, and without all her makeup on, I was able to see her face for a change. Though pale, her skin was clear and smattered with a precious few freckles. I imagined if she were able to be out in the sun like her sister, she'd be a mess of freckles and it made me a touch wistful I never had the chance to see her with a bit of tan to her skin. She could have been a magazine example of a California Surfer Girl in another lifetime. Instead she looked how I always imagined the White Witch to look in The Lion, The Witch and the Wardrobe. Her cheekbones were sharp and high and she could throw ice from those eyes when she wanted to, even though she kept it banked inside of her most of the time. She had this air of capability surrounding her, and while I knew it came from everything she'd been through, I wished she had retained some of that wide-eyed innocence I saw in her when I first sat across from her in a restaurant and told her she had a problem with her heart. I was grateful Merry didn't have Sophie's edge to her but she also didn't have the passion I admired Soph for having. She was a ship without an anchor and was swept along with the currents and through the maelstroms, hoping the boat stayed in one piece.

I feel like somewhere along the line, I messed up and screwed up both my kids. Sure, in a perfect world there are things I would change about how I handled Sophie in light of Merry's illness, and Laney's death. And I would definitely change the way I handled Merry. As a single dad of all girls, I felt like I was behind the 8-ball most of the time no matter what I did. I had to work to pay for the insurance and healthcare costs for Mer, and in being away so much between work and her condition, I alienated Soph.

It was nights like this one, outside building a fire for my baby girl and her best friend that I could forget about everything I screwed up, and just be grateful to see her standing across from me, the fire light glinting off her skin. She looked so much like Liv, and even though I'm no church-going man, I closed my eyes for a sec, and sent a silent prayer to the heavens in the hopes Olivia could look down and see her daughter. And I hoped she'd be proud of me too. We had been through hell, and I knew there was a pretty solid chance we would make a return trip or two over the coming years, but we were both still here, and for the most part, we were happy.

*****

All too quickly, my high school experience came to an end. Graduation was on a Saturday morning and I took inventory as I sat in my room after my shower. My cap and gown were hung neatly on my closet door, and I brushed my hair, contemplating what to do with it so I wouldn't be sweltering in the heat of the day. I glanced over at the bed, where my outfit was laid out. More daring I suppose than what I would normally wear, but with temps in the mid 80's and the sun showing no signs of going anywhere, I didn't want to overheat. It was a mint green sleeveless crepe pantsuit, with a deep V in the front, and cream buttons. It was flowy and light and it terrified me to wear it, but my dad presented it to me and I wasn't about to tell him no. I planned on wearing a cream tank top under it, so my scar wasn't so out there. Unfortunately, there was still going to be a solid 3 inches of deep purple showing, as well as the scars on my arms and neck.

"Hey there baby girl, did you try on your outfit yet?" My dad called from the hallway outside of my room. Ugh. Mint wasn't a color I wore regularly anyway, because it made my skin appear even paler and sicklier than normal. I hadn't thought it possible, but putting it on and looking in the mirror made me realize how horrible I looked. Time to face the music, I told myself and opened the door to see my dad waiting there.

"Well, I hope I don't scare any little kids today. Might make a scene at graduation." I laughed with my head down so he didn't see how I felt.

"Oh Mer. Look at you! You went and got all grown up on me. Stop fidgeting with the top so I can take a look." He voiced as he spun around me, brushing a piece of lint from my shoulder.

"Dad, people don't need to see Frankenstein's scars." I muttered still trying to pull the top up so less of my chest was showing. I felt exposed.

"Hey, stop for a second and look at me." He grabbed my shoulders and looked at me. "You have no reason in the world to be ashamed or embarrassed about your scars. Most people on this earth will never go through what you have. You wear those scars as badges of honor. And if anyone asks, just tell them the truth. Half of them won't believe you anyway." He calmed with those words, but it was just us in my room, and not us out in front of my classmates. I wasn't sure I would ever feel comfortable enough in my own skin to be out and proud about my scars. They were a constant reminder to me; not that I was a survivor, but that I was flawed. That there was something wrong with me that couldn't be fixed. He left the room to get the car, and I braided my hair quickly so it was out of the way, and grabbed my sunglasses. Took a deep breath, and left the room for the last time as a high school student.

My story changes here. Since I was child, I lived with my father, in his house and never dreamed I would live elsewhere. Partially because I didn't think I would live long enough to consider living elsewhere, and also because I thought I wouldn't ever be able to, physically. I decided to go to the same school Sophie did, UB, because it was nearly around the corner from my house and because I wasn't sure what I wanted to do. Whatever it was, I wanted it to be as cheap as possible. I won a minor war with my dad, and in August of 2002, I moved onto campus with Bets as a freshman in the class of 2006. Of course, he was in constant contact with the college, and while they didn't usually take requests to place particular students together, based on my handicap, they made an exception.

That grated on me. It still does. There were definitely concerns about my ability to make it from class to class, as I wasn't able to drive, and the college covered two campuses. One in North Amherst and the other in Buffalo. Relatively speaking, they weren't far apart, and there were shuttle buses between them, but for someone who walked slower than molasses in January, planning my schedule around the time it would take me to move from place to place was a huge challenge.

It was an amazing time for me. I was free for the first time in my life. These people didn't know me. They hadn't been around me ever. I could be anyone I wanted with them. I realized once I left the confines of my childhood home, exactly how little responsibility I had been given. I had to manage my own laundry, which entailed stairs and carrying load after load to and from a communal washroom. As strange as it sounded, I had always tossed my laundry down the chute, and then of course, threw it in the washer and dryer, but then my dad would always truck the baskets up the stairs for me. Now, I had to rely on Bets to do it for me, since the 4 flights of stairs in the dorm weren't the sort of exercise I could manage on a regular basis. We worked out a pretty decent arrangement. I would fold the laundry if she would do the laundry. Do you have any idea how many pairs of socks this girl had?! I can laugh about it now, but at the time, I was dumbfounded trying to pair what felt like 50 pairs of identical socks together. And she was incredibly specific. I needed to make sure that the socks I was pairing together had the same amount of wear to them, and that they were the same sizes, even though they were the same damn socks.

We got into a rhythm living with each other, and I have to say, we still never argued. I don't know why that was. Betsy has always been the person I'm the most myself with, but after being friends for so long, it was still so easy to be her friend. I was able to help her with the homework she struggled with, and she put up with my constant flip-flopping all night long. I had periodic doctor's appointments, and either she or my dad would pick me up and take me to them. I was now with one of the larger cardiology groups in Buffalo, and was being monitored much more closely now that I was not at home any longer. I wore a pedometer to clock how much I was walking on a daily basis, and had to email that data to the doctor so he could track how that activity was affecting my heart.

And for the first time, I went on dates. Needless to say, I was a late bloomer in many ways, and dating was awkward for me. Bets told me to 'rock out with my cock out' which made me laugh, but made me uncomfortable as well. I

162

had kept my heart condition a closely held secret for so long, that to be open and honest about it was foreign to me. For the first couple dates with guys whose names I admit I can't remember now, I kept it a secret and realized quickly I had little in common with them. I kept up on local sports and that was a help when it came to a first or even a second date, but beyond that I didn't play sports, I didn't have hobbies outside of reading and gardening, I wasn't one of those incredibly confident girls, and my best friend was essentially my only friend. While I had gotten less plain and more skilled in my makeup application so I didn't look like quite the Goth I did in high school, I wasn't bringing much to the table relationship wise. There were a couple guys willing to at least ask me out, but I didn't make it much farther than 2 or 3 dates with anyone. Mainly because once the physical component came into it, I got a bit gun-shy. It was hard to let go of the self-consciousness with these guys whose sole college goal was to make it through as many coeds as they could. I just didn't feel like they were worth it.

The first three years of college breezed by. I had a blast just being a college student, and there were even times I forgot I was sick. I have to say, I got incredibly lucky when it came to class scheduling. I officially declared as an English major after my sophomore year. It was a degree that combined my love of reading and writing, with my inability to handle work of a more laborious variety which would come from being in a lab environment and around chemicals. I had begun writing short stories and articles for the school paper. I had no clue what I would be able to do as a career after college, because I knew there was still half the hurricane left once you made it through the eye of the storm.

Sure enough, the summer after my junior year of school, I was out in the garden weeding on a gorgeous July day, and I passed out. I had been home alone, and my dad was at work, but I was fortunate that the little boy next door was outside on his swing and saw me collapse on the ground. He screamed for his mom, and she came out to see what was going on, and found me on the ground next to my roses. She called 911, and started CPR on me, which kept me alive until the paramedics came and shocked my heart back into action. When I had gotten to the hospital, they discovered I had another heart attack. Much like the first one, it came without any warning, and I hadn't noticed that the lightheadedness I had attributed to being out in the sun was a sign of something more insidious.

It didn't take a genius to realize the back half of the hurricane was finally here. My dad rushed in, apologizing for not being home. The neighbor from next door had stayed with me till he got there, and he kept thanking her. The roller coaster ride had begun again. The week in the hospital. Dad calling Sophie and Betsy. Sophie being too busy to come see me. Betsy trying to sneak in a male stripper. (At least she said she did, and that's all that matters!) Once released, the back and forth with the cardiologist trying to figure out what happened, and how to prevent it happening again.

Turns out my body had gotten used to the routine of being at school, and being somewhat active, and when I came home and lolled around, the little bit of activity I did in the hot sun triggered my heart to flip out. Damned if I did, and damned if I didn't, it turns out. I kept hearing the same damn phrase from the doctors throughout the years. It wasn't something they could predict, but it wasn't something they were unaware could happen. Now, because of the most recent heart attack, my cardiac output was nearly as poor as it had been prior to myectomy. By the time everything was said and done, it was time to go back to school. That didn't go over so well with my dad. Actually, he got pissed off, and yelled that I had some sort of a death wish, all because I wanted to finish and get my college degree.

For the first time ever in my life, I walked away from him, and got into Bets' car and told her to take me to school. I couldn't even talk to her to tell her what happened because I was shaking like a leaf, but once we got back and I was able to have a good cry about it on her shoulder, I felt slightly better. I know that sometimes the decisions we make affect others, but for most of my life to this point, I hadn't been given the chance to make any sort of decision at all. I was always led down a path that was cleared for me before I got there. I had to finish school. If it was, in fact, the last thing I did, I was going to finish school.

Jeff

I was getting daily updates from Betsy on how she was doing, and she told me that she was fine, but she was different than she had been over these past 3 years. Said she was quiet again. Resigned again. I wanted to call her, or go and see her, but that best friend of my daughter told me to just let her be, and give her a chance to make the first move. Sure enough, I got the letter in the mail about two weeks after Merry walked out of the house. I've read it so many times over the years that I know it by heart, and it's tearing at the folds.

Daddy,

First of all, I love you. Second of all, I HAVE to do this. If I do absolutely nothing else in my life, I need to finish this. I've never felt as alive as I have here. I feel normal for the first time. I know better than most people how fragile life is, and we both know I won't have the opportunities others have. I've asked for nothing in this life, except for this. I need you to understand that I need this for me. And besides, it's not like I'm running out after college and getting a job or going to grad school. We both know I'm coming home and you'll have to take care of me for the rest of my life. You need this school year to prepare for that. You're not getting any younger after all. I know Bets has been giving you updates. I'm fine. I promise.

Love, Mer

Damn that girl. Hard as hell to be mad at her when she put it like that.

Still worried like the dickens about her, but damn it, I couldn't be mad at her

anymore. Leave it to her to make a joke about her living at home for the rest of

her years. Even though I didn't want that for her at all, I don't think there was any

question about her going out and getting a regular job. This episode made me

realize we had gotten complacent and thinking she was doing so well that we

forgot how quickly things could change. I hadn't thought about her getting this far

and not making it. It just didn't seem possible for her to have gone through all of

this and then not make it.

*****

God, what I wouldn't have given to be normal. To be ordinary. I admit, college provided me an anonymity I hadn't had up until that point. I could tell people about my heart, though I chose not to, because I finally had the chance to blend in with the freaks, geeks, Greeks and beautiful people in a way I never could before. I *loved* college. The ability to finally be somewhat independent. For someone who spent her formative years cooped up in a house missing school, unable to play sports, unable to be a kid, *this* was freedom. And while it was liberating for me to be in a classroom, sit in the student union and people watch or walk from class to class, it also made me angry. Furious, in fact. These people had NO idea what they had. No idea what I would give to have what they did. When you want to, you can hear so much by just sitting there listening. You can hear the gossip, the weekend replays. The hook-ups, the rehashing of the big game. You hear the happy and the sad and the angry and the mundane. It made me realize how much I hadn't done. How much I couldn't do. And finally, how much I would never do. I spent the first 3 years of college thinking that I was better. That I had turned a corner, and in a snap, I learned how fragile my health was. I learned to appreciate every second of this life. I've learned to love the mundane and the thrilling equally. I didn't believe I was living with a death sentence. We were all born to die and we've been dying since we were born. Some of us will just get there quicker than others.

I made it to the final semester of college. I had fought to attend college and live in the dorms, and as my time wound down there, I realized I was ready for it to be over. I loved college. But it only reminded me of everything I wasn't and would never be and it was time to get back to the reality of my situation.

Nate

When I first saw her, my heart stopped beating. I felt like I got kicked in the chest and the air left my lungs. I understood what it felt like to get hit by lightning. I wondered briefly how bad it would hurt to pass out and hit the tile floor in the Student Union. The whole world moved in slow motion, and I couldn't help but stare at her as she crossed from the entrance of the union towards the inner bowels of the building where she'd be swallowed up by the glut of other students.

It's not that she was just pretty; she certainly was, in a pale, delicate sort of way. She moved slowly, giving me time to really see her. It's not that she appeared at first to be anything other than completely ordinary. She kind of reminded me of a snowflake. White tinged blue from the cold, and something that would get lost in a crowd of a million other snowflakes. But when you saw her isolated by herself, she was heartbreakingly beautiful. Her piercing grey-blue eyes passed over the masses in the Union, like a fly fisherman casting his line in the middle of a raging river. She furrowed her brow when she saw me gaping like a fish caught on that line, as though surprised I took the bait. She glanced away, irritated to be caught looking and I inhaled sharply. And just like that, the tenuous thread that held me snapped and set me free.

Looking back, it sounds poetic. I've never been a poet, but it's how I felt. She moved in slow motion, but she was there, and then she was gone. I told myself I had to meet her.

*****

There I was, at the start of the spring semester, stuck in one of those rooms with no windows, in the dungeons of Clemens Hall. HE kept looking at me. The guy from the Student Union. And in an obvious way too. Of course, he happened to be in the only class that I had to take to graduate, Creative Writing. (Which to this day is rather ironic, considering I was an English Major and had yet to take ANY writing class through 7 semesters. If you want to pay boatloads of cash to read books, sign up to be an English Major.) I liked sitting in the last seat by the door, in case I wasn't feeling well, so I could surreptitiously sneak out without making a scene.

Who am I kidding? I never could sneak out of anywhere, because I moved at a glacial pace so as not to turn 5 different shades of blue. My health had devolved rapidly. I was counting the days until Spring Break when I had scheduled the surgery to have a pacemaker installed, like it was some sort of car part on backorder. It was the last-ditch option prior to having a ventricular assist device installed, which was the last option before a transplant. Scary thought for me.

I'm sitting in the back like I always did, reading before class like I always did, when I got this eerie sense that I was being looked at. I look up, and see that guy sitting next to me, looking at me. Couldn't mistake that he was, because there was nothing but a bare wall behind me. Of course, he caught me looking and looked down at this desk where he had a notebook opened to a blank page. I shook my head and went back to reading my book. And again, felt the weight of him staring. I had gotten used to knowing when people were staring at me. Not looking up this time, I took a sidelong glance at him, and saw he had the most serious look on his face as he stared at me through his eyelashes. These incredibly long eyelashes. Figures. Guys always get the awesome eyelashes. He had these stormy sea-colored eyes, that weren't quite green, not quite gray, and certainly not what I would say were your run-of-the-mill hazel. They reminded me of a cirrus cloud in an angry sky just before a tornado. I have to say; the eyeballing was starting to irk me a bit. Did I have something on my face? Or worse, did I look like a blueberry again? I hadn't been running around, and my breathing was pretty ok, and my heart rate was within the normal range, except when I looked over at this guy staring at me. And I thought to myself, stop this. It's probably something stupid, like he's read the book I was reading, or had some random comment about the Pink Floyd shirt I was wearing, or something along those lines, because I did NOT get stared at the way he was staring at me. I looked like his mother's half-sister's second cousin. I didn't want to be stared at. It made me feel uncomfortable, like I was a mannequin on display. It was giving me a bloody complex, for Christ's sake. I looked over at him, straight at him, and said,

"Can I help you with something?" I said to him, in my most haughty and 'leave me the hell alone' voice. He looked down, sheepish, and then up again through those eyelashes (seriously, how the hell is THAT fair?!)

172

"I'm sorry, I don't mean to stare. Well I do. But I didn't mean to make you uncomfortable. It's just, well this is going to sound like a line, but you have the most beautiful eyes I've ever seen." Wait, what? Did that just happen?

"Um, thank you?" What the hell else was I supposed to say to that, 'thanks they're real', or 'thanks I've had them since I was a kid'?

"You sound like you don't believe me." Great . . . another chatty Cathy. I felt like telling him that I didn't need another friend; that the job was filled, but thanks for the interest.

"Well, it's the first time anyone has ever commented on my eyes, to be honest." You know, because ending anything with 'to be honest' is always honest. Even though it was in this instance.

"That's a shame. You should be told that you're gorgeous all the time," he stated matter-of-factly. WTF. Where was this guy from? I felt like asking if he was blind, because pale-to-the-point-of-being-see-through-blondes weren't in fashion, especially those who weren't wearing form fitting, revealing clothing, and who gave off 'don't talk to me vibes' to everyone she met.

"Um, thank you again. I should get back to my book now." Yeah, had no idea how to end that conversation, so I did the best I could. I was almost miffed. Like, who did this guy think he was? I had been able to pull off the brush-off once I realized that dating wasn't all it was cracked up to be, and this guy was bucking the trend.

The professor walks in, and class begins and the discussion centers on naming conventions for characters in stories that we were going to be writing throughout the semester. I wasn't terribly comfortable with the idea that I had to write something for a grade that wasn't an essay. In fact, I would go so far as to say I hated the idea that something I had written creatively would be up for discussion. I wasn't a big fan of criticism to say the least. This prof was rather exuberant, and I had learned in the course of the program, it was the exuberant ones who were royal pains in the asses, because they wanted you to participate instead of just paying attention and listening. The professor, whose name escapes me now, starts going around the room, asking everyone what their name is, and why they were named what they were. Oh. HELL. No. Nope. Not going to do this. So of course, we get to the last row, where my chatty friend and I were sitting and he stands up (seriously, who IS this guy) and says,

"My name is Nathaniel Holden Carter. My mom said she named me after the author Nathaniel Hawthorne and a character in a book she read when she was younger." I almost wish there was a camera in the room, so my expression of utter disdain could have been documented.

"Mr. Carter, did your estimable mother advise you which character in which book she named you from?"

"Yeah, The Catcher in the Rye. I haven't read it though." If I had any notions of finding this man attractive before this, they pretty much went out the window at this point. The professor moved his gaze to me.

"And you, miss, our final participant in today's exercise. Please tell us your name and how it came to be."

My heart started pounding from the adrenalin running through my veins at the affront of the professor coming to me. I don't like talking in front of people. It's not my forte. "My name is Merry Olivia Cameron. And I don't have a story to tell about the origins of my name."

"Oh well, Ms. Cameron, you know as well as I, there is ALWAYS a story. Please now, the class is waiting with bated breath to hear. Please, go on."

Well fuck. I wanted to throw my book in his smug little face. I felt myself blushing, and started to get angry. And I thought to myself, well, if you can't opt out, perhaps you should make him feel badly for asking. "Merry. As in Christmas, not as in Virgin. My mother's name was Olivia. She died in childbirth with me, and in order to memorialize her, my father gave me her first name as my middle name. As for my first name, he wanted me to forever be a reminder of something good coming from my mother's death. Since "Happy" isn't a good name for a little girl, he named me Merry." The whole time I said this, I glared at the professor. I wanted to convey the utter discomfort he made me feel for sharing something so private with a bunch of people I didn't care about, and wouldn't see after I got done with this class.

Of course, he was thrilled to have someone give him an answer like that, and he spent the remainder of class exhorting us with tales from literature of aptly named characters. I scrunched down in my seat, unwilling to listen to what he had to say, because I was so mad at myself. Why the hell hadn't I lied? I hated being put on the spot, and feeling my heart race. I felt so stupid, and so upset, and most of all, I felt like I had betrayed my family for telling something so private. Up until that point, what happened with my mom was something I didn't discuss. I didn't talk about Laney and I didn't talk about what was wrong with me outside of one-on-one situations, because it wasn't anyone's business. I didn't want people to feel bad for me. I didn't want to be a topic of conversation. And most of all, I didn't want to let anyone in, because in 15 years, so much had happened and I didn't want to keep going through it over and over again.

After what seemed to be hours, class ended, and I pulled on my jacket and started walking out the door as quickly as I could. I had learned in 3 1/2 years here, there was an art to maneuvering through the halls inside the campus without having to make my way outside in the weather. Luckily, I was done for the day, and I could make my way to my dorm room. I was waiting for it, and still almost missed it because I was so focused on getting the hell out of there.

"Hey Merry! Wait up a second." GAAAAAHHHHH, it was the gawker from class. And here I thought I made a clean exit. He caught up to me easily, and I was surprised he was taller than I thought. Why the hell did that matter, I thought to myself angrily.

"What other classes are you taking this semester?" Small talk. Awesome. Walking and talking. Yet another thing I sucked at. Maybe I could be short with him and he would leave me alone.

"Early and Late Shakespeare. Chaucer. Heaven, Hell and Judgment." And I can't even walk quickly to get away from him. Damn it!

"Sounds like you're an English Major." Captivating, he was not. What to do, what to do?

"If you'll excuse me, I have to run to the ladies' room before I head back to the dorms." Maybe he'd take the hint that I wasn't a big talker.

"Maybe I'll see you at the commons on Wednesday and we can grab some lunch?"

"Sure, maybe you will." Great, now I had to find a new place to sit and kill time. I broke off, and made my way into the ladies' restroom just to get away. My heart was pounding again and I was out of breath. I wanted to blame it on the class. I wanted to blame it on my internal anger. I wanted to blame it on my quickened pace and the chitchat. I didn't want to admit it was because Mr. Nathaniel Holden Carter of the stormy sea eyes was looking at me. And not just looking at me. But maybe, for the first time that I noticed, truly seeing me. Which, was something I definitely didn't want. I didn't want to be seen as the chick with the fucked-up heart. The chick covered in scars. The chick with one friend to her name because she spent her formative years self-sequestered. I wasn't exactly a good candidate for his next conquest and I definitely didn't want to be the token pity friend he felt sorry for and told everyone about to demonstrate what a great person he was. I didn't want to admit to myself that I was interested; because there was no way in hell I would LET myself be interested. I kept telling myself that. He was just another jock. I could just tell. And jocks and chicks with broken hearts don't mix. It was just impossibility.

Nate

I joked around in the introduction about not knowing where my name came from, but of course I read the book. I wanted to understand why my mom thought she should name me after this guy. And I still didn't get it. Holden Caulfield was an angsty jaded fool who didn't care about anything but doing exactly the opposite of what he should be. He was a spoiled cynic, and once I was old enough to read the book, and understand it, I asked my mom what she was thinking. Her response wasn't what I was expecting, but it made sense. She was young when her and my dad met, and I was an oops baby. He left before I was born, and she named me after the character in the book, because having me was exactly the opposite of what she was supposed to be doing. I was a contradiction. My mom made sure I had every single opportunity she missed out on because I came around, and I appreciated it. Obviously, more so once I got old enough to realize the difficulty she had raising me as a single mom.

She made sure I knew what it meant to work hard. That I knew what it meant to treat everyone how I wanted to be treated. Made sure I knew how important it was to learn as much as I could while I had the opportunity and to use that to get to where I wanted to be in life. We were by no means well off, and in any other city, I could have been an outcast because I didn't have the right clothes or lived in the right neighborhood. I was focused and driven in high school, and lucky enough to be athletic and popular. And that's all it was. Luck. It was a means to an end and much like my education, I used it to get into college on scholarship. I was originally planning on going out of state. But when it came down to making the decision, I couldn't pull the trigger. It was just my mom and I, and not only did I feel I couldn't leave her, I realized that I didn't want to. She was more like a friend than a mom, and since she had me so young, we were each other's best friends.

I know how that sounds, like I'm some pretty little momma's boy. I heard it all through high school. My friends thought my mom was hot (and I can admit it now that I'm an adult that my mom is a good-looking woman), and I was definitely protective over her. But because of her, I had greater goals and aspirations. I didn't want to struggle like she had to after my sperm donor father left her. I am who I am because of what we went through. And I wouldn't change one bit of it.

Sorry, this isn't about me. Went off on a tangent there. I seem to do that when I think back to when I first met Merry. Back on track now. She was a sphinx in class. She never took notes and she didn't seem to pay attention until she was asked a question, and then she would speak up and know the answer. She knew every little reference the professor mentioned. She showed up at each class with a different dog-eared book, and spent the time before class and on the break during class reading. She never seemed like she wanted to be there at all. She seemed almost resentful of the infringement on her time.

But my God, she was stunning. It was the strangest thing. Other girls were prettier. But she had this look, this withering look, as though everyone was beneath her. Her eyes were so infinitely expressive, which was only worth noting because her face never let on what was going on in that mind of hers. I would never have said I believed in love at first sight before I saw her, but afterward, it was the only explanation for how I felt. I had never met anyone that affected me the way she did, with no effort on her part at all. If anything, I think she was going out of her way to avoid me, and I wasn't sure why. She didn't dress like most of the girls I knew dressed. Jeans and tees with thermal shirts underneath, varying shades of converse on her feet. More often than not, she'd have a sweater or sweatshirt on, but she usually took it off when she first got to class, only to throw it on within the first 15 minutes after class started. Some days, she'd sit there with her hands balled into the sleeves of what she wore and hunched into herself as though trying to curl herself into a ball. The minute class was over; she got right up, and started walking slowly down the hall. There were times when she would close her eyes and wince, like she was in pain, and then realized where she was, or that I was looking at her and go back to being a sphinx. I couldn't quite figure her out, and I kept hoping that once I did, she would become like most of the other girls I had dated and I would lose interest. I needed to figure this girl out, because I couldn't stop thinking about her.

*****

The pain was getting worse as the weeks passed. I would go to class, and then back to the dorm to try to sleep because I was constantly tired. Betsy would look worried as I put on the oxygen mask and turned it up as much as it would go, but I brushed it off saying I was like those football players when they visited Mile High in Denver. Sometimes you just needed the boost. In reality, I needed it all of the time. The only time I felt decently was when I had the oxygen cranked to the highest level, and the minute I had to be off of it, I felt like I was on the edge of passing out and only by sitting completely still and not exerting myself, was I okay.

I'd notice Nate looking at me, and I kept trying to make it clear I didn't want him looking at me, but it never worked. I was so annoyed by him and I didn't understand why. He was witty, and somewhat sarcastic, but only in the most playful of ways and never cruelly. He was incredibly nice. Incredibly good looking. There were times when he looked at me that his eyes looked nearly bottomless; how I imagined a marsh looked on a cloudy day. When his hair grew out from being cut, it had a curl to it that angered me, since my hair was never anything but pin-drop straight even when I made an effort to curl it. God help me on the days when he styled his hair. On the days he didn't shave, I could see some reddish hair in his stubble. For some reason, it made him look younger, instead of older like it did with most people. Some days, he dressed like he was modeling for J. Crew with corduroys and a dress shirt under a cable knit sweater and a golf cap, and others, he looked supremely comfortable in worn jeans and a faded tee shirt with sneakers. Every once in a while, he'd show up with glasses on and I had to stop myself from audibly sighing in class when he spoke. I was never the type of girl that drooled over the guys on the cover of magazines, or fawned over a football player, but there was something about him that made me forget that I was sick and covered in scars and a generally unfriendly and miserable sort of person. A blind man could see the appraising eyes of the other females in the class on him.

But he didn't seem to notice them. Just me. I never thought of how I looked most of the time. I just accepted it as a matter of fact, and for the most part, I wore long sleeves and jeans all the time to cover up the pale skin and the scars. I didn't want to bring attention to myself by wearing something cute or trendy. I realize now that by not caring, I was bringing attention to myself in a different way. He made me so self-conscious. I hated that I couldn't be unaffected by him looking at me, and talking to me. I just ignored him as much as I could.

Of course, my creative writing professor had other ideas. In the third week of class, he announced we'd be forming teams that would remain in place through the entire semester. The teams would be assigned based on our last names and be comprised of two members. Guess who was going to be my new school partner? Made me wish I had taken my mother's maiden name!

<u>Betsy</u>

It made me laugh to see Mer so flustered when she got back from class the day she got partnered up with Nate. She was so pissed! This is the girl who doesn't let anything bother her, or if it does, you'd never know it, and here she was throwing shit around our dorm room and swearing her head off. Once she calmed down, put her oxygen on and told me what was wrong, I had to bite back a smile. Finally, I thought. This was the one. This was the guy that I had been telling her about for all those years. The one who would sweep her off her feet when she wasn't expecting it.

For the briefest of moments, when the professor announced the groups, I thought Merry was going to blow a gasket. She turned red, which is only significant to mention because she's always so fair, and looked like she was going to get up and walk out of class. Then, she composed herself, and just like that, the storm passed and she went back to being a sphinx. Part of me wanted to tell her she was so much prettier when she was actually expressing herself, but I didn't know her well enough. Yet.

We pushed our desks together, or rather, I pushed mine towards her because I always sat next to her in class. The gist of the project was that we would be given a writing prompt weekly; a single sentence geared to getting us to write. We each had to write a minimum of two pages and then submit it to the other person for evaluation. I should probably mention I wasn't an English major; I was an engineering major, unofficially minoring in English. I loved to read, but took the writing class because I figured it couldn't be that hard, and because I'd be graded on my effort not the quality of my work. After all, who can grade you on what you think, I figured.

Immediately upon pushing my desk towards hers, she looked at me. I could see her eyes were darker today, nearly gray instead of the gunmetal I had become accustomed to seeing. She had taken out her notebook and a pen, and seemed to be waiting for me to say something to her.

"Come here often?" Yep. That's what came out of my mouth. And damn that girl, there wasn't even a small smile at my stupidity. I was puzzled as to what I could do to get to know her. "Sorry, that was pretty corny I know. I just never know what to say around you." Perhaps honesty would work.

"Why do you need to say anything to me at all?" she mumbled, as she looked around the room as if to find a way to escape. She sounded hoarse, almost as though she was losing her voice, and I kept thinking how sexy she sounded without even trying. Without even wanting to be. Could she be so blind as to how she affected me? And I didn't even get it. I didn't understand what it was about her.

"Because that's what happens when you meet someone you want to know more about. You talk to them. Try to learn more about them. Share war stories. That kind of thing," I said with a smile. And still. . . no smile from her. What did I have to do?

"Well Nathaniel Holden, I don't know that you'd want to trade war stories with me. As for learning more about me, there's not much to learn. I'm probably the simplest, plainest person you'll meet in your life. You're better off wasting your time with someone who's more interesting." After this speech, the longest one she had said directly to me at one time, she closed her eyes again, furrowing her brow.

"Is something wrong? Can I get you anything?" She looked like she was going to faint right there on the desk, and I'd have to catch her before she fell. She looked up at me with disdain and shook her head no.

"The only thing wrong is the fact we have to do a group project in a creative writing class. It's asinine. I have no idea how this professor finds a group project in a creative writing class to be rational," she said wincing.

'Hey, are you sure you're okay? We can get out of here if you want, I'm sure the professor won't mind," I said, worriedly to her. She looked like she was in some serious pain and I was starting to get worried.

"I'm. FINE. Let's just get the logistics of this whole thing worked out so I can get this done and over with as soon as possible." With that, she seemed to shut down the idea that we would be cordial through this whole thing. Or rather, that she would be cordial through it. I was positive there was something else going on with her that she wasn't saying, and knowing what I know now, I'm amazed she was able to withstand going to class, let alone carrying a full load of classes in preparation for graduation.

*****

I wasn't *trying* to be nasty to Nate in class. I was in so much pain; so much more than I had been before, and I could barely concentrate in class let alone be friendly and personable. I barely made it back to the dorm room, and was lucky enough to make it back there before Bets got back from her class, so I could compose myself. It was a week before Spring Break. I kept telling myself that if I could hold on till then, the doc would implant the pacemaker, and I could then go on my Merry way (pun intended.)

I was starting to become scared. Scared that now that I was this close to graduating and accomplishing something I was told I was never going to make it to see, that I wouldn't get there. I was terrified my heart would finally give out. I was determined to make it through graduation, and determined to walk that stage. I was barely eating because it hurt so damn bad. My thoughts were dark and I wasn't sleeping. I kept thinking, what happens if I close my eyes, and they don't reopen? I couldn't do that to Bets at school. I snuck in naps where I wasn't sleeping, and wasn't fully awake, but just enough to recharge my failing batteries and give me the energy needed to keep going until those next few precious stolen moments.

I wasn't going to put what I'm about to put in here, in here. I don't know if anyone would have thought that I had considered ending things at several points throughout the years since I was diagnosed. When I first had open heart surgery, when I had the kidney issues, and again and again when I was just so fucking tired of being tired. A slight adjustment of my medication, and I could have slipped off, and no one would have been the wiser. A pillow placed ever so slightly over my face, when my oxygen mask was conveniently not on. A fall down the stairs. A big pot of coffee to rev my heart up until it crapped out on me. I could have come up with any number of things. And I considered every single one. Time and time again. But I didn't kill myself, as much as I wanted to.

I don't mean to speak lightly of the ending of my life, or suicide in general. I think if anyone could speak frankly of life and death, it would be someone who has been so close to the end of their life that they could understand how blurry the line between the two realms is. I understood the war the doctors were waging against me. Because wasn't that what was happening? My doctors were fighting a war against the evil little bastard who resided inside my chest and I was caught in the crossfire, and I don't honestly believe if my father or my best friend or my sister even would blame me if they had any idea how much pain I was in. Physical pain was a good portion of it, but every time I took a pill, or my doctor cut into me, or I had to get another scan, it was an assault on my mental health. There were days I felt like I was going crazy. Lack of oxygen, lack of a life, lack of my health; it was all weighing on me and I couldn't move and I couldn't breathe and I just didn't want to be here anymore. I had stitches and staples, acid reflux from all of the pills, I couldn't eat what I wanted, and I couldn't drink what I wanted, I couldn't go dancing and I couldn't drive a car. I was a sack of flesh with bones and blood and I just wanted to cry and not be here anymore.

It's pathetic how pathetic I felt.

Each time my heart weakened and I got worse, I began to fear that I was disappointing Laney and my mom and Mr. and Mrs. Jay for not being more than I was at that moment. And if I killed myself, I could only imagine the wrath I would face if I made it to heaven. I don't know if I believe in God, and I don't know if I believe for one moment that I will be saved if I were to die in any way, let alone by my own hand. Fortunately for all involved, including myself, my fear of the unknown is enough to prevent me from going down any of those paths.

Betsy

Merry wasn't doing well. She tried to hide it, but she was clearly in pain. She never once complained and never once said anything, and was the same old stubborn pain in my ass as she ever was. But something was definitely wrong. She was almost constantly on oxygen when she was in the room, something she previously only needed at night after long days. She kept massaging her shoulder and her collar bone, as though rubbing it would make it feel better. When she took her makeup off at night, or re-polished her nails, the blue that was ever present in her eyelids, lips and nails was deepening. She was always able to play it off prior to this as a trick of the light if she was ever caught without her war paint, but there was no hiding the deep blue that was present. Without the oxygen, she would gasp for air, and then when I'd ask her about it, she just said she had to walk the stairs since the elevator was slow, or she just walked too quickly from her last class.

But that wasn't it. If it were just her being physically unwell, I could strong arm her into the doctor, or call her dad as I had done so many times before. This was different. She looked desperate. She wasn't much of a crier ever, but there were nights I'd wake up to the unmistakable sound of sniffing and quiet sobs.

Everything came to a head one night right before spring break in March, when I found her sitting up on her bed, head against the wall with her eyes closed. For the briefest of moments, I thought she was dead because I couldn't see any movement in her chest. She had taken her makeup off for the night, and you could trace the blue blood vessels on her eyelids and cheeks much like seeing a meandering river from a plane. I nearly ran over to shake her, and make sure she was still alive and breathing when she opened her eyes, and looked at me.

"Ever wonder what it's like to be dead, Bets? Not the act of physically dying, but what happens afterwards?" she whispered as she rotated her neck and rubbed her shoulder for the 18 millionth time in the past 2 months. "Like I wonder if it's just like an elevator and I'll be taken up to heaven and Mom and Laney will be there to greet me. Only will it be weird that I'm how old I am now, and they'll be how old they were then? Will Laney still be my older sister then? Shit, what happens if I get on the wrong elevator and I'm shipped down to hell? Oh wait, too late, I'm already there. It can't get much worse than this," she said, with a furrowed brow as if the idea puzzled her.

"Mer, why are you thinking about dying, when we have midterms coming up and spring break around the corner?" I tried to laugh it off and act like the question didn't bother me, but it did right down to the core.

"I think I was right. I do think I pissed someone off in a former life, Bets. Think about it for a sec. Neither mom nor Laney had to go through all of this. Just one minute they were there, and the next, poof. Gone. It makes sense," she said, looking past me, as though she didn't want to see my reaction to her thought.

"I don't think of it like that, Mer. I think we're all given what we can handle. I think it shows you're stronger than your mom or Laney was, because look at everything you've been through and you're still here," I said desperately to her. I didn't like how this conversation was going, and I couldn't figure out what I could say to turn it around.

"Who gives us all we can handle? God?" she laughed derisively. "I've read the damn bible. I've read damn near every single major religious text I could find over these past 15 years of being fucked up from my stupid heart. I'm sorry; I can't buy into the idea that I was chosen to go through this, when some serial killer gets to be healthy and live until he's 90. Or that my mom and my sister were taken so young when there are people out there who have never done a damned thing for anyone in their lives and get to do whatever the FUCK they want and I'm stuck here attached to a fucking machine to breathe with a heart that sucks. I can't do anything. I don't get to live a life like everyone else gets. I don't get to fall in love; I don't get to go for a run. I can't even go to the damn mall without having anxiety or flashbacks of having a fucking heart attack when I was 5. I'm going to college, and for WHAT? I can't work. I can't hold down a job. I'm a fucking drain on you and my dad and my only living sister hates my guts and I can't even have a pleasant conversation with anyone without thinking how goddamn lucky they are to be in their skin and how they don't even realize what I would do to be them. I don't want this life anymore Bets. I don't want this anymore."

I don't know if she realized tears were soaking her shirt. I don't know if she realized tears were dripping down my face. I dropped my bag and my purse on the ground, and walked over to her bed and sat down next to her, and put my arm around her.

"You know, Carrots, if you weren't here, your dad would have to put up with Sophie by himself. That would be terrible for him. And, after Mrs. Jay died, I know you made Mr. Jay feel better. He loved you so much. You were his favorite and you weren't even related." I took a deep breath here. "You are NOT a burden on me. You're my best friend. You've taught me so much over these last 15 years that I couldn't even begin to thank you for."

"Like what? How to spend hours in a hospital when you're not even sick? How to sit still and not be able to do all the stuff that a normal kid gets to do because your best friend is practically an invalid?"

"You taught me to appreciate the little things. You taught me to notice things that if I wasn't sitting still, I'd never have seen. Like how the drops of dew on your roses catches the light and you can see images in them. Or the butterflies that flit around the flowers you put there especially for them. You taught me that there was so much more to life than going to the mall, and watching TV or any of the superficial things that kids do that mean absolutely nothing once they get older. You taught me to live life deliberately, without fear of what would happen today or tomorrow or down the road, because none of that was promised to us. And most of all, you taught me to learn how to shut up and listen. Mom still thanks you in her prayers every single night for that. She tells me so every time I call her. 'You tell my Merry-girl that I thank the baby Jesus for her every night for teaching you some self-control.' I so wish I was joking, but I'm not." I rolled my eyes for effect, and I could see the tension in her shoulders had released, and the biggest storm had passed over us. "I know this sucks. And I know if there was anything in this world I could do, including prostituting myself on a street corner so you weren't in pain any longer and your heart was fixed, I would do it. I would hold it over your head until you outlived me, but I would do it. Can you imagine the stories I'd have? Me tottering around in some CFM heels with a sign saying 'I'm hooking for my friend, because she wants to know what it's like to live on the edge.'" At this, Merry burst into laughter with tears still coming from her eyes. The laughter made her grab her shoulder again, which made her laugh harder, and even though it hurt her, I was happy.

It's true what they say. The hardest thing in the world for me was watching my best friend go through hell on earth, knowing full well there was next to nothing I could do but to keep her spirits up. Days like that were few and far between thankfully, but my own heart dropped into my stomach when they came because I knew the pain had to be horrible for her to think like that.

*****

One more class. That's what I kept saying to myself. One more class before I was off for a week for spring break, where I would be holed up in a hospital. Part of me thought it was so sad that I was looking forward to it. No beaches, certainly no bikinis or drunken exploits in some coastal town with a couple thousand of my closest friends. Just me, a few good books and a comfy hospital bed. I look back now, and I realize I stopped believing in any future after that last semester of college. I was angry. Angry at the world for how unfair this was to me. Angry at myself for not being able to just suck it up and deal with it the way everyone thought I was. (and 'everyone' at the time was what, all of a handful of people who even knew about what was going on?) But most of all, I was angry at the idea of what could have been.

I stopped dreaming of what I would grow up to be when I was 6. It wasn't conscious; I realize that now. I just wanted to grow up. But before that, I dreamed of fairytales, and of tomorrows and of how I would grow up and meet Prince Charming and we'd get married and live happily ever after. There was no option for happily ever after once you've had a couple of heart attacks, an open-heart surgery and a kidney transplant with a side of dialysis. Maybe if any of that had led to my heart being fixed, maybe if I were feeling well for longer periods of time, maybe then I'd have believed there was something more for me than this.

But this was what I had to look forward to. I wanted to make the best out of it, and for the most part, before college, I did. I had a few moments then, sure.

But the three years of college where I was as healthy as I had ever been, served no purpose other than to demonstrate the vast difference between me and everything else. College was a place for futures. Where they are discovered, formulated, built and changed. Where you could figure out what you wanted to be, or what you didn't want to be. Where you could find yourself. My future was decided so many years before and after getting to within 2 months of college ending; I finally realized what a waste it all was. It made my temper short, which was odd because I never used to have a temper. It made me short and snarky with people I came in contact with, even Bets. I didn't want to talk to my dad on the phone, because inevitably the conversations centered on how I was feeling, was I okay, did I need anything. My life had become less about me, and had become nearly all about my heart. It was what kept me alive, but it was also what kept me from being everything I could have been. Everything that I desperately wanted to be and never would be.

I walked into class that last day before spring break having done my homework, but not prepared to talk about Nate's piece from last week. I contemplated skipping, not because I didn't feel well, (even though I didn't), but because I just didn't want to deal with it anymore. My surgery was first thing the following morning, and I just had to get through this class before I was heading to the hospital. School was in the way, Nate was in the way, everything was in the damn way of me hopefully feeling better after tomorrow. Combine that with a raging headache, and I was just not in the mood to be anywhere around people. But of course, Nate didn't get that message. Nothing I did kept him from asking how I was doing, asking how my week had been, asking if I needed anything, and generally, just being smiley and happy. It was so bloody annoying. I know it was made worse because I wasn't feeling well, but good God it was grating on my every last nerve. I kept telling myself just to get through this, get through class, and you can go home and get away from all of this.

I wanted to see Merry before spring break the way you crave coffee in the morning. That feeling that you weren't fully functioning until you took that first sip. The way it washed over you and made everything right with the world. I had read over her homework piece from the last week, and it was so poignant and so infecting that I couldn't wait to tell her how incredible it was. Even though I was getting used to her hands-off attitude, there were times it felt like there was more behind that mask of hers. Like she wanted to tell me more and didn't know the words to use to tell me what was on her mind. I wanted to respect her privacy, but I also had a feeling all was not well in her world.

I pulled my desk up to hers and waited with my toe tapping for her to arrive. It was weird; she was never late to class. It was the first time she hadn't beaten everyone in the class to get here. When she finally arrived, I was taken aback. She looked. . . I don't know how to describe it. She barely had any makeup on and I only noticed that because I could see a bluish tint to her skin through the little bit that was there. When her eyes scanned the room, it seemed like the act of the moving the muscles hurt her. She had nothing with her but a small purse that she was barely hanging on to, and a slim folder, which I assume held the homework. She didn't sit down as much as she fell into her desk chair, and only the rubber soled bottoms of the bright yellow Converse she wore kept her from sliding down through the desk and under it. As it was, she was so far slunk down in the seat; her head hit the back of the chair with a soft thud.

"Hey there sunshine, can I get you anything? Water? Pepsi?" I asked hesitantly, knowing she rebuffed these questions each and every class.

"I can't drink Pepsi," she said hoarsely as she pulled herself upright. Seemed like she had lost her voice completely, because she went from normally having this totally sexy porn voice, to sounding like a 20-year smoker. Whatever had been going on with her over the first 2 ½ of the semester had progressed and sitting in class next to her like this was like waiting for something bad to happen. You knew it was going to, but you just weren't quite sure when it would.

"Can't drink Pepsi? What about coffee? Coke? I'm a Pepsi guy myself. The caffeine allows me able to be around other people without wanting to bite their heads off." I was trying anything in my power to keep her talking and trying to keep her focused on something. She turned and looked at me; and for a minute I feared she was going to say something sarcastic that I wouldn't have a quick response to. She looked almost haunted, as though she wasn't there with me.

"I can't have caffeine at all. I don't drink pop. Don't drink coffee. I drink water. Sometimes herbal tea. But that's it. Hey Nate?" To hear her pose a question to me, something she hadn't ever done to this point, made me feel like I'd gotten through to her. Finally.

"I don't think I can stay through class today. I have to go." And with that, she pushed her way up out of the chair and staggered towards the door. Since we were still a few minutes before class, the professor hadn't gotten there yet; I grabbed my jacket and pushed my way out of the door right after her. I was glad I did, because I was able to catch her before she collapsed in the hall. I sat on the ground, holding her in my arms, and after what felt like an eternity of me calling her name; she opened her eyes, looked up at me, and swore softly.

"You know you didn't have to faint if you wanted to get my attention, Merry. You've had it since the first time I saw you," I said with a smile on my face. "While I'd love nothing more than to sit here holding you like this, I'm thinking we should get up off the floor."

"Don't think I can walk. So tired," she said and started to close her eyes again.

"No, no sweetheart, come on open those baby blues. Is there someone I can call to come help? Should I call 911?" By this time, I was starting to get a little worried. No one was coming down the halls. I was starting to figure out where I could carry her to get her some help, when she patted her pocket.

"Phone. Bets. Call Bets," she whispered. I reached into the pocket she patted, and found a listing for a Betsy in the phone, and hoped the call would go through where we were in Clemens. Of course it didn't, so I scooped her up, and fast-walked through the halls and into the elevator, which took us to the ground floor. Still cradling her, I walked to the window, and adjusted my grip on her so I could hit the button to call Betsy.

"Girl, aren't you supposed to be in class right now? Don't tell me you decided to skip right before surgery?"

"Uhhhh hi. I'm Nate and Merry left class and fainted in the hall." I didn't know how else to say it.

"Where are you right now?" All of the sudden, the cheerful tone went business-like. I told her where we were, and she advised me she would be calling 911, as well as Merry's doctor and that if anything else changed with her, I should call her back immediately but to keep talking to her. I ended the call, and looked down at the girl in my arms who felt like she weighed next to nothing.

"Hey there sunshine, your friend sounds like she's worried about it. She's calling an ambulance for you. And your doctor. I just have to keep you safe and warm until then. Hope you don't mind." I felt like I was babbling, but I wanted to keep talking to her to try to keep her awake.

"Always worried. Like it's her job." She winced as she said that and started to adjust in my arms, and I loosened my hold so she could.

"It's good to have people worried about you. It means that you've made an impression on them that they care about what happens to you."

"Pain in my ass. They should just let me go." She winced again, and for the life of me, I couldn't figure out what was wrong with her. She tilted her neck back, and her shirt gaped a bit and it was then, I saw the scar on her neck, and the start of a scar on her chest. Whatever she had been through, it had been serious, I remember thinking to myself.

"Let you go? Where, on Spring Break? You and I should go somewhere once we graduate. Somewhere warm away from these Buffalo winters. What do you think?" I felt like I was starting to babble, but it was then I noticed the sound of sirens approaching. Before they got there though, I saw a small blue car peel through the lot outside, screech to a stop in a handicap spot and a tallish brunette rush out of it leaving the driver's door wide open.

"How is she?" Looks like there was no messing around with this girl.

"She's in and out. She almost collapsed walking into class, and then just said she had to leave and got up and walked out. When I followed her, I caught her right outside as she fell. She didn't hit her head or anything. Said she's tired." Looking down at Merry in my arms, she looked like she could have been sleeping, if it weren't for the pinched look on her face.

"Hey there Carrots, if you wanted to get the hottie's attention, fainting was definitely the way to do it," Betsy said in a cheerful voice, which betrayed the worry on her face.

"Shut the hell up, Peas," Merry whispered, her eyes still closed. She seemed uncomfortable and was fidgeting in my arms, but there was no way I was letting go until the EMTs showed up. I could hear a commotion outside, and it seemed as though the ambulance had finally arrived after what felt like an eternity.

"Mer, I'm gonna call your dad okay?" Betsy said this as she walked towards the doors to hold them open for the EMTs. I heard her talking to them, and while I didn't understand most of what she said at the time, whatever was wrong with Merry was something serious that had been going on for some time.

"Should have let me crack my head," Merry whispered as the EMT came over.

"Now why would I do that?" I said to her, as I laid her gently on the floor and placed my jacket behind her head.

"Never gonna hear the end of this from Bets. Probably planning our wedding in her head now," she said as they covered her mouth with an oxygen mask. And just like that, they lifted her up and whisked her into the back of the ambulance. I stood there and looked down at the spot on the floor where she was laying, and reached for my jacket.

"Thanks for calling me. I appreciate it. How did you know to do that?" I heard Betsy ask through the haze of processing what just happened.

"She told me to." I held up her phone that I still had. "That was probably the scariest thing I've ever witnessed." I went to give her the phone, and she held her hand up.

"Hold onto it. It'll give you an excuse to visit her at the hospital. Call me later tonight. I'll try and explain as much as I can." She paused at that. "You care about her, don't you?"

"Hard not to, even though she pushes me away." It was somehow easy to admit that to this girl I didn't know. "I'll let you go, and I'll give you a call later, and we can make arrangements to get the phone back to her." I thought she was going to say something else, but she just waved and ran back out to the car, and drove off.

*****

I woke up in the hospital mortified. Absolutely, horrifically, ashamedly mortified. Bets was sitting in the room with me (as apparently, I'd been admitted) reading a book and as I came to, she put this shit-eating grin on her face. Knew it. I just knew it.

"Damn girl, he's beautiful. And he's totally got the hots for you. He carried you all the way from the basement without even blinking. You're going to owe him one," she smiled like a pleased serial killer at me. Part of me hoped this was her way of keeping my mind off my precarious health, but I knew better. This was the opening she was looking for.

"What the hell happened to me?" I croaked as I tried to adjust myself.

"Oh, just the usual, your oxygen levels sucked because your heart sucks and once they got the O2 cranking in you, and ran all the usual tests, they seem to think you'll be okay for the surgery. The reason why you've had all these headaches and the aching in your shoulder is because you weren't getting enough oxygen to your brain and your muscles. The doc seems to think you should have been on oxygen 24/7, instead of just a few hours a day like you have been. And in a wheelchair, not walking. Oh yeah, and not in freaking college. And having the surgery months ago like they told you to. They were amazed you were able to function at all with as crappy as your vitals were. But I told them you had been brain damaged well before this. Your doc mentioned the pacemaker would kick start your heart when it starts to lag behind where it should be." And this is why

Bets was my healthcare proxy. One of the smartest things I ever did. Minus the sarcasm. Expected it, but could've done without it.

Nate

I paced in my living room for hours, until I thought it would be a good time to call Betsy. I think I saw every single minute pass from 3 o'clock when I got home from school, until 8 when I finally decided it was okay to call. I could tell immediately when I called that everything was better, just from the tone in her voice. I didn't know what I expected to hear about Merry, but I didn't think I would hear that she had a congenital heart condition. Merry was doing much better than the last time I saw her, and was resting comfortably when she left for the night. Betsy seemed extremely well-versed in the medical lingo, and I had to stop her several times to ask questions about what she meant by this or that. I can laugh about it now, but I took notes, with horrible misspellings just to make sure I got down everything she was saying. Merry was scheduled to have a pacemaker implanted the following morning, and would be in the hospital through the weekend, so I could come up and visit her as early as Saturday afternoon.

I was still pacing when my mom got home from work. She was a nurse and worked days mostly, but put in a ton of OT so I wouldn't need to work while I was in school. I wound up bouncing some of what I heard from Betsy off of her, and got the impression from my mom the condition she had wasn't minor. In fact, if she was having a pacemaker put in, my mom thought it had progressed to the point where medication wasn't able to help as much anymore.

It made sense. Why she was so hands-off. Why she was so pale. I figured that was likely what her mom died from, if it was congenital and her father was still around. (At this time, I didn't know about Laney. Knew nothing of Sophie.) I just couldn't imagine living like that. And I certainly couldn't imagine not having my mom around.

I hemmed and hawed about visiting her on that Saturday, and what I should bring to her. I didn't want to risk bringing her chocolate or wine because I doubted they let heart patients have those. Flowers seemed like the way to go, and I must have spent an hour in the florist, before I decided to say screw it and went with a bouquet of red roses. When I walked down the hallway, and knocked on the door to the room they told me she was in, I almost turned around and left, except I heard a feeble 'Come in' from Merry.

The room was darkened, and a TV played on the wall across from her bed. She had the room to herself, and was by herself. When my eyes finally adjusted, and I could see her, I sighed quietly.

"So now you know," she said, still pretty hoarse. She had tubes running from both arms and wires connected to leads on her chest. She wore no makeup, and for the first time, I could see how see-through her skin was. She looked like a child lying in the bed, and as I came around the end, I sensed she was embarrassed that I knew what was going on.

"Yeah well, having a gorgeous blonde faint in my arms and then rushed to the hospital required an explanation. How are you feeling sunshine?" I wanted to sound happy, but I felt so horrible for her. What kind of life had she led to this point?

"No idea why you call me gorgeous. And I don't like being called sunshine. You sure you didn't bump your head when you grabbed me?" She grumbled without the hesitation that had been present just a few days ago.

"Nope, no head trauma here! And I call you gorgeous because you are, or did you forget that I said that when we first talked in class? As for the sunshine part, I don't know. You remind me of the sun. The blonde hair, the blue eyes." I shrugged as I set the roses down on her bedside table and sat in the chair next to her. "You never answered. Maybe you're the one with the head trauma. How are you doing?" She huffed at this, and I have to say, I was pretty pleased to see her attitude coming back to her.

"I'm fine. I'll be out in a few days, once everything is all squared away and the doc is sure my pacemaker is adjusted properly. What did Bets tell you?" She wouldn't look at me when she asked, and I realized as well as being embarrassed she was nervous. I couldn't figure out why, because it wasn't like we hadn't spoken before. Her hand kept picking at the blanket next to her leg, so I grabbed it through the bars on the side of the bed and held on to it. It was cool to the touch, so I started rubbing it between my hands to warm it up.

"She told me you have a bad heart," I said as I kept holding her hand. I looked up at her, and saw she was looking at me with that sphinx gaze again, so I continued. "She said you'd been through a few surgeries throughout the years, and they were hoping this one would be your last for a while. And she mentioned a ton of shit that I didn't understand at all, so I asked my mom."

"Wait, you talked about me with your mom? Why? Does she think I'm some sort of freakshow now?" Merry interrupted in that gravelly voice that sounded suspiciously like she was about to cry, and tried to pull her hand away from me.

"No. Not at all. She's a nurse on the surgical floor at Roswell Park. I didn't understand what your friend was telling me, so I asked her what it all meant. She actually thinks you're pretty hardcore because you're going to college through all of this. And then, when I told her that you were a pretty little blonde, well, she started to understand why I was interested. She can't wait to meet you. I told her I would wait until you were out of the hospital to take you to dinner though," I said with a smile looking back at her, still holding onto her hand.

"There is something seriously wrong with you, isn't there? You don't get it. I'm not some normal college chick looking to be your next conquest. I'm not looking to do anything more than graduate in May and go home to live with my father until my fucked-up heart gives up and I die. There's no dinner. There's no date. There's no us," she said vehemently, pulling her hand out of mine finally.

"I think I'll wait till you're off the pain meds before we figure out which restaurant to go to. You're not vegetarian or anything like that right?" I paused here, figuring she'd have some smart-ass comment, and upon receiving nothing but an open-mouthed stare, continued. "I'm a big steak guy personally, so I was thinking we could find somewhere that had good steak."

"You're insane. There's something wrong with you," she stated flatly.

"Nope. Nothing wrong with me. Last time I checked you were the one in the hospital bed, sunshine." At that, I rose from the chair with a smile, and grabbed the roses from the bedside table, and walked out to the nurses' station to see about getting them in water. I'm sure Merry thought I was leaving.

Betsy

I walked into the hospital to see Nate leaning on the nurses' station, charming the pants off the night nurse. I held off going into Mer's room, just to see what was going on, and was pleased to see he had these beautiful blood red roses in his hands that he was getting ready to place in a vase.

"Well hello there handsome. Are those for me?" I couldn't help but tease him because he was so clearly enamored by my best friend. He looked up, as though surprised anyone was speaking to him, and a faint blush filled his cheeks.

"Shit, was I supposed to buy flowers for you too? If Merry throws these back in my face, you're more than welcome to them," he replied with a rueful smile on his face. Looked like Merry was in quite the mood.

"She giving you a hard time? She's not good in hospitals. You should have seen her after the kidney transplant. Refused pain meds so she didn't ruin the kidney Sophie the Dramatic gave her. I'm betting she's not having any this time either." I watched as he kept adjusting the roses in the vase, like he was nervous.

"Who's Sophie the Dramatic? And why wouldn't she take pain medication? Does she not feel pain like the rest of us humans?" He asked with an incredulous look on his face. He was so damn cute, I'm telling you. I walked him over to the little sitting room near the nurses' station, and sat him down.

"Merry hasn't taken pain meds since her first open heart surgery. She took them for the first heart attack, mainly because she wasn't quite 6 yet, and they wanted her to be comfortable. Once they started cutting into her, she told everyone she didn't want them anymore. It got to the point where her dad and I would crush them up and put them in her food when we knew she had to be in pain. Tells us she'd rather feel the pain, than to mask it." I shrugged at this, as it was something I no longer argued with her about. He seemed so stunned. "And Sophie is her eldest sister. She's 9 years older than Merry. And a raving bitch. I hate her ever-loving guts. Although she did give Merry her kidney, which is about the only redeeming thing she's done since I've known her. Oh wait, she gave Merry her Laney doll too. But that's it." He looked like I had hit him with a bat.

"And who's Laney? I'm sorry, I feel like I'm missing a bunch here. Kind of like when we talked the other night . . . it's all going over my head!" Poor guy.

"Laney was Merry's sister. She died when Merry was 5. Same condition Merry has. Same condition Merry's mom had. She was riding her bike in the driveway and just collapsed and died. Laney was only 9. Merry ran to the neighbor's house for help, but it was too late. She was already gone. She was the closest thing to a mom Mer had." I said softly. "I met Merry at Laney's wake." I knew Merry was going to be pissed if she found out I told him, but he needed to know what he was getting into. He sat back in the chair, and looked down at the flowers in his hands.

"Wow. I don't even know what to say. It explains quite a bit about why she's so," he paused.

"Combative? Stubborn? Difficult? Absolute pain in the ass?" I interjected.

"Closed off, I was thinking. I told her I wanted to take her to dinner and introduce her to my mom, and she sort of flipped out on me and said her only plans were to graduate and go home and die." Damn that girl.

"Nate, I'm going to be honest with you. Mainly because you're the only guy that's ever been interested in her that's truly been aware of her condition. But also, because you don't seem to be like other guys she's dated before." I stopped here, trying to figure out how to say what I was thinking the best way possible. "Merry's condition is serious. It's been serious for a long time. She can't do most of what someone else with a normally functioning heart can do. There's quite a bit she's missed out on because of her heart, and because of that, she feels like there isn't much she can do. I've known her so long, I didn't have to crack the shell she has now and I'm kind of grandfathered in. She doesn't have any other friends, because she refuses to make any. She had to fight her father till he agreed to her coming to college, and live in the dorms. He only allowed it to happen when I told him I would go with her and we would dorm together. She dated in the first couple years she was here, but then she had her second heart attack over the summer, and she stopped." I was nearly certain this was going to scare him away, but I didn't want him to not know, and then figure it out afterwards and walk away.

"Why are you telling me this? You looking to warn me off?" he asked.

"I'm telling you this, because my best friend has a broken heart. And if you fuck with her and make that worse, they will never find your body." I stated with the smallest smile on my face. "I'm not kidding. She's been through hell, and for as much venom she spews, she's fragile. I wouldn't hesitate to do anything for this girl up to and including felony homicide because she asks me for absolutely nothing. Consider this your one and only warning." I waited a moment to see how he reacted, and seeing nothing that worried me, continued. "Tell me, what's your plan for winning her over?" He laughed a little as he looked into the bouquet in his hands.

"I find myself amazed by the way your mind works. I don't know. Same thing I've been doing. Just keep showing up, putting myself in her face. Just keep being here for her."

"If I may be so bold, might I make a few suggestions? The roses were a good idea. When she's not completely down and out like she is now, she keeps some pretty incredible gardens at her dad's house. You should see them. I keep telling her she should send them into one of those home magazines, but she doesn't do it for the praise, she does it for the peace it brings her. Since she isn't able to do the things you normally do with someone, you're going to have to be a bit more creative for whatever you plan next. She loves to read. She loves music. She loves all genres of both books and music, and she has more books and records than anyone else I know. She likes watching movies, but if given the choice, she'd pick the book over the movie any day. Oh. And between you and I, she loves pizza." I hoped that by giving him this information, he would be able to put the pieces together and surprise her, but I wasn't holding my breath on it.

"Pizza huh? Good to know. I offered to take her out for steak." He laughed a little at that.

"She's been on a pretty strict diet ever since she was a kid, so as not to piss off her heart and her kidney. Pizza and double-stuffed Oreos are her weaknesses. Her father would kill me if he knew, but we had a standing pizza date every time she slept over my house, which was every other week until we graduated. Now we get it at least once a week at school." I looked at my watch and realized how late it was getting. "I should get in there before she calls my mom wondering why I'm not here. Do you want me to take those into her?" I asked, knowing the answer already.

"Nope. I'll take them. Let's go." With that, he got out of the chair and held out his hand to me to help me up.

"Hey Nate, if you decide blondes aren't to your liking, you can always check out what this brunette has to offer," I said with a wink, taking his hand and getting up. He laughed, and we walked towards Merry's room. Walking in to the darkness, I saw she had Jeopardy on, just like when we were kids. I paused our progress in the door, waiting for it.

"'Logically, it's the middle book of Dante's Divine Comedy.' What is Purgatorio?" There were few things I could count on in this life, but Merry knowing her Jeopardy questions was one of them. I motioned him in, and I was pleased to see her sitting more upright in bed, with some red Jell-O in front of her.

"Well hello there! It's just like Friday nights back home!" I exclaimed, noting she wasn't looking at me, but at Nate next to me.

"Yeah, minus the pizza. Oh yeah, and that whole 'home' thing. And the whole surgery thing and being in the hospital. Let's not think for a second that just because I'm here so damn much that it's like home," she threw back at me, spooning Jell-O into her mouth. I grabbed the other spoon on her tray table.

"Please tell me this other cup is for me. You know how much I love cherry Jell-O," I said as I reached for it.

She reached to snatch it away and set it further away from me on her tray. "No, you don't deserve Jell-O. You've been plotting. I know you've been plotting, because HE hasn't said a bloody word." With that, she looked at me darkly, and then back at him.

"No idea what you're talking about, sunshine. I met Betsy in the hallway and she kindly assisted me in arranging your roses. I just came back in to make sure you didn't need anything else before I left for the night," Nate came back with ease.

"Why do you insist on calling me sunshine? Ugh, you are so annoying," Merry snapped. Nate smiled, and I realized he seemed to be enjoying himself. I was right. He was smitten with her.

"I'll leave them here so you can see them, and be reminded of me. I'll see you tomorrow." With that, he left the room, and I was left sitting next to Mer. I did not expect what happened next. Out of the blue, I felt a slimy something hit my face and slide down into my lap.

"What the hell, Mer?!" She threw Jell-O at me. A day after having surgery. I'm not saying I love having Jell-O thrown at me, but it was a sign of her feeling better, which was worth the mess.

"What the hell, Mer?" she said in a high-pitched voice, obviously mocking tone. "You KNOW what the hell. It's bad enough that he played knight in shining armor and I have to deal with that. But I don't need you colluding with him in some skewed attempt at setting me up for a Happily Ever After. STOP," she said vehemently.

"You know, that speech would've had more effect if you weren't shoving Jell-O into your face." Oh, how I loved seeing the fire in her eyes.

"I am not doing this. I am not starting anything with him. I am not going to be responsible for dying on him once he becomes attached. He's like a puppy dog for Christ's sake. I don't need a puppy. It's not happening," she announced. For someone who was so calm all of the time, this situation riled her up. It made her prettier than normal if that was even possible, giving her some color she didn't have on a daily basis. I said something that has weighed on me since I first began to understand how her health would affect her life.

"What about me? It's ok for you to break his heart, but not mine?" I said half-jokingly.

"Bets, you and I are like peas and carrots. Besides. . . I couldn't get rid of you if I tried. You know too much." Her mouth smiled, but it never reached those baby blues of hers. She was so illogically infuriating, so fucking stubborn. It was that spine that kept her alive and was the best part of the Merry I loved, but also kept her from being so much more.

"Before you have a coronary," (I expected THAT dirty look) "just give him a chance to talk. Maybe there IS something more there. Something not apparent from the interactions you have had so far."

"Bets, he can't cure me. He can't fix my heart. He can't make me better. And I don't think of him like that. Not at ALL," she declared haughtily.

"Uh huh. Sure you don't. Totally believe you. 100%. You're not dead, Mer. You're still female. Unless you're into chicks. No, I would know if you're into chicks... For all you know, he can give your heart a reason to keep beating."

Wow, I hadn't ever gotten that look before.

"I don't make it a practice of living a cliché so I would greatly appreciate it if you'd stop dropping them on me like rain. And you know better than to throw that at me. He has no fucking clue what he's interested in. I'm just the shiny new toy to play with," she corrected. "It would never work. He's not going to go for someone that can't go to the goddamn beach or on vacation or whatever the hell it is that normal people do." She stabbed her spoon into her newly empty Jell-O cup with a huff, and knowing it would piss her off, I grabbed the other one quickly and grabbed the extra spoon I had set back on the tray and began to slowly eat it, making a show of savoring it.

"Bet you wish you hadn't chucked that last little bit at me right about now, dontcha?" I smirked, wiggling my eyebrows at her.

"If you weren't the only person on this earth I was friends with, I would hate you right now. I would seriously hate your guts. This is stupid. Why are you backing this horse, and not any of the others I dated before him?" she exclaimed. "This is some serious bullshit right now! I don't need this. I just want to finish school."

I interrupted here, "And do what, go home and die? Seems like a brilliant plan. I'd ask if you were on drugs, but I know better so instead, I'll just say it's well past time the blonde in you made an appearance." I finished up the Jell-O, smacking my lips just to be a jerk, and I could sense her boiling next to me. "Listen. I get why you're all hands off with this guy, although I have to be honest, I would love nothing more than to get hands on with him. He's not going anywhere. I have no idea why he likes your stubborn ass, but he does, so I would imagine you better get it through that thick skull of yours that you're going to have to deal with him. It could be worse."

She looked at me and grumbled, "How could it be worse?" I looked back at her, unsurprised at the question.

"He could be hideous. At least he's smoking hot," I quipped back cheerfully at her. She growled back at me and that was pretty much the end of that conversation. I think back on it now, and I wonder if Merry knew then how different he was than any of the other guys she dated. And that the difference was what was pissing her off.

*****

I wanted to get out of the damn hospital. All I wanted was to get back home, and not stress out about Nate visiting me in the hospital. It wasn't enough that I generally looked like hell in class, with my nun-like clothing coverage, and pale, clammy appearance from the strain of walking back and forth so they could figure out what my pacemaker was supposed to be set at. I looked like complete shit in the hospital, in those decidedly un-sexy grayish white hospital gowns that did nothing but wash me out more than I was combined with stringy, dirty hair, and no makeup. Not that I had even tried to be alluring, but hearing that he would be coming back to visit me made me want to get out of Dodge as fast as possible. My doc wouldn't let me leave until Monday, so I was stuck getting a visit from Nate on Sunday afternoon.

I know now it was different with him, and I know that's why I was pushing back so much. This last health episode made me realize I likely wasn't long for this world without a new heart. They could keep cutting me open, pumping me full of drugs, but none of that was a solution. They were a stopgap measure and eventually the docs were going to run out of options. It was demoralizing and I felt sorry for myself. It was hard not to. And here was this guy who wanted to get to know me, and for what? To what end?

Before he came on that Sunday, I figured I would just be honest with him. It was logical once he knew how badly off I was, that he wouldn't want anything to do with me. We could be friendly until school ended, and then it would be done with.

But damned if he didn't surprise me. He walked into my room right before dinner with a gym bag, and proceeded to close my door, open the bag, and pull out plates, plastic solo cups and napkins. I tried to ask what was going on, but he just held his finger up to his lips to keep me quiet, and kept pulling things out of this bag. Next, he pulled out a carton of milk, and poured two glasses (skim milk, what guy drinks skim milk?!) and then placed a small box of pizza on my tray table. You could have knocked me over with a feather. If I were standing, of course.

"We'll have to eat this quick since you probably aren't allowed to eat pizza," he whispered, grabbing one of the plates. "Do you need me to cut it up for you?"

"Uh, no. I'm confused," I replied.

"Well, you like pizza, right? And most women I know prefer skim milk, so I figured since I can't bring a bottle of wine into a hospital the milk would work with the pizza and what I brought for dessert," he said with a full mouth of pizza. "Come on start eating so you don't get busted by the nurses!" I grabbed the plate, and started devouring the pizza. I have to say, whether it was because I was in the hospital, or that I hadn't had any in a couple weeks, it was the best I'd ever had. It was exactly how I like it. Well done, lots of cheese, and extra garlicky. I ate the piece quickly, and he motioned to ask if I wanted another, and I thought, 'what the hell, why not?' and nodded. He served us both another piece, and when we were done, cleaned up the mess, and then brought out a package of Double Stuf Oreos from his magic bag.

Well shit.

I wish I could have captured the look on Merry's face on camera that day. When I walked in, she seemed determined to speak, and then as I kept pulling things out of my bag, she just looked stunned. It was kind of awesome to surprise her like that. She didn't say much after the pizza and Oreos, and I left shortly afterwards, in case she was tired. I got a call from Betsy the following day saying Merry was out of the hospital and considered showing up at her house. I figured that might be a bit creepy and stalker-like, so I did nothing.

That following Friday night of spring break, I was lazing around the house not doing much. I considered going out with a couple of buddies, and idly wondered what Merry was doing. When the doorbell rang, I thought it was strange since Mom was at work, and I wasn't expecting anyone. I opened it, to see Merry standing on my porch.

She showed up at my house. At my front door. I probably looked like an idiot gaping at her, but that didn't take away from the fact that she showed up AT MY HOUSE. She asked if she could come in, and I don't think I said anything to her, just sidestepped and let her in. I remember the conversation like it was yesterday.

"Hope I'm not bothering you, or keeping you from something," she said as I led her to sit in a recliner.

"No, nothing. Actually, I was just thinking about you. Wondering what you were doing tonight, when you knocked on my front door, just like magic!" I replied.

"We have to talk, Nate. I don't know want to be a bitch, or come across like I'm making assumptions, but this can't go any further," she started.

"What, this? Here at the house? I wasn't planning on taking you up to my room, or anything. I just figured the living room was the best place for us to sit and talk." I joked with her.

She sighed and looked like she was explaining something to a small child and it wasn't getting through, "Nate, seriously. You and me, it's just not going to work. My condition isn't going away. I've had two heart attacks. One open-heart surgery, kidney failure, followed by a kidney transplant from my oldest sister. My heart isn't getting better; it's getting worse. The pacemaker is second to last option the doctors have before I'll need to have a heart transplant," she said, before getting up out of the chair. She took off her jacket, and then the long sleeve navy blue shirt she had on, and finally, slowly but with resignation before the nerves could get to her, the white tank top she wore underneath. The scars I had only gotten glimpses of before this were starkly purple and raised angrily against the chalky tone of her skin. One on her neck, one down the middle of her chest, and the new one under her collarbone where the bump of the pacemaker could be seen. Another on her abdomen, and marks on both her arms. She was thin, almost to the point of being too thin, but with sinewy muscle apparent which was surprising considering she wasn't able to exercise.

She took my breath away, and I don't think she realized it.

"This scar on my neck is from kidney dialysis. These marks on my arms are from years of IVs. This one, down my sternum, is from when they cut my heart open to remove a piece when I was 15. It looks like this because the wires they used to put my ribcage back together popped through the skin a half a dozen times and I had to keep getting my skin fixed. This scar here on my stomach? That's from the kidney transplant right before my 17th birthday. Here's where the pacemaker sits, right below my collarbone." She paused again, and for a brief second met my eyes, and then quickly looked down. "My dad and Bets, they've been there since the beginning of this, and if I could, I'd walk away from them so they don't have to put up with me. I can't drink caffeine because it speeds my heart up too much. I have to monitor what I eat constantly because of the meds I'm on. I take twenty-some pills a day, and will for the rest of my life. I can't drink a beer or have a glass of wine. I can't even get a tan because my medication is contraindicated for sun. I can't go to the gym, or to the beach and I can't have kids. You don't want to deal with this. All of this. You don't need to and I won't let you. I'm not worth all of this trouble, Nate." She went to grab the tank top she had shed, and I don't remember getting up. I don't remember crossing the space between us. I just remember kissing her. At the time, it seemed to be the only way to shut her up. I just couldn't help myself when it came to this girl.

*****

I figured if I went and had a logical, adult conversation with him, he would understand. I looked at myself in the mirror every single day and I hated what I saw. I hated being nearly albino. I hated the scars that crisscrossed my body like a toddler with a magic marker going to town on a wall when their parents weren't watching them. They weren't badges of honor to me. No one wants a constant reminder of the flaws they have, and my scars mocked me every day and showed me how different I was. If I could have, I'd have covered them in tattoos, because at least then, I could tell a different story.

After having lived with this for so long, I didn't want to see anyone else sucked into the worry vortex. I saw how it wore on my dad and Bets. I saw what it did to my relationship with Sophie. I couldn't let it happen with Nate. I had Bets drive me to his house (which apparently, she knew where that was, and I still don't know how) and I left her car saying I would call her when I was done having my conversation. She was pissed at me, and didn't say anything; just nodded that she heard me. I had never stripped down in front of anyone who wasn't a medical professional or Betsy. But my words hadn't been enough to this point, it seemed. He needed to see evidence of what I was saying; that this wasn't just me being a bitch. I started the speech I spent the week carefully planning out in my head, and started taking my shirt off. I was certain once he saw my scars; he'd be disgusted like I was.

And then he kissed me. While it wasn't my first kiss, it was the first one that ever made me forget what I was saying. Forget what I was doing and forget where I was. I forgot I was sick, for the first time since I'd been sick. I forgot I wanted him to see me how I was, a terminally stubborn, terminally ill heart patient. I forgot everything and just kissed him.

All too soon it ended, and I looked up at him, and of course, he had this HUGE grin on his face. He looked like a little kid who was just given a toy that he'd been asking for.

"It was the only way I could get you to stop talking," he said sheepishly. "You're probably freezing standing there without your shirt on, and as much as I truly admire the picture before me, I don't want you to get sick because of it." I was still stunned. I forgot I had my tank top in my hand, and only realized I was standing there without a shirt on when he backed away from me, and his warmth was gone. Feeling him next to me like that made me realize how cold I was, and I fumbled getting my shirts back on, while he stood back and watched with the smile on his face. Once I got situated, I fidgeted, trying to figure out what the hell I was supposed to do now, when he broke the silence by lifting my chin so I was looking at him. Those moss green eyes had never looked clearer or deeper than they had at that moment.

"None of us know how much time we have left on this earth, Merry. We aren't promised anything. But I'll take whatever time you give me. It doesn't matter if you get sick of me in a couple of weeks, or a couple of months. I just want to be around you," he said, putting his hands on my hips.

"Nate, why? Why would you do this to yourself?" I pleaded. I simply didn't understand how anyone could be such a masochist; especially knowing what I put Bets and my dad through.

"Because, you ARE worth it. Don't ever think you're not. Come on sunshine, everything happens for a reason," he said matter-of-factly. I must have made a face at that, because he laughed, and said "Why do you hate me calling you sunshine?"

I finally extricated myself from him, and sat on the couch. "When I was a kid, we had an elderly couple who lived next to us. Mr. and Mrs. Jay. I don't have any extended family to speak of, and they treated us girls like members of their family. Mr. Jay and I used to garden together. It was one of the few things I could do, provided I wore SPF 2000 and sunglasses and a hat," I paused here to look at him. "He always looked up at the sun, squinting, and I asked him why. He said Mrs. Jay reminded him of the sun, with her blonde hair. He would sing 'You Are My Sunshine' to her, and they would dance around their kitchen. He called me sunshine, much like he called Mrs. Jay sunshine when they first started dating. The afternoon before he died, he told me that. He and I loved roses, and we had planned to plant one in my garden when he died. The roses you brought me were the same shade as the rose bush my dad planted there for me."

"So, the nickname is perfect then. Since I'm not the only one to think so, I'll keep using it," he quipped.

Nate, when you read this, after. . . I think I fell in love with you at that moment.

I became a college graduate in May of 2006. I had officially crossed off the only item I ever placed on my bucket list. My dad was beyond ecstatic and insisted on making graduation a big deal, and he and Nate's mom planned a party for Bets, Nate and I at our house in late June after the ceremonies were over. It was funny, I fully expected my dad to hate whomever I decided to bring home (if that ever happened). It was the exact opposite. He LOVED him. I don't know what Nate did, or what Nate said, but they were buddies from moment one. It's amazing to me how Nate just fit right in with everything. Nothing shocked him. Nothing phased him. The only thing he got excitable about was me, and hockey. Life with Nate was easy. He just fit in like he had always been there, and it was becoming harder to think of what life was like without him being in it.

So, I haven't mentioned Sophie in a while, with good reason. I hadn't talked to her much. She was up for partner in her firm, and whenever Dad and I would have dinner at the house for one of the holidays, she was always busy. I dutifully called her regularly, but wound up speaking to her voicemail instead of her. I sent her birthday cards, and Christmas cards, and 'thinking of you' cards, and received an occasional card here and there, with a check enclosed in lieu of a present. I know Dad talked with her more than I did, but when I asked how she was, he'd just say 'Fine' in a short, clipped tone, so I dropped it. I assumed she wouldn't make it to the graduation party because, why would she?

About a month after the English department graduation for me, and the Business department graduation for Bets, and the Engineering department graduation for Nate, I looked forward to having the people I cared about, and the ones who cared about them at my house for a party. I was stressed out about how I should dress, as Bets insisted on making it a garden tea party theme. I finally found a vintage style blue floral dress that didn't make me look like I was an old lady. I paired it with a wide brimmed, white hat with a matching blue ribbon and as I got dressed, and looked in the mirror, I heard a gasp, and turned to see my dad standing in the doorway, tears in his eyes.

"When your mom and I were dating, she had this big floppy hat she would tie around her chin like she was Scarlett O'Hara. She always dressed so spiffy, with tailored, bright dresses. You're the spitting image of her, Mer. She would be so damn proud of you today," he got out, before giving me a hug. "I'm glad you did this, baby girl. I know it was hard, but I'm glad you made me let you go." He cleared his throat, and left, saying that Nate was downstairs waiting for me. I threw on the sandals I chose to wear, hoping I wouldn't trip over the slight heel I wasn't used to wearing, and made my way to the stairs, where I saw him waiting for me at the bottom. The way he looked at me made my heart skip beats, but not in a way that scared me.

<u>Sophia</u>

It had been five years since I saw Merry in person, and driving with Adam up to my dad's house, I realized I was nervous. My baby sister was no longer a baby. Since I had last seen her, I had moved up the ranks in my firm, and was close to being named partner. I had met the love of my life, and today, I was going to introduce him as my husband. She was 16 the last time I saw her. And now she was 21, a college graduate. An adult.

I realize how that sounds now. I had kept Dad and Mer out of my life for so long, despite their attempts to rein me in. I was about to walk into my sister's celebration, one she never dreamed she would see, and be all 'Surprise! Here's my husband!' I kept my relationship with Adam quiet. Not because I was ashamed of him, in any way. And not because I was ashamed of my family in any way. But because I wanted something for me. I wanted the wedding to be mine, with no concern if Merry was going to be able to make it, or whether or not she would be able to partake in any of the events that go along with a wedding. I wanted it simple. Quiet. Adam and I had dated for several years before he proposed, and he understood my need for simplicity. It was wonderful to not have to explain myself. He just got me. He smoothed my rough edges and he made me happier than I had been nearly all my life.

When we walked hand in hand to the back of the house, I was struck by how lush everything was. I hadn't remembered it like this growing up, and it was stunningly beautiful in how it flowed together. The colors were vibrant, and the scents of whatever it was I was looking at were powerful and intoxicating. We stopped at the end of the path by the back corner of the where the garage met the edge of the back porch, and I saw this tall, lithe champagne blonde standing next to and talking with my dad. She had her arm wrapped around the waist of a man dressed in a blue polo and khakis who was clearly love-struck, as he couldn't take his eyes off of her. He kissed the side of her head and held onto her similarly, and laughed with my dad. My dad caught a glimpse of me, and must have said something to the blonde, because she turned around, and started coming towards me.

I barely recognized the woman in front of me. Not until she gave me a hug and said 'Hey Soph' in that hoarse alto voice I hadn't heard in over 5 years. Dear God, she looked just like how I remembered my mom.

"Mer. Wow, look at you." I held her at arm's length, and saw the scars the dress didn't hide, and the pale skin that had a bright sheen to it from the sunscreen I knew she slathered on regularly. Our hands next to each other were like day and night; hers a shiny, milk white with just the faintest of pink tinges to it, and mine, tan and freckled. She looked like an adult, but without having any of the normal signs of aging I thought I would see at this point, just from the stress she'd had in her life. She was so angelically beautiful.

"Hi, I'm Merry," she said, holding out her hand towards Adam and I realized I must have missed some discourse while I was looking at her. Adam introduced himself, and I found myself awash in a wave of sadness that I would never see her in a bridesmaid dress, leading me to him at the end of an aisle.

"I have someone I want you to meet, Soph. Nate, can you pull yourself away from my dad and come here a sec?" she called over to the man standing next to my dad, now holding a beer. He came over, eating up the space between them easily with his long legs, and immediately put his arm around her. He was attractive, and not someone I would have thought would have been interested in my sister. He seemed like one of those popular, life of the party kind of guys. "Nate, this is my sister Sophia. Soph, this is Nate," she said with a blushing smile on her face. Mer never blushed. She was never happy. She was never, ever anything emotive. Stoic and quiet and contemplative. But smiling? Who was this girl and where was my baby sister?

I went to shake Nate's hand, and instead, he pulled me in for a huge hug, one I didn't expect. They were so happy. You could just see it seeping from them, infecting everyone around them with an illness anyone would have been thrilled to get. A part of me was jealous. They hadn't missed me at all. Their lives went on without me. And the rest of me? It took everything in me not to start sobbing right there. I'm sure it was the pregnancy hormones, and since I wasn't yet showing, Adam and I had decided to hold off telling Mer and Dad so as not to upstage her special day. When I was hugging Nate, I felt Merry grab my left hand from behind his back, and knew she discovered my engagement and wedding rings.

"You got married?" I heard her whisper. I pulled away to see her eyes filled with tears. "When did you get married?" I felt Adam's hand on the small of my back, as though reassuring me.

"We got married in March. It was a small ceremony, just us in the Dominican. I knew you were in school, and Dad mentioned you weren't feeling well, so we went ahead anyway," I said nervously. I don't know why I felt so timid with her, because I never used to be. Maybe I was changing in my old age.

She looked at both of us, and I could see the change come over her. It was like a veil had been dropped over her face. "I'm happy for you, Soph. I'm only sorry Dad and I couldn't have been there." And like that, our interaction was over. Like a balloon in a child's grasp, she slipped away from me, and I was left feeling like I had missed a chance. I sensed Adam wanting to say something, and he bided his time until we got to the car.

"You know; we could have waited. Could have included them, Soph. I wouldn't have minded at all," he started, as we drove away from the house.

"No. We couldn't have. Not without there being some sort of medical drama. You don't understand. The Merry you saw today? I've never seen her before. This isn't her. She's been sick and in and out of doctors' offices and hospitals for the last 15 years. In March? She was having surgery again after she collapsed at school. I didn't want that at my wedding. As much as a piece of me regrets she wasn't there, the rest of me is happy because it meant the day was truly about you and I." I shook my head, clearing the sadness I felt from my brain. It was done and over with and I couldn't change it now if I wanted. I wouldn't see Merry again until after my Robert was born, and rings I hadn't thought she would ever see on her own finger. We had come full circle, it seemed.

It is true. You reap what you sow.

*****

I married Nate on a sunny October afternoon 5 months after we graduated, 10 months after I met him, underneath my willow tree with the rustle of the autumn breeze as the only symphony. It was a small ceremony. His mom, my dad, Bets by my side, her parents, and Nate's uncle. Sophie was unable to attend, as she was on bed rest. My dad joked around that bed rest for Sophie was probably like a normal working day for most of us, and I detected a smidgen of resentment in his words.

For my part, I decided not to think about it. I had more than I ever thought possible for me to have. I had gotten the fairytale I thought I would never see. It was a whirlwind and I was still having a problem understanding how I went from sick and miserable and alone, to feeling well and having Nate and being happy. Our courtship was swift, or as Nate insisted on calling it, 'expeditious' saying he didn't want to wait another moment to call me his own. He had proposed shortly after our joint graduation party, and to look down and see the ring on my finger felt strangely, incredibly normal. Like it was always meant to be there, even though we had known each other for only a short time. I had been swept off my feet, and Nate would joke around that I was stuck with him, and there was no turning back.

Funny, I wondered if he had considered that he was now stuck with me, and what that entailed. I had been in relatively decent health since the pacemaker surgery, but knew that it was only a matter of time before the beast in my chest decided to rear its ugly head. He had found a job with a great company in our area, and we had been searching for a place to live. I'd have been happy in an apartment the size of a dorm room, but it would seem as though my father had planned out something more for me.

I hadn't known it, but my mother had life insurance and the proceeds of that insurance were put into trusts for each of us three girls upon her death. My father was the steward of those trusts, and upon Laney's death, divided her portion between Soph and I. He advised me the night before I got married, and what I thought at the time, was my last night in my childhood home. I was overwhelmed. Grateful, of course. But overwhelmed to learn that I was now the recipient of a rather large sum of money I only had because I didn't have a mother or a sister. I wanted to say no, to tell him to keep it or donate it or burn it for all I cared. But I realized that I brought nothing to my impending marriage with Nate. I had no job, and would continue to have none unless I could make something of my writing, which I knew was a long shot at best. I could provide suggestions on landscaping design but wouldn't be able to build anything for a customer should I find one. So, as much as it hurt, I gratefully accepted the money and put my pride aside.

After the small service, we had a small, catered dinner on the back patio under a tent lit by candles and small twinkling lights. It was perfect. I kept pinching myself, unable to understand that I was truly there. I had found my Prince Charming.

Jeff came up to me as I was leaving the house, the night before the wedding. I thought I was in for some sort of 'dad' talk. Instead, he handed me a thick envelope, and pulled me to the patio and sat me down.

"I don't want you telling Merry any of this until you guys get back from your trip. I just gave her a check which was the proceeds of her mom's life insurance and I thought for a sec she was going to give it back to me. She kept it, telling me that now she could help pay for things once you guys got an apartment since she can't work. I don't want my baby girl worrying about where she's going to live, and I know you're gonna provide for her. But this has been the only home she knows, and up until she met you, she would tell me she was going to die here." He paused for a second, and tried to compose himself. "That envelope there is the executed deed to the house, at least on my end. You'll need to go to the lawyer's office and get it signed on your end. Both of you."

"Jeff, you can't give us the house. Where are you going to live? You just paid it off, I thought?" I stammered, the words barely forming in my mind before rolling out of my mouth.

"Nate, I remember starting out with Liv, and not having much money, and bills up the ass and wondering how I was going to be able to afford a house with a baby on the way. And one night after a particularly bad day at work, I stumbled upon this house. It hadn't been lived in for a few years, and it needed some work. The previous owners had passed away, and his father was selling it.

When I found out how much it was going for, I knew I couldn't afford it, and I thanked the man, and began walking away. He called me back, and we walked to his house, and sat on his back porch with a beer, kinda like we are right now. He asked about my wife, and I told him about my baby daughter on the way. He mentioned that his son and his son's wife had planned on having kids, and never wound up being able to before they had been involved in a bad wreck that they didn't make it out of. He asked me how much I could afford to pay, and I told him a number. He looked me up and down, and told me he would sell me the house for $10,000 less than that number on one condition." Jeff looked out over the lawn, across to where his next-door neighbor's house was. "That condition was that I raise my babies in this house, and let he and his wife dote on them since they hadn't yet had any grandchildren of their own. We shook hands on the deal, and I rushed on to where we were living at the time and told Liv I found us a house, and a set of grandparents for our babies to boot. The Jays' celebrated each of my girls being born, and mourned with me when Liv died. They mourned with me when Laney died. And up until Elsie and Chet died, they doted on my girls."

"He sounds like a pretty amazing man. I'm sorry I never got to meet either of them. For that matter, I'm sorry I never got to meet your wife or Laney. But I still don't understand why you'd give me your house," I said raising my beer to my lips and taking a swig. I couldn't believe what I was hearing.

"Chet loved all 4 of my girls, Nate. But he loved Merry the most. I'm certain she would tell you the same thing if you asked her. She was the apple of his eye, and she loved him almost as much as she loves me. The two of them built this backyard. Every rock, every bush, every flower and bed. I got caught up in the fever and helped her as much as I could along the way, but this was always her project. The only thing that was here was that willow, and Mr. Jay planted that himself for his son when they moved in. He told her when she was just a wee bit of a thing that he planted that tree for her, and she loves it because she loved him. Merry loves this house. And she loves this yard. She always said that with as little as she could do in this world, at the least, she could make herself a little piece of heaven right here." He stopped and looked at me. "Nate, I can't fix Merry's heart. I can't make her healthy enough to have kids. I can't make her healthy enough for her to go out and be successful like her sister is. But I sure as hell can give my baby the piece of heaven she built as a wedding gift."

And with that, it was done. I couldn't argue with his logic, and I couldn't decline a gift that I knew would mean the world to Mer. I promised that I would keep it a secret until we came back from the road trip we were taking as our honeymoon, and I did. The look on her face when we walked into the emptied house, which had been freshly painted for us, was more than priceless. I couldn't have asked for more than that at that moment.

<u>Sophia</u>

My mom had a life insurance policy that was paid out to the three of us when she died. When Laney passed, there was a small amount from the policy my dad had for each of us girls, and he added that amount in to the grand total and split it between Mer and I. We were to get it after college, once we turned 21. Only I didn't take it. I let it sit there. At the time, it was for selfish reasons. I was going to let it accrue as much interest as possible, and then use it to put down a payment on a house once I got done with law school. And then, right before school ended, Mer had the first open-heart surgery. I thought about taking the money then, using it to pay down the student loans I had, but I left it. I got done with law school, and got hired right away and put my nose to the grindstone and that's when Merry needed the transplant. Still, it sat. I never asked my dad why he didn't dip into it to pay for the medical bills. He never complained. Not once.

He came to me after Merry graduated from college, and right before she got married, and he had a check for my share of the policy. He told me he was giving Merry hers, and wanted to give me my share. I looked at it, and grabbed a pen and signed the back and handed it back to him.

"She needs this more than I do. Just don't tell her, okay? I don't want her to know," I said as he looked at me. I knew he was going to give her the house. He asked me first if I minded. What could I say? I understood why he wanted to do it. She didn't have a job, there would never be two incomes in the family and with my half of the insurance kicked in, she would have enough money to provide a small cushion on top of Nate's salary. It was the least I could do for her, although if you ask my dad, I'm sure he'd have disagreed on some level. I was starting to understand him more as my pregnancy progressed. I understood why he put everything into Merry and left me to grow up virtually on my own. Some kids learned to swim when you dropped them into the pool. And some, no matter what you did, there was just no chance they were ever going to get in the water without a life vest, for whatever reason.

I have always been grateful to be a strong swimmer.

Nate

There are things you don't learn about a person before you live with them. It was obvious when Mer and I got back from our honeymoon that she had been a satellite travelling in a slow orbit around her little world. She was this complete and self-sustaining ecosystem, and for the first few months after we got married, I wondered if my infatuation had been misplaced. I loved her and I felt like needed her in my life, but I don't know that I truly believed she felt the same way about me. She alternately fascinated me and frustrated me. She wasn't ever emotive, and we never argued or even disagreed. She would just shrug and accept whatever it was that I was saying. I'm not trying to say that I love conflict, but the back and forth interaction we shared in that crappy basement classroom in Clemens was virtually gone.

One evening, Mer was out back on the porch with her dad, and Bets and I were in the kitchen cleaning up after dinner and I let it slip that I was frustrated. Betsy turned, and leaned against the counter wiping her hands with a dishtowel and sighed.

"Nate, I wish I could wave my magic wand and fix it. She can be difficult to get used to, even for the most accepting of souls."

"I guess I'm not sure what to do," I hesitated here. "She's just so compliant all the time. She's down for whatever, and it feels like I'm driving the bus too much."

"Let me tell you this. She doesn't want to play games, and she's learned being a spectator is more important than participating. She watches EVERYTHING, and she absorbs everything the same way a sponge does. It took me a long time to realize that she wasn't just okay with me driving the bus; she preferred it. She's never been someone who wanted to drive. And because she doesn't have the life experiences that the rest of us had, in some respects, she doesn't know what she's missing. And in others, she knows all too well what she's missing and has chosen not to focus on it so that she's not sad or depressed about what she can't do." She paused here. "I love Jeff like he's my own father, and I would do anything for the man. Sophie wasn't much of a big sister to her, and while part of it had to do with the age difference, it also had to do with the fact that Soph and Mer are as polar opposites as they come. Jeff did the best he could with Mer. Mer has this fear of doing something to hurt herself, and in doing so, hurt him. He's gone above and beyond to help bring a sick little girl through treacherous waters to this point. But, he's also stopped her from doing things on the off chance that it would harm her. It's quite the Catch-22. I don't blame him for it, but it's why I've always tried to push the boundaries a little with her, with Jeff's unspoken approval because he knew I would never go too far. We ate pizza when she wasn't supposed to. I brought her sponge candy in the hospital when she was there for the kidney transplant. She and I would go to the playground late at night when we were in college and I would push her on the swings, or we would go on the teeter-totter together. It sounds silly and childish, I know, but she'd never done it before. If I hadn't suggested it, she never would have gone. We used to take these drives on the backroads in the northtowns and just blare the music and sing and dance in our seats. And we'd go driving in the cemetery where her mom and Laney are, and bring lunch and sit there under the oak tree and have lunch with them. And I'd let her drive my car, because she couldn't have a license with her heart the way it is. Not like she could kill anyone other than me and we were going slow enough for me to jump out if things got bad.

"Her first vacation was with you. That was a huge step and she was terrified of disappointing you before you guys left. I know it sounds like I'm making excuses for her, and I also know that there have been times when I've been frustrated with her myself. It's taken me a long time to understand how to work around her internal governor." She stopped and looked out the window at her friend. "Being her friend has given me a different perspective on life. I'm grateful for the things that I wouldn't have cared about if not for her. I'm not saying you're not," she held up her hand here, "but you have to stop and look at it from a different point of view. Think of what your life would be like if you couldn't do what you do now. If you couldn't be the Nate you are now. And then think of how to do something else instead. Mer has had a ton of time to sit and contemplate her fate and learn how to deal with her lot in life. If you want to be with her, you have to figure out a way to take your perspective and make it work for her too. You're a smart guy. I have faith in you." With that, she threw the towel next to the sink and walked towards the door. I know you gain more than a wife when you marry a woman, but I didn't know how important my wife's best friend would be to me.

I suppose I thought once I came into Merry's life, she would be happy and we would be happy and everything would be great. I realize how naïve that sounds. I hadn't put much thought into what the rest of her life was like outside of being sick, and I know now that being sick wasn't just a calendar entry like it was for most of us. It was a lifestyle. It was discipline and it was something so ingrained that there was no beginning or end. She was just Merry. Once I got to that point, I began looking at her a bit differently. I still thought she was the most beautiful thing I had ever seen, but now, I could see how difficult that beauty was to come by. I could see tiny facial expressions which were only there for a fraction of a second that allowed me to read her mood a little bit better. I began to see a smile in her eyes where I had only seen a glance before. When I would get home from work, I could see which book was out and it gave me a hint as to what she was interested in or what mindset she was in that day. To say she was a voracious reader was an understatement, and I could barely keep up with her. I'm not ashamed to say that I would google the book to learn of the plot so that I could talk with her about it over dinner. I'm sure she thought I was as much of a reader as she was, but in reality, I just wanted to understand her better. And music. Man, she loved her music. I thought at first it was strange that she had so much Pink Floyd, but then I remembered her doll and figured it had something to do with Laney. She played it a lot during the summer, which made sense knowing that was when Laney's birthday was. And when they lost her. Not that she talked about Laney ever. I don't think she had it in her to talk about how she felt about the loss of her sister without breaking the façade she had so carefully built.

She enjoyed relaxing to jazz and she told me once that jazz was always happier or sadder than she was, and when you think about it, it made an odd sort of sense. She would sit reading a book in an armchair with the slightest of smiles on her face as she listened to Thelonious Monk or Ella Fitzgerald. And then the next day, I came home to her playing Guns 'n Roses, and sort of bopping around to Sweet Child O' Mine as she dusted and I had to stop and admire the picture in front of me. It was so free and so loose and so unlike her.

But the most surprising thing I discovered about my wife's music taste is that she loved punk. Like, LOVED. I got home early one spring afternoon and could hear music coming from the backyard. Once I got back there, I was treated to the site of my sedate, yet sexy wife singing along to The Ramones – I Wanna Be Sedated while she crawled along her rose bed weeding in her floppy hat. Laughing and leaning against the house to watch the picture in front of me, the song changed to Rancid's Time Bomb, and she proceeded to grab the hori hori knife and sang with it like it was a microphone. Damned if she didn't know every word. I kept watching and I was cracking up when she finally heard me and turned and was startled. She had the cutest mad face and that made me laugh even harder until she stomped her foot at me and threw her hat in my direction. It was astonishing to see her with such a fury on her features.

One sticky night in the middle of July, we were sitting in the sunroom after dinner, and there was a vicious crack of lightning followed by a deep grumble of thunder. Merry was out of her chair, moving faster than I had ever seen towards the screen door and outside before I even knew what was happening.

The wind was whipping up and the first heavy drops of rain had begun to fall from the angry sky, and she just stood there, eyes to the now-charcoal sky. She saw I had followed her out and she grabbed my hand and I threw my arm around her as we stood in the rain.

"The angels are bowling tonight. Isn't it incredible?" she whispered in my ear. "Laney used to go to the bowling alley with my dad, and sit with him and all of his buddies as they drank and smoked and bowled on Friday nights. She was their little mascot, and they would always let her throw a ball or two during practice before the league started. And now she bowls for me during the summer when she knows I miss her most of all."

There wasn't anything I could say to her that night, as we got soaking wet and watched the lightning streak across the sky. We eventually went inside and we never spoke again about the angels bowling, but from that evening on, when the thunder rumbled overhead, she'd grab my hand and we'd venture outside to spend time with her sister for a few brief moments.

*****

Life is about balance. Happy and sad. Healthy and sick. Living and dying. I had always experienced the latter of each. Sadness over the losses in my life. Being sick to the extent that there were times death would have been welcome. And learning to deal with the idea of dying, while other people were living. Until I met Nate, I had resigned myself to the idea that I would just exist until such time as my heart gave out. I knew how close I had come time after time, and wondered each time if this was going to be it. I had never felt like I wasn't worried. Never felt like I was going to be happy or healthy or living. Really living.

And suddenly, I was happy. How the hell was this real? How was this possible? And oh God, what did I have to do to stay like this for the rest of my life? I had found the love of my life something I never believed was possible. My father had given me the greatest wedding gift of all time. I had the most amazing best friend in the world. And even my sister was learning to be happy, and had started her own family.

Sophie had Robert just before Christmas in 2006. I almost shared my birthday with my nephew! And then, in short order, she was pregnant again and baby Jeff joined the family in March of 2008. I had never seen her so happy and so unlike the Sophie I had known growing up. She and Adam threw themselves into being super parents and I watched, amused at the extent they went to for the boys. It was nice to see Soph put effort forth into being happy, instead of being driven. Not that she wasn't . . . she had in fact, made partner and was happy running her little fiefdom.

The years were passing, and before I knew it, July of 2010 had rolled around. I remember looking at the calendar thinking, there's no way. There was no way Laney had been gone for 20 years. And in August of 2010, she would have been 30. There's just no way I've been without her for so long. I still had my Laney doll sitting on my childhood bed. There were days when Nate was at work, I would go into the room and look out the window like I did on the year anniversary of her death and hope I could bring back the vision of the ruddy-haired girl smiling with her rain boots on. But the vision never came. I forgot how her voice sounded, and no matter what I did, I couldn't imagine her as an adult. Couldn't dream of where she would be right now. In my head, I still talked to her every single day, wondering if she could see me and if she knew I was happy. I dreamt of her most in the summer months, and there were times when she would ride her bike away from me down the street and I just kept yelling for her to stop. If she stopped, she would still be here, and we could fix our hearts and everything would be okay. And after dreams like that, I woke up with my chest heaving and feeling my tear-soaked pillow underneath me.

Her room had long been packed up, and been turned into a little library for me, with a comfortable armchair and an ottoman, with shelves lining the walls. I would sit in there reading or not reading when the weather was cold, until Nate got home from work and we could begin our evening. But when the weather was warm, I was back to where I was as a child. Under my willow. No longer reading the pilfered books of my sisters, I turned back to the classics, and blew through Shakespeare, and Dickens, Twain and The Bronte Sisters. I had always been a voracious reader, but I became insatiable. I was fortunate Nate was always willing to listen to me chatter on about a plot point, or what I thought was going to happen in this book, or with that character. It was a huge relief to me to learn he had read The Catcher in the Rye, and there were many evenings where he and his mom and Bets and I would sit around chatting about books like our own private book club.

It was too good to be true, wasn't it? I knew before Nate did that my heart was having a hard time when I woke up dizzy a few mornings in a row in the summer of 2013. While I wore socks constantly because my feet were always cold, my hands were becoming increasingly icy, and the slight blue tinge I hadn't seen since before the pacemaker was back. I chalked it up to the summer humidity affecting my oxygen levels, since I was spending so much time out in my gardens. There were some moments where I was starting to get the blackness coming into my vision when I was outside working, and had to stop what I was doing to prevent myself from passing out. I kept thinking I was wrong; it wasn't my heart. I was happy, I felt fine. It was something else. Anything else. One night right after Bets left, I slipped in the kitchen. Or at least, that's what I told Nate. In reality, I started to black out and dropped to the floor, where the pain of the fall to my knees shocked me into consciousness.

I had fallen into my old habit of telling everyone I was fine. And in doing so, I was trying desperately to convince myself I was. It all came to a halt when I would kiss Nate goodbye for work, and my lips were ice cold on his. He finally called me out on it, and asked me if I thought I should call my doctor. It was the last thing in the world I wanted to do.

In short order, I was back at the doctor's office and scheduled for the plethora of tests to see how everything was going. My pacemaker battery was supposed to last some 5-10 years, and it had been 7, so I was hopeful it was just going to be as simple as replacing it. I suppose I should have known better.

Nate

I hadn't been to any of Mer's doctor's appointments before, so I didn't know what to expect. They had all been minor appointments, yearly physicals, blood work, and weren't anything she said I needed to concern myself with. This one was different. This was going to be at her cardiologist, and they were going to detail out explicitly what was going on with her heart from the last time they saw her. She insisted all I needed to do was to drop her off or sit in the waiting room, but I wanted to be there. I needed to be involved in this. Part of me wanted to be angry with her; as though she didn't tell me she wasn't feeling well because she didn't want me to worry. When I broached that topic, she promised me that she didn't keep it from me. It was more that she had just gotten caught up in living and didn't think about it. I didn't understand that, because I couldn't personally imagine forgetting that my heart was prone to malfunction. She was still on all her medication, she still watched her diet, and we were careful when it came to physical activity, so I couldn't say she was neglecting her health.

I had just started getting a greater understanding of what all had gone into getting her to this point, and it terrified me. I had taken to using my lunch hours to research HCM, and what I found astounded me. I had never heard of it before Merry, and to read that there had been some pretty well known people who had died as a result of it, or from complications stemming from it was shocking. I had no idea there were so many athlete deaths from it, and to see that it wasn't something that was tested for, even in today's day and age; well, it sickened me. I read through the various treatments, and it didn't take a heart surgeon to point out that Merry was nearing the end of the line when it came to treatment options.

On the morning on the appointment, I was a bundle of nerves. Mer was composed, but then again, it took a lot to rile her up. I think my nerves amused her. I wasn't amused by her amusement, to put it mildly. I suppose that was the difference between someone who had been dealing with it directly for 23 years, and someone who had been dealing with it for 7 years, second-hand. I had known she would have a physical exam, and then a discussion with the doctor detailing the results of the tests she had gone through. Her calm demeanor had always struck me as out of place in a world where people got upset when their coffee spilt, or their favorite show got cancelled. Here she was detailing her symptoms to the nurse in terms I had only just begun to be familiar with, as I was sitting there bouncing my foot, and looking at the clock on the wall wondering how she withstood the anxiety of not knowing what was happening. When the nurse left and she had begun to get dressed again, she asked me if I was okay.

We were in a doctor's office awaiting news which could tell her the heart that had been beating in her chest for nearly 28 years was finally giving out, and she was asking ME if I was okay?

God, I loved this woman. I couldn't imagine losing her.

For the first time since I had touched her all those years before, both my hand and hers were freezing as we were led into the doctor's office down the hall from the exam rooms. Merry's doctor was nondescript and I don't know that I could tell you what he looked like that day, other than he was younger than I expected and looked tired. Once the niceties got out of the way, followed by a small rebuke from the doctor about Merry not calling sooner about her symptoms, he finally got down to the details.

Her heart was weakening.

Her pacemaker had been calibrated based on how her heart was, and now, in order to keep her heart working at a sustainable level; it would have to be recalibrated and adjusted to account for the demands of her failing heart. There was a ton of technical terms I didn't understand, but what I didn't hear is what struck me most.

"Sorry if I'm late to the party, but there has to be something else we can do here. There has to be another option beyond the pacemaker. What about the ventricle assist device? What about a transplant?" I interjected into his soliloquy. I saw Mer smile sadly at this, and wondered if she already knew what he was going to say.

"Mr. Carter, Merry's physical condition combined with her medical history provides us with a difficult, complex situation. The likelihood of success for a heart transplant is considerably reduced here, because she's already been through one organ transplant, and based on the tests we've run, the transplanted kidney isn't as effective as it was when it was put in, due to the medication your wife has been on." Holy shit, you've to be kidding me. This isn't happening. He turned back to Merry. "That being said, the LVAD is also not a viable option, in my opinion."

"I was afraid you were going to say that," Mer said flatly, closing her eyes.

"Merry, you knew this was something that was a distinct possibility. I think the time to adjust the pacemaker is sooner rather than later, so you can maintain some sort of standard of living," the doctor replied.

"Cardiac rookie here, folks. Why can't she have the LVAD?" I interjected. Merry turned to me, and I gripped her icy hand tighter.

"The reasons for not going with the LVAD are similar to those for the transplant. I just don't believe based on her history of pleural effusions and cardiac infections that it's a good idea. After surgery, she would have an open wound in her abdomen for the power cable and even with the most stringent of care, the chance for infection is extremely high. She's already immune compromised more than your average heart patient because of the kidney transplant. Her heart simply cannot withstand another instance of pericarditis. There is also an increased risk of stroke because of clotting, and once we treat the clotting, she's then at a greater risk of bleeding out." The doctor paused here. "Merry, I don't need to tell you what the score is. Since you've been with us after the transplant, we've been chasing the dragon, to put it bluntly. The goal was never to cure your condition, as it's not possible even with the medical advances since you were diagnosed. The goal was always to treat the symptoms to the extent we were able to provide you with some sort of life outside of the hospital. I am still inclined to want to place you on the transplant list, merely because once we go through the adjustment of your pacemaker, there isn't much else we're able to do medically or surgically for you other than that. But to be honest, I truly can't see that being a viable option for continued life expectancy. You'd likely never leave the hospital." That was it? There was nothing more they could do?

I felt as though my own heart was being ripped from my chest hearing this, and couldn't understand why Merry just sat there. I held it in, until we got to the car, and drove home. I told her I needed to take a drive to clear my head, and she nodded, as though understanding it was something I needed to absorb. I walked out of the house like a zombie and made it to the car, backing out of the driveway before I started sobbing like I had never done before. I pulled over a street over from our house, and just cried thinking about not being able to fall asleep next to my wife, my head on her chest listening to her heart beat as I had every night since we were married.

Jeff

I only knew it was Nate calling because I saw his number on the caller ID. Otherwise, I don't think I could have told you who was calling me, because all I heard was crying. After a few seconds, he composed himself enough to tell me that Merry had been to the doctor, and there wasn't anything else they could do for her.

My heart dropped. I knew there was going to come a point where they were going to run out of treatment options for her, but I suppose I always believed there would be something they could do and that Merry being Merry would withstand it, like she always did. I told Nate to come on over to the apartment I was living in at the time, and in short order he arrived. If I hadn't known better, I would have said he was sick. Or drunk. I brought him in, grabbed him a beer, and we sat down to go through what had been said.

"I had to leave. I had to be alone and figure out what I'm supposed to do. I have no idea what I'm supposed to do," he said over and over. I had been there, multiple times over this past two plus decades, and knew the helplessness he was feeling.

"What did Mer say?" I finally asked when he calmed down. Knowing my daughter as I do, I was pretty sure what he was going to say.

"That she knew what he was going to say. She wasn't surprised. She just sat there. I don't understand how she could just sit there, and act like nothing was wrong!" he cried out. That's what I expected him to say. And exactly how I expected her to react.

"I think Merry figured to be gone long before this, Nate. She's been dealing with this for damn near her whole life. This is her normal. Doesn't mean she wasn't upset by it. In fact, I'm gonna bet she was more upset for you, than she was for herself," I replied. I wasn't sure if anything I would say would make him feel better.

"Nate, when she was 5, and they first diagnosed her, and she had the heart attack, they said there wasn't much they were able to do for her other than fill her full of pills. They told me to take her home, make her comfortable, and hope for the best. I called every single cardiologist in a 3-state radius to find out what I could do to keep my baby alive. And we got her to a doc locally that was willing to work with her pediatrician to see what they could do for her. And then she had to get the open-heart surgery, and I thought for sure I was gonna lose her. And she came through that. And then the kidney transplant. And then the second heart attack. And then the pacemaker. And through all this, she sits there, and she accepts what's happening to her, because she wants to make it easy on all of us who love her. It's not that nothing is wrong. But I'm sure she thinks it wouldn't do us any good to see that she's upset, when we already are." I took a swig from my beer, wishing it were something stronger. I still don't know how I never turned into an alcoholic with everything, but thankfully I never had the urge to bury the problem in alcohol. . . if anything, the pain of dealing with Liv, and Laney and Mer made me all the more grateful for the life I had been given.

Nate took a deep breath. He looked like he was going to start crying again, and seeing as how it was the first time I had seen him doing so, I wasn't quite sure what to do. When a man cries, it's usually because all of the other options to deal with letting his anger and sadness out just aren't enough.

"How do you do it? How do you stand by and watch her go through this, and not be able to help her?" He asked finally. "She warned me. She told me she was going to die, and went through a laundry list of things she was never going to be able to do and told me that I didn't need to put up with everything that she had to. That she wasn't worth it."

"Well, let me ask you this. Is she worth it?" I already knew the answer, knowing how he felt about Merry.

"Of course she's worth it."

"Then you just take it one day at a time, Nate. They've been telling me she's going to die for 23 years. And for 23 years, she's defied all those odds. She's lasted this long because she takes things as they come, and if I had to bet; I would say she's going to be more worried about you through this, than worried about herself. I'd take her lead on this one. If she's worried, she'll tell you. Until then, we just have to roll with it." I'm sure I sounded much more strong and confident than I felt, because I knew when it came right down to it, my own heart would break into a million pieces if Merry didn't beat the odds this time.

*****

I had my pacemaker adjustment at the beginning of September of 2013.

For the first time in my life, I woke up in the recovery room agitated, and had to

be sedated. From what the nurse told me, I kept saying 'No Laney, it's not time

yet.' I begged her not to tell my family, because I'm sure that wouldn't have gone

over too well. Especially Nate. He would have freaked out. He had come back

from his drive after my appointment, and gave me the longest hug. I don't know

where he went, or what happened while he was gone, but he seemed more settled,

I guess.

I had a hard time with this surgery. More than my others. My heart and

my pacemaker always seemed to work relatively well together when I first got it,

but this time was different. From what I was told, my pacemaker was more

programmed to make my heart pump harder, in an attempt to resynchronize my

heartbeat in a manner conducive to a normal heart's function. It would be shocked

into working. My heart was pissed about this. Really pissed. I was in and out of

the doctor's office for weeks after the surgery, as they attempted to figure out how

to manage the pain I was having, while still managing the rest of my symptoms.

Between the antibiotics, the painkillers I hadn't wanted but were forced to take,

the anti-rejection meds I was still on, and with the rest of the heart medication, I

had no idea how my transplanted kidney was still working. At times, I could

swear it was trying to revolt, much like the rest of my body was. Through it all, I

was lucky I had my dad, Bets and Nate all trading off taking me to my doctor's

appointments with a minimum of hassle on any of their parts. The three of them formed this sort of task force that was driven to keep me as happy as possible while making all of this as easy as possible. It was wearing on me though.

It wasn't until mid-November that I was finally considered stable. Almost 2 full months of weekly appointments, being bed-ridden and generally being a drain on those around me. My dad had taken to stopping over for lunch on a daily basis, and I was certain there was some sort of agreement that I wasn't to be left home for more than a couple hours at a time, because Nate would leave for work at 8 and Dad would show up at 11 and stay until 2-2:30. Then Nate would get home from work around 5:30 and on the rare nights when he'd go out with his friends, Bets would stop over. Actually, more often than not, I didn't mind this time I got to spend one on one with them, because I felt as though I could physically feel the sand leaving my hourglass. I couldn't spend time outside, so I was essentially housebound and the few hours I was home by myself, I felt frantic. I started writing this then.

Thanksgiving was normally a low-key event, and usually meant that Bets would come over and cook for Nate, Dad and I, and then her mom and dad would come over for dessert. This year, for some unknown reason, Sophie invited us over. To say I was reluctant was an understatement. I wasn't feeling well, and while I loved my nephews and they were generally good kids, the idea of having them running around me was a bit off-putting. Combine that with Sophie's personality, and you could legitimately say I would have rather gone anywhere else.

It was Nate who convinced me we should go. I don't know why he thought this would be a good idea, but because he never asked me for anything, I agreed. I was nervous. I had a bad night the night before. Bad dreams had plagued me more often than not since the surgery, and I was learning to take sleep where I could get it. Sophie scheduled dinner for 3pm, so I snuck in a nap before we went over to her and Adam's.

This is another one of those things I had just about decided I wasn't going to write about. Mainly because it hurt me worse than anything else I had been through in my life with the exception of the continued absence of Laney. It felt like punching a bruise to actually write this down on paper and remember what was said, but I promised myself when I started this that I would write down things that changed me. Things that made me who I am, and how I am.

We arrived early for dinner, and were greeted by Adam who said Sophie was in the kitchen. Nate got me settled on the couch, popped his head in to say hi to Soph, and then he and Dad and Adam began chatting about the football game. I must have dozed off, because the next thing I recall was Soph calling us all to the table to eat. Nate helped me into my chair, and I recall commenting on how wonderful everything looked. I think I missed something, because I was certain Sophie was getting ready to say something, when Adam spoke up and offered to say grace.

I had the impression that something was off. I wasn't sure what, but something wasn't sitting right with Sophie and I wasn't sure what it was. Adam finished with grace and we began to pass dishes around. I was having a hard time lifting the heavy platters and bowls and one slipped and hit the gravy boat, which tipped and slopped gravy all over the table. I was embarrassed, and Nate being Nate, immediately went to the kitchen to grab something to clean it up, while I apologized to Sophie. Nate was used to my inability to manage heavier or awkward objects and had taken to serving me when we were home, just for the sheer fact I wasn't able to manage it as easily as he could. It was becoming the norm around my house, and when he was busy serving Robert, I just grabbed the platter to do it myself.

"Wow, there's a shocker, Merry ruining a holiday," I heard Sophie mutter. I looked up from wiping gravy off of the tablecloth in front of me, not sure if I heard her correctly. Nate must have heard the same thing, and said in a cheerful voice that he had it nearly all cleaned up, and there wasn't that much spilled and it wasn't a big deal. Big mistake.

Sophie calmly stood up from the table. "You know what Nate? It is a big deal. Did you know I haven't had a normal family holiday with Merry in attendance since she was 5? She's either in the hospital or too sick, or we need to be conscious of what Merry needs and we need to be quiet or we can't eat this, and can't do that. Just ONCE, I wanted a normal meal and a normal holiday, and we can't even have that now, can we? Not without the princess fucking it up for everyone." My dad started to speak up and Soph cut him off. "No, Dad, this is my house and my thanksgiving and do you think she could even offer to help me out? Nope. She has to go lay down because she's too fucking tired from doing NOTHING her entire life. Guess what? I don't get to be tired. I don't get to take a break, and I sure as hell still have to be a functional, progressive and PRODUCTIVE member of society even when I don't feel well. She has no concept of what real responsibility is. She just leeches off of everyone around her."

Tears were rolling down my face and I was shaking as I set my napkin on my plate full of food. Nate looked like he was ready to punch Sophie, my dad and Adam were horrified, and luckily, my nephews were too busy playing at the kid's table to realize what had just happened.

"I'm sorry I'm such a burden to you Sophia. Don't worry; you won't have to concern yourself about that for too much longer. Nate, I'd like to go home now please," I managed to get out before I started sobbing. Nate grabbed me and walked me towards the closet where our coats were, and all I could hear as we walked out was my father saying Sophie's full name like she was a kid again.

<u>Nate</u>

I have never once wanted to hit a woman before that day. I have never once wanted to destroy something for harming someone I love, but I swear to you, if I weren't more concerned about my wife, I'd have committed a violent felony. Sister-in-law, or not. Sophia has no idea what Merry goes through on a daily basis, and I don't even think if she knew it would matter to her. That's what happens when you're selfish and cold.

And yes, Mer, that's what I think of her. You don't treat your sister like that.

Jeff

I have nothing to say about what happened at Thanksgiving, other than that I didn't raise my daughter to act like that, no matter what she wants to believe. There is no excuse for beating up on a terminally ill woman like that, let alone a terminally ill woman who happens to be your only sister. I have no clue what the hell got into her.

<u>Betsy</u>

Nate called me as they were on their way home from the bitch's house. I ran over there with some food because I knew Mer wouldn't eat otherwise. I have to say, I'm surprised it took so long for Soph to lash out like this to be honest with you. I expected it years ago.

I beat them home, and was in the kitchen when they got there, and Nate brought Merry in. I hadn't ever seen her like this. We had been through everything together that two friends could go through, and I had never seen her like this. She was more than devastated. She looked empty. A broken, empty vessel. Nate settled her onto the couch and then came in the kitchen and told me that she sobbed like he had never seen her sob before. "'She hates me, Nate. She hates me because I'm here and Laney isn't. She hates me for killing Mom. She hates me' is all she kept saying, Bets. I thought I was going to have to take her to the hospital. She kept clutching at her chest like it hurt while she sat there and cried. I swear, I want to kill Sophie for doing this to her."

Yeah, well you're not the only one, Nate. I get first dibs.

<u>Sophia</u>

It was a baby girl from what the doctor told us. She had a condition that was "incompatible with life." Funny, isn't that what Mer has? And here she is still kicking after everything she's been through. We were advised to terminate the pregnancy because she wouldn't survive outside of the womb, and even though I went to 4 doctors, they all said the same thing. Maintaining the pregnancy would result in a still birth, or the loss of the child shortly after. One doctor alluded to my age as a cause for concern should I have chosen to continue through to her due date.

Her name was Eleanor Anne. She will always be Laney to me though. In the end, I couldn't bring her into this world as a full-term baby, because I couldn't continue to carry her and know I would lose her just like I lost Laney before her. And I couldn't in good conscience put her through what I've witnessed Merry going through for her entire life. I saw her. Before they took her from me, I saw her. She was tiny and she was perfect and for one hysterically long moment, all of the breath left my body and all I could think of was what if they were wrong? But, the doctor came through after they took her from us, and said that her heart and her lungs were malformed and she wouldn't have been able to breathe outside of me.

The irony of this situation is striking to me. My mom, Olivia, died because of a malformed, defective heart. My sister, Laney, died because of a malformed, defective heart. My baby, Laney, dies because of a malformed, defective heart. My sister, Merry, is dying because of a malformed and defective heart. And here I am, the only one of us girls with a perfect heart and it keeps breaking over and over again with all of these losses. It's not true what they say, about what doesn't kill us makes us stronger. It makes life harder. It makes us harder. More brittle. More fragile. It makes it tougher to let people in and to let people love you for the fear you'll lose them too. You either let people in, and break into a million pieces, or you keep out all but a select few. I tend to think of them like roses that I've selected to tend to in the garden of my heart. I've come to accept that it won't be full and lush, because some of the roses that I've loved have died and have become bare spots where I've put cairns reminding me of what was once there.

I wonder why it was only the females in the family afflicted with this. Why my boys were healthy and happy and completely and utterly normal. I had them checked when they were born, and again every year after because I kept thinking, what if they have it? What would I do then? Would I be like my dad? But, I'm lucky. I laugh at that. I'm lucky my boys are perfect. And I'm lucky that the girls I tried to have died before they could go through what my sisters and my mother went through. Luck can kiss my ass.

I think it was probably a bad idea from the get go that I held Thanksgiving. My emotions were raw. I thought having the family over and having some semblance of normalcy would help me feel better, but when Nate and Merry got there and she just flopped down on the couch, she set me on edge.

Did I know she was as bad off as she was? No. Of course I didn't, because no one told me. Which is my fault, I'm aware. I've made myself the outcast in our fractured little family, and I couldn't expect them to keep me updated on every little thing that happened to her, but it seemed to me, this was a pretty big thing to keep a secret. When she dropped the platter of turkey onto the gravy and it went everywhere including all over Mom's tablecloth, I saw red. I should have just gotten up and walked away but I snapped. I'm human. I snapped and I regret saying what I said, but it's said and I can't do anything about it now.

Do I believe that?

Do I have to answer that? I am aware Merry can't help what's wrong with her. I'm aware that I have it extraordinarily lucky in comparison. But she's been the focus of everything since Laney died, whether she wanted to or not. Just once, I wanted a normal family holiday where we could forget that we didn't talk for much of the year and that Merry was dying and I lost another baby and my dad was going to lose another daughter. I just wanted to pretend for a minute I was normal. That everything was fine. And the minute she dropped that platter, the illusion was shattered. To further continue my honesty, I didn't feel bad about it until she said that I wouldn't have to put up with her for much longer, as they left. As my father oozed disapproval, and my husband just sat there and kept quiet, I dropped into my chair and started crying myself. I kept hearing my father speak, but I didn't hear a word he was saying. I just kept thinking, 'I'm going to be an only child', and 'Isn't this what you wanted Sophie?'

No. It's not what I wanted. What I want I can't ever get back, and that's the fucking problem. I want my mom. I want my sister. And I want Merry to live until she's old and gray, tottering around with a cane as my grandchildren play around her. But guess what? It won't happen. People don't come back. Mothers die. Sisters die. Babies fucking die. And the guilt I have will weigh me down for the rest of my goddamn life, more than anyone ever realizes. What I said was true. I don't get to be sick or tired. I have to be functional and productive because my family depends on me to be that way. I don't get to take days off.

Oh God, I know I'm going to hell. And while the angry road leading me there is paved with the best of my intentions, I know it never came across that way. I know Merry will never forgive me. As well she shouldn't. I don't know if I can ever forgive myself.

*****

I've realized now that coming down to the end of this life of mine, that I've been fortunate in many ways. I could have had no familial support. I could have no friends. I could be alone. I've never been made to feel different by my best friend or my now husband. I've done that to myself, no doubt. I've had the support of Bets and Nate and my dad, and Bets' family and Nate's mom, and that's more than most people have.

Do I wish things were different? Depends on what you mean. At this point in my life, I've come to realize how delicate the balance is. If my mom had lived, if Laney had lived, would I have met Betsy? Would I have met Nate, and learned that despite all of my scars, I was deserving of his love? I can't tell you which I would choose. I never knew my mom, and though I see the relationship between Bets and her mom and a piece of me craves something like that, whether between my own mother and myself, or with a child of my own, I know it was never to be. I knew Laney for 5 years. She was my best friend and my closest ally, and her death brought me a best friend, and my closest ally. My heart brought me every single step towards Nate, whether by beating, or by failing to beat as it should.

Do I wish for less pain? I'm not into pain for the sake of feeling pain, and I don't know anyone who would want to go through the surgeries and treatments and medications and sickness the way I have. But the pain makes me feel alive. There will come a time when I won't be in pain anymore and that's how I know I'm finally, really dying. I relish the pain in a way, because as long as I'm hurting, I'm living. Maybe not to everyone else's standards but to my own, such as it is.

If there were anything for me to wish to be different, it would be my relationship with Sophia. After Thanksgiving, Nate and Betsy decided I wasn't going to be subjected to the 'evil one' as they designated her to be. I laughed. I had to. If I didn't, I probably wouldn't have started crying. I had this horrible feeling that I was going to get to heaven and Laney was going to be disappointed in me for not trying harder. That thought colored my sleepless nights, and I still don't understand how Nate slept through my restlessness. I remember hearing my dad lecture Sophie when I was in the hospital for the first heart attack.

"Sophia Joy, blood is thicker than water. One day I won't be here, and you'll only have each other." Those words resonated through me then, and still do now, all those years later. I wondered which one of us forgot that first. I wonder if my dad realizes I'll be the one who isn't here. The thought makes me catch my breath, and Nate looks over every time I do to make sure I'm okay. I smile, and I say I'm fine, even though I'm dying inside. My heart is dying and I'm afraid the pieces of me that are left behind once I'm no longer here won't be enough to keep my broken family together. Will Betsy still come with her mom for book club nights? Will Dad and Nate still watch hockey together, screaming at the TV? Will my nephews even remember they had an aunt, albeit one as pathetic as I am?

I don't have much more to write now. It's almost like I can feel the time ticking away inside of me, like a watch that hasn't been wound in a while. But there's still so much I have left to do! I have to make arrangements. How does someone go about planning his or her own funeral? I don't even want a damn funeral! I don't want people looking over me as I lie there made up in a casket. I don't want an obituary detailing my life for people who didn't know me. I don't want a graveside scene where my family is crying as I'm lowered into the cold ground. I want none of that! I know funerals are for the living, as I'll be dead. It's hard to write that, even though I know it's always been the end to my story. I guess I always hoped for the fairy tale ending and to be saved from this, which is just stupid. This is the path I've been on since I've been a kid. Now, it's just a matter of when and where that end will come.

So how can I do this? How can I take this burden off of them? I don't know how to leave them. And I don't know how I can make this easier for them. I want a party. I want all of my favorite foods, all of my favorite music. No black. Pictures in a slideshow of everyone together. Stories and laughing and happy tears, instead of sad.

I don't know if this is even possible.

My name is Merry. My favorite color is midnight blue; the color of the sky in the stillest part of the night when the stars peek through. I like pizza. Okay, I love pizza. Extra cheese, light on the sauce, well done with lots of garlic. I love to read and I live vicariously through the characters in the books I read, whether it be Chaucer or Bronte or King or Rowling. I like to watch movies that other people don't watch because they're obscure or terrible or serial killer documentaries. I watch them because they remind you of all of the terrible, awful things this world is truly capable of producing. I'll take an apple pie over a cake, and Oreos and skim milk over just about everything.

I'm a person. I have a bad heart. But I don't have a bad heart. I'm capable of loving and hating and crying and laughing and even though I'm leaving this world faster than most everyone, we are ALL dying. I've spent my years sitting back and watching the time slip through the hourglass while you all rushed around fulfilling dreams you used to have or were told to have. I've been fortunate enough to watch a rose bud come alive and open into the most beautiful, perfect flower. I've been lucky enough to then see that flower lose its petals as they dried and slipped from the grasp of the stem onto the ground and become the mulch that protects the roots, so the rose can bloom again next year. I've seen little boys and girls learn to ride their bikes, and then learn to drive a car, and learn to love and be loved.

I am so much more than my bad heart. I've fought so hard to get to this point, and now that I'm here and I love my life, I'm leaving it.

Nate

Christmas of 2013 was a quiet affair. Jeff was going to split time between our place and Soph's, and was taking over the gifts Mer had bought for the 4 of them. I had kept my mouth shut on that. I didn't think Sophia deserved anything personally, but Merry insisted. My wife is a better person than I am.

I wanted to get Merry something different for Christmas this year. I kept feeling like we had this cloud hanging over us, and I wanted to take the somber vibe that had settled over the house and shake it up some.

So, I bought her a puppy. Not just any puppy, but a puppy that had been designated to be a service dog, and had flunked out of that for whatever reason. Bets and Jeff knew, and Bets was thrilled to keep the puppy at her house until Christmas morning. I knew she'd have a hard time giving the little blonde cotton ball that purported to be a golden retriever back to Merry. He was incredibly cuddly, and much like Merry, was content to just be there watching his surroundings. I guess he wasn't an ideal fit for a service dog because he was a scaredy-cat and the runt to boot, which was perfect for Mer.

I woke up on Christmas and met Bets outside to grab the puppy and bring him in to Merry. I had thought about having her open up a big box with him in it, and then decided I would let the puppy wake her up. Bets and I snuck back up the stairs, and set the little fluff ball on the bed, where he gamboled over the covers and started sniffing Mer's face.

No reaction. Merry had a rough night, and had just gotten back to sleep around 6 that morning, so I wasn't terribly surprised she didn't wake up. Her face looked paler than normal and she had dark circles under her eyes more often than not lately. What happened next surprised me. The puppy looked back at Bets and I, and then flopped down with a huff and nestled next to Merry. He yawned and then fell asleep next to her. We kind of looked at each other and shrugged, and went downstairs for coffee, waiting for Merry to wake up.

*****

I had this dream, where I was sitting under my willow in the back yard and the sun filtered through the branches, flashing intermittently over my skin as I read a book. I could feel the warmth, hear the leaves rustle in the breeze, and see freckles develop on my skin as the sun crossed through the sky and the hours passed. I set the book by my side, and watched the bees touch upon the flowers that sprouted from the beds I had built all those years before. I could see the butterflies flit through the garden, with seemingly no purpose or path, and wondered if they worried about a strong gust of wind or a sudden storm, or if they just meandered their way through life concerned only with where they would light upon next. As I sat and watched one in particular make its way through the multitude of flowers and plants towards me, I wondered what it would be like to just be like that. The butterfly came closer and closer still and finally rested on my arm and began to walk slowly up towards my elbow, and shoulder, and finally made its way to may face where it tickled my nose. This had never happened before and I was terrified to move for fear it would leave me.

And then I woke up, still feeling that tickling sensation on my arm and face and looked down to find a mass of golden blonde fur lying next to me. When the mass began to move and turn around to get comfortable, I found myself looking at the most perfect furry face, with smushed closed eyes and a little wet nose.

My butterfly was a puppy!

Betsy

Nate and I were downstairs for about an hour when we heard Mer rustling

around upstairs and start to make her way down. She held the puppy in her arms,

and it wasn't hard to see she was already enamored with him. Her eyes were shiny

and she held him against her chest, and the puppy, for his part was un-puppy-like

and just kept curled against her with his head on her shoulder, content to be carried

around.

"You got me a puppy?!" she exclaimed as she made her way to give Nate

a kiss good morning. "He was curled up next to me asleep when I woke up. He

doesn't seem to want to do anything but lay with me!" She sat down in her

recliner and the puppy just stayed where he was.

"We thought it was a good idea to get you a companion for when

someone isn't here with you," Nate said, smiling at her. "He was deemed to be

too shy and timid for the service dog program he was in, and Bets found him up

for adoption. What are you going to name him?"

Merry seemed to think for a minute, her lips pressed to the fur of the

puppy's neck, and looked up and said, "Azrael."

"Azrael? You sure about that, sunshine?" He thought about it for a

minute. "Wait, isn't that the name of the angel of death?" Nate asked

incredulously.

"Azrael means 'one whom god helps' in Hebrew. In Judaism, he's the

highest-ranking commander of God's angels. And in Islam, he watches over the dying, and receives the spirits of the dead to deliver them to heaven," Merry

replied.

"Don't even want to know how you know that, babe. But if you're sure

that's what you want to call him, then Azrael it is." I wasn't sure if Nate realized

it at the time, but the fact that Mer was able to rattle off the etymology of the name

so swiftly meant that she was back to reading the religion books again. I don't

know if she was searching for an answer, or searching for salvation, but the last

times I had been aware of her interest in this topic was when she was struggling in

her last semester in college. Right before she collapsed outside her class. I wasn't

sure what to think of it. Was it a good thing? Or was it a sign she was preparing

for something more?

*****

Winter turned into spring, and spring turned into summer. A beautiful summer, warm but not too warm. Just enough rain to make my flowers bloom bright and strong, with the sun peeking through any clouds that dared cross its path across the sky. I passed the 24th anniversary of Laney's death as I always did, sitting against my willow with Azrael, watching everything and seeing nothing all at once. It had become difficult to walk much, but I made the trek outside nearly every day with the help of my now nearly full-grown shadow who followed me everywhere, and a hand carved cane Betsy brought back from Epcot for me. She insisted it was to solidify my crotchety writer status, rather than of necessity, and I appreciated the gesture and the support more than she realized. I'm not sure how much Nate has been sleeping, because every time I woke up, he was asking if I was okay, and if I needed anything. Stairs had come to be the bane of my existence, and much like my father nearly 24 years before this, Nate had taken to carrying me up and down them to prevent me from straining myself any further than that I was.

Straining myself. It's kind of funny now. I remember being a kid and feeling so small being carried up and down those stairs by my dad, and wishing I could be let down to walk them myself. And now, I never wanted Nate to let me go, for fear it would be the last time.

Summer turned to an Indian summer, with fall pushing against it trying to get through. I was grateful for the continued warmth outside, because it meant I could stay outside longer, sitting either on my patio, or if I was having a good day, under my willow. I kept thinking of Mrs. Jay, towards the end when she was bundled up against a perceived chill, even when the sun shone brightly in the sky and the mercury decried the coming autumn. I had become her, in many ways. The cane. The multiple layers of clothing. The constant watchful eye on my loved ones. I understood now. She knew she wasn't going to make it through the winter, I think. Just like I know deep in my broken heart I won't make it to see another Christmas.

I had an appointment scheduled with my cardiologist on Friday, October 10th, and Nate wasn't able to take me, even though he said he could cancel his meeting. Bets was free, and cheerfully offered to take me to the appointment and then for a girl's pizza lunch. In fact, she insisted upon it, saying Nate had been hogging me in that playful, teasing voice she used with him, when she was trying to hide her worry from him. The day loomed gray and dark, much like the first anniversary of Laney's death and I kept looking for the chestnut-haired child in rain boots as we drove to the doctor's office.

The appointment went as all had, with the vitals and the questions. This time felt different. Like the nurses knew a secret, and were sorry they couldn't tell me. While Bets waited for me in the lobby, my doctor slowly and methodically went through the steady and constant decline of my vitals. My oxygen levels were borderline; my circulation was starting to shut down. Was sleep a problem? Yes, sleep was always a problem. Not because of this shitty heart but because I didn't want to die in my bed for my husband to find me. Appetite? Negligible, at this point. Headaches? Yeah, from constantly trying to figure out how the hell is a 29-year-old dying on her family. It wasn't fair.

The questions were finally over with, and the doctor looked at me, and just said he was sorry, and in his opinion, I should be admitted to the hospital or at the least, have Hospice come to the house to make my 'transition' easier on everyone. He was sorry? He wasn't the one dying.

"So that's it then? I just go home to die now?" I felt the tears starting to pool in my eyes, and even though I knew this was coming, it still felt like a shock. It was too soon.

"Merry, I'm sorry. Medically speaking, you're looking at a week, maybe two if you were in the hospital. I'd prefer it if you were in the hospital, just so I know you're not in pain. I can give you the contact information for Hospice, if you'd rather be at home." He stopped speaking at this point. I don't know if there was anything else for him to say.

"The one thing they've never told me through all of this is what to expect. How I should expect to die," I said hoarsely, trying to imagine Nate finding me dead next to him when he woke up in the morning.

"Well, one of two things will happen. You'll either pass in your sleep. Or you'll lose consciousness, and they won't be able to wake you up."

"Will I know? Will I have a warning?" I asked, hoping there was some way I could.

"Merry, you know your heart better than anyone else. You know what your normal is. You know what's abnormal. With as functional as you are at this point, I would venture a guess and say you'll be able to tell, at least a little bit. Is there anything else I can do for you?"

Yeah. You can stop my heart from breaking, doc.

Betsy

I realize now why Merry used to say BLD and ALD. Her life changed so swiftly in those few hours from the time that Laney collapsed until she had heard she had died. It had to have been difficult for a 5-year-old to grasp the loss. I know I didn't for many years after that. I know it's hard now to fathom what my life is going to be like without Merry in it. I've had these conversations with myself over these last few years. Saying to myself, Merry is going to die. And then I lose my composure and begin crying. Because she's always been there. It's been a blessing in many ways to have a best friend who literally cannot do anything, because she's always available. She's never not picked up the phone. She's never not wanted to see me and I don't know how that's even possible because, well, I can be me. When she was in the hospital all those times, and I was sitting and waiting for her to wake up, I kind of muttered something to myself about how I needed my best friend here with me to deal with the fact that my best friend was undergoing major surgery. I needed her steadiness, her absolute strength to help me deal with her being sick. Her backbone. Her understanding.

She's been a high-rise built on an earthquake table. You know what I mean, right? They shake the shit out of buildings on an earthquake table to see what makes them fall, what makes them fail and for the past 25 years, she's been shaken every which way possible and she's still standing. But, this last doctor's appointment didn't just shake her. It took the cracks from all of the other times she's been shaken, and it destroyed her foundation. She's lived for so long patching up the cracks and dealing with a façade that had seen better days for sure, and this last appointment just about leveled her. I never realized how much I depended on her attitude to maintain my optimism. Oh sure, she's had some episodes in the past where she got low and needed a boost, but never before did she come out of an appointment and look like she did after this last one.

Merry knows her heart better than anyone. She has ignored warning signs and symptoms in the past, but I think that was more her ignoring the rest of her rather than ignoring her heart. She's been so attuned to the beating and beat-skipping and hiccupping and fluttering to not know there wasn't anything else that could be done. I think deep down she always believed she was the smallest margin ahead of the game in terms of what they were able to do for her. She believed that as time went on and her heart worsened, they were going to come back to her with some magic potion or some new solution that was going to keep her going until they could find the next thing that was going to save her. And when they told her there was nothing more they could do other than to make her comfortable, I'm sure that resonated with her because they told her father that so many years ago. Did she believe them at first? Or did she think she could find another doctor and find another solution if she just tried hard enough?

I can't remember much of my life before I met Merry at Laney's funeral. I can't imagine my life without her in it. That I'm going to have to, sooner rather than later it seems, makes my heart hurt. Maybe I finally understand what she's been going through all of these years.

Nate

Our first dance was to a Dave Matthews Band song. Angel. Merry

picked it and I liked it and went with it. Didn't think too much about it at the time.

I'd have danced to Black Sabbath or Megadeath or anything at all had she only

asked.

When she got back from her appointment, she got in the house and I

knew immediately something was wrong. She didn't have to tell me; she just

looked at me with tears in her eyes. We didn't talk about how much time the doc

said she had left. It didn't matter, because any way you looked at it, it was never

going to be enough if it was anything less than however long I live. Throughout

the night, she sat in her chair and just watched us feign normality around her. Jeff

and Betsy were there, and Bets' mom stopped over to bring us dinner and stayed

for a bit. I think everyone was trying to act like there was nothing wrong, when

our worlds were imploding around us. It was strange, now that we knew things

were coming to a close, how aware I was of everyone around her and how few

people that really was. How could the world not know how incredible she was?

How hard she had fought?

Later, after Betsy and Jeff went upstairs, I went to pick her up to carry her

up to bed and we just stood for a moment. If I could have stayed like that forever,

I would have. I'd have given anything to stay like that forever, and I was just

about to say so, when I heard her voice, that gravelly alto sing breathlessly in my

ear, "I swear, I'll be your angel, when I'm gone." I felt her bury her head in my shoulder as she cried silently in my arms. She lifted her head after a bit, and those gunmetal eyes were filled with tears as she just stared at me. My chest felt like it would explode and I brought my forehead to hers and just held her. There wasn't anything I could say to her that she didn't already know. There wasn't anything anyone could say that could make losing her any easier.

*****

It needs to be today. If I die on Sophie's birthday, she will likely piss on my grave. I always said she was a witch, and being born so close to Halloween only confirmed that for me.

But I know it will be soon. I'm feeling things in my chest I haven't before. A sluggishness followed by a quick triple beat. My pacemaker is probably going batshit trying to do its job, and it hurts to breathe. I think my broken heart is tired as it nears the end of its marathon.

As the sun sets, I find my eyes are tearing up at the idea I won't be here to see it rise. I know I won't. I've had a week since the doctor broke the news to me. Nate knew it wasn't good when he got home that day. I couldn't hide the tear stains on my face, and the fact that Bets and my dad were both there with me. Both of them insisted on staying with us. Until the end. I wanted to tell them they didn't have to, but I couldn't bring myself to say the words. I'm scared. Scared of dying. Scared of dying and leaving them here. My dad called Sophie to tell her she needed to come see me, and her and Adam stopped by with the boys. There wasn't much left for either of us to say. There were instances where I started to talk, and Soph would just say it was okay and look away. Even though it wasn't, and it never would be. I think she was trying not to cry, but that might just be me wishing it to be so. The boys were enamored by Azrael and she and I found ourselves watching them playing with the dog in the backyard by the willow.

Both silent. I wanted to tell her I would tell Laney she said hi, but I didn't. The mood was already somber enough.

Bets and my dad finally went to bed. I gave them each a hug and a kiss and told them I loved them. There weren't enough words to say to them, and not enough time to say them anyway, so I kept it simple. They looked like hell. I think everyone is just exhausted from this deathwatch. Nate came over and much like we have in the past, he knelt on the floor in front of my chair, wrapping his arms around my waist with his head on my chest. Can he hear my heart dying? Can he tell? How do I say goodbye to the love of my life for the last time? How can I thank him for loving me, when I thought for sure I was unlovable and unworthy? I'm sure he sensed my tears because he whispered to me,

"I wouldn't trade a single second of this life with you for a thousand years of a life without you."

Please God, or whoever or whatever is out there, make this stop. It's bad enough to be in physical pain, but to know that I'm leaving behind the people who love me is . . . it's what's killing me. It's quite literally breaking my heart.

We sat like that for what seemed like forever. Nate wanted to carry me off to bed, and for the first time ever, I said no. There is no way I could make it back down the stairs. I explained I wanted to stay down here tonight, as I was comfortable watching the night outside and I didn't want to keep him awake. I asked him to leave Azrael with me, since he liked sitting on my feet. I'd like to say that he loved my company, but my feet had been so cold lately that I'm sure he used them like an ice pack on his fur covered belly.

Nate gave me one last, long look and one last, long hug and kiss and left the room on my promise I would call him should I need him.

Nate. . . did you know? Did you know it was the last hug? The last kiss? The last look? I hope beyond all hope you know how much I love you madly, and I will miss you like crazy from wherever I am.

And If I'm wrong, I'm going to feel stupid in the morning when they find me outside. I just don't think I'm wrong this time.

Watching the clock tick each second of my life away, I wonder if this is how a condemned prisoner feels. Only I don't know the hour of my death. A refrain of 'soon' plays through my head, and I finally inch my way forward to the edge of the chair. Azrael seems to know something is coming, and gets up to wait for me by the back door. I'm glad I won't be alone out there.

The walk, once made easy by youthful legs and a heart not yet scarred by years of living this life, took all of my strength. Azrael clung to my side, while I hobbled outside without my cane. I needed my hands to carry these pages. I guess you can call my scribbling just that now. The point this story began and the point this story ends will be the same. Tucked against my willow, this time in autumn with the yellow-tinged leaves skittering in the slight breeze of the Indian summer. This time, I lay with my back against the tree, looking up to that beautiful midnight blue starry sky with Azrael next to me, curled tight against my side keeping me warm.

I'm rambling. So much left to say.

I love you all. Thank you for being my world. Thank you for letting me love you. I'm sorry. I tried to make it.

I get to be with Laney now. I get to meet Mom. I finally get to see my Laney now.

My heart is full.

Now I lay me, down to sleep

I pray the Lord, my soul to keep.

If I should die before I wake,

I pray the Lord my soul to

Betsy

It was a hysterical shriek from Nate that let me know the inevitable had arrived, and Merry was gone.

Nate woke up early, and went downstairs. No Merry. No Azrael. Merry hadn't been mobile much in this past few days since we left the doctor, and liked to sit in the sunroom overlooking the backyard she had loved since she was a kid. To find her missing must have been terrifying for him. He ran from room to room, calling her name, and becoming more frantic as he went. He finally noticed the sunroom door cracked; not quite latched. He went outside, and as the light of the morning filled their backyard, he found her lying against her willow with Azrael lying next to her, his head on her lap.

My friend, so beautiful in life, walked to lie down at her favorite place on earth so as not to leave her husband the task of finding her lifeless body in their house. And her shadow lay with her, so she wasn't alone. I truly hope he was the harbinger of her soul up to the heaven she was so uncertain of ever seeing. She held on her chest a thick folder containing a sheaf of papers and a pen, and 4 letters.

My God. I can't believe she's gone. She's my best friend; my adopted sister and I can't believe I can't call her. I can't believe she's gone.

Nate

I wish it had been me. I wish I had been there. I want her here. I just want her here with me. I can't believe she's gone.

Adam

When my Jeff called to tell us Merry was gone, I didn't know what to say. I took the phone from Sophie when it became apparent something was wrong, and I heard him speaking, but I don't have any idea what he said because all I could do was watch my wife. She just sat down at the table, and looked down at her hands. I saw tears fall onto her freckled hands and on the tablecloth under her head. I walked behind her after I hung up the phone and wrapped my arms around her shoulders, and I could feel her convulsing, but without any sound. And then just as suddenly as I heard nothing, I heard this roar coming from somewhere deep inside of her that I hadn't known was there. The boys came running in as the sobs wracked her body and she just sat there bawling like I had never witnessed before. Not even when she lost the babies. I'm sure it terrified the boys but she couldn't seem to stop.

Sophia

I had always thought I would feel a sense of relief when Merry finally died. It's not as though we didn't know this was coming. But now that she's gone. . . there is a piece of me that died with her. I don't mean the kidney. She's my sister and I don't know that I understood what that meant to me or should have meant to me. I'm no longer a sister. I don't know that I was worthy of being her sister.

My dad used to tell me that still waters run deep when I would make a nasty comment about Merry and how quiet she was all the time. I used to get so angry when he would say that, as if the inverse, me being effusive, meant that I was shallow or somehow less than she was. I spent my life trying to do more and prove to my father that just because I hadn't been sick didn't mean that I wasn't strong and substantive in my own way. But I disagree with my dad. She was never still waters. She was a rogue wave, and she destroyed me and now she's gone and she won't ever come back.

Oh God, she's gone.

Dear Nathaniel Holden,

There are so many things I want to say to you. So many moments I want
to relive, so you know how I saw you, how I saw our lives together and know how
much I love you. I don't want to say I love you with all of my heart, because it
was never going to be enough to fully express how much that is. There aren't
words that can describe it, as least not words of my own.

You gave me more than I ever believed I had any right to. More than I
ever believed would be possible. You were with me through the hell I walked in
and made it feel like it was no more than a walk on the beach instead of walking
on hot coals. You dealt with more than anyone who wasn't sick should have to go
through, and you kept the positivity going even when it became clear things were
going south. I still don't know how you did that. You gave me moments of such
pure happiness that I was finally able to envision heaven. I know I'm glossing
over so much. . . the trips to the hospitals, the surgery, long nights unable to sleep
and of course, the constant cloud that hung over everything we did.

I never told you this, but Bets and I had a conversation the day you
showed up at the hospital after I had the pacemaker installed. I had decided that I
simply HAD to tell you this couldn't work. She told me to give you a chance; that
maybe you'd give my heart a reason to keep beating. It was ridiculous to me at
the time. I went to meet you, determined to stop whatever was going on. And you
just didn't care. I think back about it now and I laugh because I was so annoyed
that you wouldn't listen to reason.

I think what I'm trying to say, is thank you. Much like your namesake, I became cynical and jaded and angry and you shocked me out of that. I think the thing that I'm saddest and angry about, is that I was right. (Sorry, I just had to get that in!)

To wrap up this letter before it becomes illegible from my crying over it, thank you for these years. Please don't lose yourself once I'm not here. You have so much inside of you that needs to be shared with the world. You were always able to make me a part of whatever it was you were doing, even if I wasn't able to do it with you. Keep doing that, until you find someone else to share your life with. And yeah, blah blah blah they won't be me, I'm irreplaceable and all that jazz. I know. It's because I'm made of awesome, but I'm a firm believer that there is someone else out there who will make you as happy as I did.

We made the best out of this too short time we had together. Remember me in the summer, when the butterflies visit my flowers, and the sun shines high in the sky. You'll feel my presence there with you, when the breeze filters through the leaves on my willow and the cicadas buzz in the heat. I told you in our vows I would love you until my dying day. And I tell you now, if there is life after this, and I need to believe there is, I will love you until then too.

Till we meet again,

Merry

Oh Peas,

I'm afraid peas will have to be served sans carrots from now on.
Because, every time you look at a carrot, you're going to hear, "Don't eat me!" in
my voice echoing through your head.

Yep. I just did that. You're welcome.

First of all, I was right, which sucks.

Second of all, did I say this sucks? I knew it was going to happen. Knew
it was a matter of when, and not if. But I learned to love being alive even when it
hurt like hell. So many little things you don't think about. I loved waking up and
seeing the single ray of sun shining through my curtains in my bedroom. The dust
motes floating in that ray made me think 'that's how I wish I could always be.'
Floating along in the sun, not caring about falling on the floor or getting vacuumed
up or sucked into the cold air return. Not worried about this piece of shit, busted
ass heart of mine. Not writing letters to my loved ones saying shit like 'It'll be
okay!' and 'We fought the good fight, didn't we?'

In reality, I'm pissed. I'm pissed I'm going to be dead when you read
this and won't be able to joke around how cliché writing these fucking letters is.
I'm pissed I have an amazing, smoking hot husband who adores me and I DIED
on him. (Not literally, because that would be bad. . . God, I hope that didn't
happen!) I'm furious that my poor dad and chronically angry sister have to go
through this again.

And I'm devastated you'll never look at another carrot the same way again.

(See what I did there?)

I know, I know. I joke with you, because you've seen me through this mess since the beginning. It's the only way for me to stay sane. Or rather, it was. Luckily, I won't have to get used to tense changes for too much longer. How annoying.

So here are some final gems as I venture on towards whatever is waiting for me once my ticker kicks. (I love the alliteration and imagery in those two words there. I keep picturing a mini-me kicking the shit out of my heart, stomping it to death.)

1. No black at my party. Oh, that's right. . . you don't know about my party. I do NOT want a funeral. No wake. No memorial service. **NO BEING SAD!!!!** Merry wants a party. One of those parties where everyone gets rip roaring drunk like at an Irish wake, telling stories about me which are likely fibs about things I never did. I want you all to play with lawn darts, throwing caution to the wind about the danger. There must be a slip and slide. I demand metal Tonka trucks in a sand box for the boys to play with. There should be shots of expensive vodka and margaritas and strawberry daiquiris and a chocolate fountain you dip Oreos and cheesecake into and trays and trays of pizza, heavy on the cheese and garlic and light on the sauce, well done. Shit, if it gets that out of hand, you have my

permission to have Naked Twister. There needs to be some loud and crazy DJ, playing all of my favorite songs, even the punk I know you all hate. It's just not a party without Rancid's Ruby SoHo, Bets. You'll just have to deal with it. You know why? Because we're all gonna die, and you may as well have fun until you get to that point. None of these things will kill you. And it would make me smile to know you guys are having one hell of a good time instead of being sad. In fact, it would make me fucking thrilled to know that Sophia is sitting there with a splitting headache listening to music that offends her sensibilities while her children get all sugared up and dirty.

That was mean.
I don't care, I'm dead.

Included in this envelope is a set of 'suggestions', so to speak, including music and places I've already contacted. Get a tent and put that sucker in the backyard and party. They know you're going to be calling. The lawn darts, Tonka trucks, vodka, rum and chocolate fountain are in the box labeled 'Merry's Party' in the garage attic right at the top of the stairs. I can feel the eye roll from wherever it is I'm at. But hey, I've taken the guesswork out of this whole thing. I don't want people to remember me and be sad. There is no one I trust more to pull this off. And while I know I didn't have anyone in my life outside of you guys, I also know you and my dad and Nate and even Sophie have others in your lives that you can invite over. Have Dad invite all of his bowling buddies and his work friends. You'll need those people in your life now. I have faith you'll make this exactly what I've (demanded!) asked for.

2. Life sucks. We both know this. Parents die. Best friends die. Everyone dies. We are only made up of things that can be used to remember us once we are gone. And we are only remembered by those who were affected by those things. So ultimately, life is nothing more than a circular argument. If we aren't doing things that are memorable, then we won't be remembered once we aren't here anymore. So in essence, I'm calling life here on earth a series of connected circle jerks.

I'll give you a moment to absorb that image.

But, as I was saying, how well we perform our portion of the circle jerk will determine how well we are remembered. And as crude as that analogy is, it's rather apt. Life starts out easy, but as the days, weeks, months and years pass, it gets harder to get that absolutely fulfilling moment where everything comes together. And then once it does, the process begins again. Sometimes it's easy to make an impression and other times, nothing we do and nothing we try works. I suppose my reason for this long and drawn out allegory is to delay the inevitable by making you laugh. I hope it worked.

3. I don't want to be remembered as Merry who had a bad heart. I want to be remembered as Merry who loved her friends and family so much it killed her.

    No, wait. Not that either. I guess I just want to be remembered.
Moving on.

4. Nate. He's going to take this hard. I blame you. It's completely your fault that I fell in love with him. He was everything I ever dreamed of, and never thought I could have. I worry he's going to forget how to live after watching me die. Just watch him for me.

5. Sophia. I don't know what to say here. I don't know how she will act or react. I hope perhaps my not being such a focus will give her peace. I fear it won't. She's been in the shadows for so long, not realizing that I would give anything to be in her shoes. Maybe she will miss me now that I'm not there. Maybe. Make her let you be in HER life. She could use some Betsy in her world to remind her that there is more to life than work and being miserable. I need to make sure the boys know all about the things Soph wouldn't tell them or wouldn't know even. I hate that I won't be there to get them in trouble. I leave that to you. Make her let you be in their life.

6. Dad. I just can't. He gave up everything for me, and I'm still dead. Every time I think of him being here without me and having to deal with Sophie the Dramatic, I start crying all over again, and I'm running out of time and tears. Please check in on him for me. I will from wherever I'm at.

7. And finally, we come to you. I have been blessed to have you as my friend for nearly 25 years. You never once (seriously) complained about wanting to do something I couldn't. You were my guardian angel in best friend form, and you did a fantastic job. From grade school to middle school to high school, college, and life thereafter, you were the sister I always wished Sophie could be to me. I can never thank you enough for what you've done for me.

I don't know how to end this. I just don't know how I'm supposed to end this letter when I still have so much to say to you. From this lifetime, into whatever or wherever I go, you'll always be my best friend. You and I, we will still have conversations in your head and even if everyone thinks you're crazy, I'll know you aren't and I'll respond. Somehow, someway, I'll give you my two cents. This isn't goodbye. This is just I'll see you later.

Love always,

Carrots

Dad,

This sucks. I can't believe this is it for me. I never wanted to say goodbye to you like this. I wanted to believe I could make it, if for no other reason than because I promised you I would fight from the start of this adventure. You've been the constant in my life, since the beginning. You fought for me, and instilled that fight in me from the moment they told us about my heart. I'm so sorry Daddy, I just can't fight anymore. I've tried to be positive about my chances of coming out of this alive, but there just isn't anything left for me to do but wait now. I know you'll get this once I'm already gone, so I wanted to make sure I told you a story. Maybe it will help. (I'll apologize in advance for any details that may make you a little uncomfortable.)

I thought it would be easy to say goodbye to everyone. I've had a pretty good idea about things would end for years. I realize that spending all this time slowly dying; I've done quite a bit of living too. Let's talk about everything they used to say I couldn't do. That list is long.

When Laney died, and they tested Sophie and I and found out I had a bad heart too, they told you to take me home, and give me medications that would make me comfortable, because I couldn't be fixed. My heart was worse than Laney's was and only because I was a calm kid was I still here. You didn't listen and took me to any doctor you could to try and give me a quality life. And you succeeded. (I didn't know any of this until Betsy's mom told me a little bit ago when I was having a bad day.)

307

I have you to thank for helping me make it out of grade school and middle school.

They told you I wouldn't make it out of high school after I had the myectomy and I went into kidney failure. They wanted you to take me home and make me comfortable because the chances of getting a kidney were slim. After being on dialysis for weeks and thinking that this was finally it, and I was going to die, Sophie gave me one of her kidneys much like you give someone a hug.

I have Sophie to thank for making it out of high school.

They said I shouldn't bother going to college. It was too strenuous and why bother when I couldn't work after college anyway. It would take too much out of me walking around campus and I missed too much high school to even bother. With the support of my bestest friend in the whole wide world I made it to class. I studied through an oxygen mask hooked up to that monster apparatus I thought would wake the dead. Bets being Bets just put earplugs in and rolled over to sleep. Only, I found out much later on, she only put one in to make sure I made it to bed and woke up in time. She checked in on me throughout the night to make sure I was still breathing, and basically acted as a nurse right there in my dorm room. I think when it comes down to it, she may know more about my condition than even I do, because she had been exposed to the caretaker side of it. She literally carried me through college both mentally and physically. She did my laundry knowing how I couldn't carry the basket of clothes, in exchange for being folding bitch. I'll tell you what. . . I think I got the shit end of that deal.

I have Bets to thank for making it through college.

They told me I wouldn't live long enough to be married. This one I decided *they* were right about. I didn't want to meet Mr. Wonderful, fall in love with him and him with me only to die on him. I thought I had put up sufficient defenses in both high school and college against the extremely few inquiries I received. My walls withstood a small number of now nameless boys and men with no issue. But, there was this one guy in my creative writing class who just wouldn't take no for an answer. He just wouldn't stop staring. I finally had enough of the looks and constant offers and invitations that I decided to set him straight about why there would be no we.

After getting out of the hospital after they installed the pacemaker, I had Betsy drive me to his house, cloaked in disapproval of what I was about to do. And I stripped off my shirts revealing the scars covering my chest, abdomen and arms from the multiple surgeries and procedures that I had been through. I calmly explained that I had a fatal heart disease that would sooner, rather than later, kill me and I would not date him because of that. He stared. . . which I expected. It was kind of his M.O.

And then he kissed me.

I had just shown this near perfect stranger scars I hadn't shown anyone outside of you, doctors and Betsy. Scars I took great pains to cover. Imperfections I hated, and that weren't viewed as the battle scars you wanted me to think they were. They were the bane of my existence and visual evidence I was anything but the normal I so desperately wished I could be. And he didn't care.

So of course, I had to marry him. My logic was sound. Despite my broken and battered heart, despite my scars, despite everything I couldn't do, he still loved me. Despite knowing we wouldn't grow old together, he still loved me. He took each and every second of our life together and made them multiply by treating each second as a precious gift.

And so, I have Nate to thank for showing me that I did deserve to have a 'Happily Ever After' after all.

So where does that leave us? Well, I was asked a question in my freshman philosophy class I'll answer for you now. Would you rather have 30 years of pure, blissful happiness, or 100 years of nothing but mediocrity? I never needed to answer that question, because for me, there was never any other option. I would take these 30 years I almost had, even if the 100 were within my grasp. None of these years have been easy. There isn't one that has passed without missing Laney, and feeling like a piece of me died with her. It's that piece of me that isn't sad about leaving you guys, because I get to see her, and Mom and Mr. and Mrs. Jay again, even though I'm leaving you and Bets, and Nate and Soph.

In the time since Laney died, I've lived every single minute as though the next wasn't guaranteed. I've loved you, Laney, Sophie, Betsy, Mr. and Mrs. Jay and Nate with every single cell of this broken, beat up and battered heart. Lately, I've questioned everything I've ever done, wondering if it was enough. And I've spent nights awake lately worrying about all of you. I couldn't have asked for more in this life. I did everything I could hoping they would either find a way to fix this heart or get me a new one so I could stay with all of you. I guess I was meant to leave this world with the heart I was born with still in my chest.

Do you remember when you used to carry me down the stairs? Right after we got out of the hospital, when I had the heart attack at the mall? I told you how much I hated it. I told everyone how much I hated it. Because I felt like I was a baby and I desperately wanted not to be. I didn't. I felt so safe, like nothing could touch me. Like I was invincible in your arms. And I would listen to your heartbeat, and beg my own to beat like yours. I would go to bed every night and ask my heart to please, just beat like yours. Because it was perfect and normal and even though it was full of love for me and for Sophie and for Laney and Mom, it kept right on beating. It was an example of what a heart should be.

You always did everything you could for me. And while I was stubborn and didn't like some of what you did for me, or rather decided for me, I know you did it with my best interests in mind. I'm so sorry I have to leave you and Nate and Bets here without me, but maybe you three can grab a beer, and sit around the campfire together and tell the war stories Nate always asked me about.

I refuse to say goodbye to you. I refuse to accept the idea that I won't see you again. Everything that comes to mind boils down to one thing. Thank you for loving me and thank you for fighting for me. I'll pass along your love to Mom and Laney.

Love always,

Your baby girl

Sophie,

    I never wanted to write this letter to you. One, because it meant I was truly dying, instead of surviving the way I have been. And two, because I don't know how to put into words what I have wanted to say without it sounding trite or canned.

    It goes without saying I never wanted this life. But, I guess I also think that because this is the one that I got, I needed to make the best of it. I think my attitude about everything from being sick to school to how I live my life in general is . . . offensive to you. Maybe that's not the word. Annoying? Irritating? It's no secret my ability to just deal with things bothers you. I guess I just never understood why. I didn't have your ambition, your drive, your need to be more, because I knew wanting those things was just going to make dealing with the everyday reality of my situation much more difficult to manage. I couldn't have those things, so they were outside of my purview and therefore, not a part of my life. I'm not seeking attention. I'm no martyr either.

    Don't you know I would have given everything just to be like you? You get to be normal. You get to be a mom. You get to LIVE. I think that's always been it. The comparison. Despite everything you've accomplished, you still feel like you have to do more. And I never got that . . . there is no comparison. You are you, and I'm me. Neither of us is better than the other. If anything, Soph, you've <u>always</u> been my ideal. You were a shining example of how to take what life gave you, and squeeze every last drop out of it until there was nothing left. I

312

sometimes wonder if the fact that I could never do that was the insult. That I was

a waste of a life to you. That you wish Laney was the one who was here, instead

of me. I've always thought you wished it was me who died that July day all those

years ago. Or better yet, that I was never born and Mom was still here. Life

would have been perfect for you then; wouldn't it have been?

Part of me wants to yell at you. To tell you this was never easy on me.

To scream and cry and throw a fit about how unfair this is. Ask why you couldn't

just be my sister instead of being this snippy, jealous, angry woman who blames

me for being sick and stealing her mother from her, and for not being Laney. Part

of me wants to end this by saying that soon; you won't have to worry about

competing with a woman dying of heart failure. Truthfully, if you're reading this,

that's already happened, so congratulations! You're free. And part of me wants to

tell you that I never had the comfort of a career and children to soothe the parts of

me damaged by all of the losses we've experienced. I only had Dad, and Bets, and

Nate to help me navigate this mess that I never wanted.

I hate this. I hate that when I think of you, I get angry. Blindingly angry.

I miss my SISTER. I miss that when Laney died, you may have well have died

along with her, for as much as you were there for me, with the sole exception

being when you begrudgingly gave me your precious kidney. I hate that I can't

call you up and talk to you like we're sisters, instead of these two strangers. That

song that Laney always played, you know the one, plays in my head on repeat

when I think of you. "We're just two lost souls living in a fishbowl, year after

year running over the same old ground. What have we found? The same old fears." I had hoped that once I got older, we could talk, really talk about everything and find some way to get past ourselves and everything we went through, but that never happened. I've always regretted we couldn't be closer than we were. Could I have done more? I don't know. I don't think so, I just don't. I am forever grateful you were there for me when I needed you. I'd never have made it this far without you giving me your kidney. I only wish I had let you know I needed you more. That I wanted more from you. I needed a sister, and when Laney died, I lost any semblance of one in you too. It's perhaps easier for me to admit now; that I'm coming to the end of this, that me being stubborn made our relationship more difficult than it needed to be. I just didn't know how else to be, Soph. I was constantly fighting this life of mine from the time we found out about it, until it ended. Maybe I didn't know how to do anything but fight. For that I'm sorry. I'm so sorry.

I love you Sophia. I'm sorry if I didn't tell you enough, and I'm sorry for whatever I did to make our relationship the way it was. I see you with those boys of yours, and I see the person you never were with me, and I'm thankful I could see that side of you before I died. I hope my passing can bring you some measure of peace I wasn't able to give you while I was alive.

Love always,

Merry

<u>Betsy</u>

I knew Merry had been writing. I figured she was writing in her diary, and was pleased she had kept doing so after I bought her that first one all those years ago. I didn't have an inkling she was writing this for all of us until nearly the end. When she came out of that last doctor's visit crying, and we found out that it was near the end for her, she made me promise her that I would take the folder that was always with her and transcribe it. She had these pages ripped from spiral notebooks in there, and slipped in between the pages were the memories she asked me, Nate, Dad Cameron, and Sophia to give to her. I asked her if she read what we all wrote, and she nodded slowly. Part of me ached to ask her to read what everyone wrote while she was still alive, but I knew that wasn't what she intended. I wasn't to edit it, unless there were major grammar issues (which she didn't expect, she told me with a small smile) and I was to print out copies for myself, Dad Cameron, Nate, Sophie and one each for Robert and Jeffrey. And then, I was to keep the master copy and hold onto it in case Sophie had any more kids.

"Put the papers in there from you guys; put everything in this folder in there, even the 4 letters I've written. It's all in order. Take your copy, read it once and then put it on a shelf somewhere and when you're really missing me, take it out and remember how much I loved you."

These are her words, unfiltered, unedited. They are so her. They positively ooze her essence to the extent that I keep thinking if I sit here holding them long enough, she'll magically appear before me.

She lived to be almost 30 years old, and died not because her heart was broken. Much like Laney before her, she died because her heart was full. She gave me a piece of herself, which stays with me to this day and will remain so until I see her again. I'll never forget her.

Merry Olivia Cameron Carter

December 22, 1984 – October 17, 2014

Acknowledgments

First and foremost, I would like to thank my lovely, rebel friend Betsy for giving me the kick in the ass I so desperately needed to write this. This book idea festered in the darkness in my head, and she forced it out into the light. While she called me a pig from hell for making her cry when she read the first iteration of this story, I took it as the highest of compliments and I am grateful she had faith in me when I didn't have faith in myself. My Betsy in the book could never come close to the real thing, but I hope I've given you a glimpse of the sass and sparkle she brings to everyone she knows.

I would also like to thank my friend Angelyn, who read this and provided me with a much-needed sanity check right before I published.

This book bloomed in my brain when I heard the Dave Matthews Band song "Baby Blue" while driving down Sheridan Drive, and their music had a starring role in the soundtrack in my head while writing this book. One of their perhaps lesser known songs provided the title to this book back before I knew how much of an impact the word and the song would have for me.

Thank you to everyone else who put up with me during the long and drawn out process of bringing this book to fruition.

About the Author

Nikki Murray grew up in Western New York. She currently resides in a small suburb of Buffalo with her husband, Rex, and a bevy of furballs. Sister is her first novel, but hopefully, not her last. You can read more at blonderoyalt.com, or find her on Facebook and Instagram at blonderoyalt or by email at blonderoyalt@gmail.com.